Pruning the Magnolia

BOOKSURGE PUBLISHERS
PRINTED IN THE UNITED STATES OF AMERICA

The resemblance of any character in this novel to any person, living or dead, is not intended. The characters, events, and locations are completely fictional. However, since we all have a dark side, each of us just might see ourselves in one or more of the people that reside in the fictional community of Falls City, Georgia.

WWW.EPISKOPOLS.COM
Books for Clergy and the People They Serve

ISBN: 1-4196-7804-3
ISBN-13: 978-1419678042

DENNIS R. MAYNARD

PRUNING THE MAGNOLIA

BOOK THREE IN THE MAGNOLIA SERIES

BOOKSURGE PUBLISHERS
2007

Pruning the Magnolia

ACKNOWLEDGEMENTS

I want to acknowledge all the Rectors and bookstore managers across the nation that have invited me to preach for them and do book signings. From Chicago to Houston and from Virginia to California, bookstore managers have not only stocked these books, but along with their Rectors, they have actively recommended them to their customers.

The list of clergy that are utilizing the books in the Magnolia Series for discussion in their congregations is lengthy, but I would be remiss not to acknowledge you in this writing. I am grateful to each of my brothers and sisters that wear the collar.

I owe a special word of appreciation to David Ward, C.P.A., and Michael Foley, of La Jolla, California. That same heartfelt appreciation is extended to Keith Kendrick, of Scottsdale, Arizona. I am equally indebted to Judy Ellis, of Greenville, South Carolina, for suggesting the title for this particular book. The cover photograph is from the home of Fay Witkin in Beaufort, South Carolina.

My wife, Nancy, continues to be one of my best critics and supporters. My sons Dennis Michael, Andrew and his wife Kristin Zanavich, and our daughter, Kristen Anne, have been steadfast with their words of encouragement.

My heartfelt thanks to each of you that have read the words that I put on paper. I am also grateful to you for recommending my books to others. No one knows better than I do that the words come through me, but they are not from me.

Steele Austin is filled with youthful enthusiasm. This idealistic Episcopal priest accepts a call to one of the oldest and most prestigious pulpits in the state of Georgia. His idealism continually conflicts with the determination of the parish leaders to keep things just the way they have always been. Steele, on the other hand, is equally determined to battle bigotry and prejudice, even when masked in tradition.

In this, the third book in the Magnolia Series, *Steele is forced to defend himself against a plot to accuse him of embezzling church funds. Not only is his integrity as a priest being threatened, but there are those in his own congregation determined to see that his new home will be a federal penitentiary.*

While defending himself against this latest assault, Steele and Randi struggle to decide if they wouldn't be better off to leave Falls City and accept a call to a new parish in Texas.

Then, an unusual pastoral crisis bonds him to one of his most vocal antagonists. Could it also mark a new day for Steele at First Church?

And through it all, the work of the Church goes on. Miracles of work and mercy do occur. You won't want to miss this, the third installment, of life in Falls City, Georgia.

"I think When the Magnolia Blooms is fabulous. I was reading it at Panera and I realized people were looking at me because I was laughing so loud."
Becky Michelfelder
Delaware, Ohio

"I thoroughly enjoyed Behind the Magnolia Tree, both laughing and crying as I read it. You say the characters are not actual individuals, but I swear I have met them. Their desire to maintain appearances and keep the status quo, yet their need for compassion and empathy, is just as apparent.
Carol Bettencourt
San Diego, California

"I read Behind the Magnolia Tree in two sittings. I couldn't put it down. I was aggravated when I had to stop. It is a fabulous read!"
Steven Scott Cochran
Sanderson, Florida

"I think Behind the Magnolia Tree is a great novel. It is quite the eye opener on how Christians can call themselves Christians and act like they do. I read the novel in two days and could not put it down. I look forward to the next one."
Jodi Marshall
Plano, Texas

"We are sharing your novels around the congregation. People are ready for the next one. Your writing is delightful and the issues are real. There are undertones of these things in all churches."
Fain Webb
Sussex, New Jersey

"I did nothing else for a day and a half but read your first novel. Then I got up at two o'clock in the morning to start the second. It is a wonderful story, beautifully written, and it moved along quickly. I didn't want it to end! The characters became real to me. I now fear getting your third book. Once I do, the world will have to stop turning while I read it. I can't wait.
Nancy Cathcart
Houston, Texas

"You need to put a warning label on your novels. May alienate spouses and injure ribs! We didn't speak to each other for two days. One while I read When the Magnolia Blooms non-stop and another when she did the same. Not quite true—we each quoted a great portion of it to each other. Thanks for a hilarious two days. Oh yes, hurry up with the next one."

Gene Holly
Las Vegas, Nevada

"I enjoyed both of your books in the Magnolia Series. MUCH better than the Mitford novels. I laughed and cried, sometimes at the same time. I hope there are more of your books in the offing."

Netha Brada
Iowa Falls, Iowa

"Not that I'm hooked, but when will book three in your Magnolia Series be available???"

Nancy Sinclair
Surfside, California

"We can't stand it! The first two books in your Magnolia Series have been passed around our congregation so much they're probably worn out. Seriously, we are all enjoying them very much. I hope that you're about done with #3."

Dick Stanley
Greenville, South Carolina

BOOKS BY
DENNIS R. MAYNARD

THOSE EPISKOPOLS

This is a popular resource for clergy to use in their new member ministries. It seeks to answer the questions most often asked about the Episcopal Church.

FORGIVEN, HEALED AND RESTORED

This book is devoted to making a distinction between forgiving those who have injured us and making the decision to reconcile with them or restore them to their former place in our lives.

THE MONEY BOOK

The primary goal of this book is to present some practical teachings on money and Christian Stewardship. It also encourages the reader not to confuse their self-worth with their net worth.

FORGIVE AND GET YOUR LIFE BACK

This book teaches the forgiveness process to the reader. It's a popular resource for clergy and counselors to use to do forgiveness training. In this book, a clear distinction is made between forgiving, reconciling, and restoring the penitent person to their former position in our lives.

BEHIND THE MAGNOLIA TREE

When the Gospel of a young Episcopal priest conflicts with the secrets of sex, greed, and power in an old southern community, it can mean only one thing for the youthful outsider, even if he is ordained. His idealism places him in an ongoing conflict with the bigotry and prejudice that are in the historical fabric of the community.

WHEN THE MAGNOLIA BLOOMS

This is the second book in the Magnolia Series. Steele Austin finds himself in the middle of a murder investigation. Those antagonistic to his ministry continue to find new ways to attempt to rid themselves of the young idealist. And through it all, the work of the Church goes on. Miracles of work and mercy do occur.

PRUNING THE MAGNOLIA

Steele Austin's vulnerability increases even further when he uncovers a scandal that will shake First Church to its very foundation. A most unusual pastoral situation cements him in an irrevocable bond with one of his most outspoken antagonists.

THE PINK MAGNOLIA

Will Steele and Randi leave Falls City? The antagonists have a new plan. A central character dies. You won't want to miss the fourth book in the series.

All of Doctor Maynard's books can be viewed and ordered on his website
WWW.EPISKOPOLS.COM

FORWARD

The people that live in Falls City, Georgia live in most every community in the nation. I have a couple of letters, one from a soldier in Iraq and another from a resident of a small village in England, that suggest these fine citizens just may have universal identities. There appears to be a common consensus from those who delight in living with the people at First Church. *Keep breathing life into them and continue to let the story unfold.*

I've been particularly pleased to learn that the various book clubs and study groups that choose the books in the Magnolia Series for their discussion are beginning to read them Biblically and mythologically. The names of the characters have been chosen with some intent. The various incidents, while resembling real life events in many congregations, also parallel some of the stories recorded in the Bible. It pleases me to know that this underlying message is now being uncovered by these astute readers.

While it has been my hope to entertain through these stories, it has also been my hope that they would lead to self reflection and, if possible, congregational reflection. More than one reader has asked me if the fictional travails experienced by Father Austin mirror those of a priest serving a parish in today's world. Let me answer that question by sharing some very disturbing statistics. Gene Wood in his book Leading Turn Around Churches offers the following observations. *Thirteen hundred Christian pastors are forced to resign their parishes every month. These pastors are forced to do so without cause and often under a cloud of rumor and insinuation. Another twelve hundred pastors voluntarily leave the ministry every month, citing stress, church related issues, family issues, or burnout.*

The wounds inflicted by contemporary ministry are felt not only by the clergy, but by their families as well. Sixty-seven percent of clergy spouses express dissatisfaction with their marriages. Clergy divorce rates have risen sixty-five percent over the past twenty years. The burnout rate is at an all time high. Only fifty percent of those ordained complete their working years as pastors. Fifty percent of seminary graduates remain in parish ministry less than five years. Seventy percent of pastors state that they do not have a close personal friend, and that, as a consequence, live extremely lonely lives. Seventy-one percent of pastors report having financial problems. Thirty percent of all pastors, through no fault of their own, are formally forced to resign their parishes at least one time in their ministry. And last, but not least, seventy percent of all churches that have forced a pastor to resign once have a seventy percent chance of doing so again.

So what does all that have to do with a series of novels on a fictional congregation in Falls City, Georgia? The answer is, quite simply, everything! If these novels can provide both clergy and people a safe way to do some self examination, then these stories transcend the realm of entertainment. If entire congregations will read them and, in the process, take a closer look at their own behavior, then perhaps in some small way the above numbers might be reversed. For this to happen, however, these novels must not just be read. They must also be discussed!

Do you remember in John's Gospel the story of Jesus healing the blind man? Jesus touched the man and then asked him, "Can you see?" He replied, "Yes, I can see people, but they look like trees." So Jesus touched him a second time. He then asked him again, "Now can you see?" The man responded, "Yes, I can see people as God sees them."

It is my fervent intent that the characters on these pages might help us begin to see one another as God sees us. The great difficulty with this challenge is that all of us can easily spot other folks that we know on these pages. Few us of will recognize ourselves. We may not see ourselves in one of the primary characters. We could be one of the silent and unseen in the multitude that simply stands back and allows evil to triumph over good. If the characters on these pages motivate us to confront the forces of evil and practice the charity that we sing about each Sunday morning, then the Church of Jesus Christ and His message of love finds renewed strength.

And now, do you smell that hint of incense in the air? Can you hear the organist begin the prelude? The bells in the tower of First Church are beginning to ring. The greeters are standing at the doors welcoming the worshippers. There are families all dressed in their Sunday best. There are young singles, teenagers, and the elderly leaning heavily on their canes. The people of God are gathering to once again hear the all so familiar story. It's a story that no faithful person grows weary of hearing. It is in the hearing that we find strength, comfort and renewal. Come on in. We're going to sing some familiar hymns, recite prayers we've committed to memory, and eat the holy food. Won't you join me? Hurry! The processional cross is in place. The candles are all lit. Here comes the choir. Let's find a seat. You'll be so glad that you came. I know that I'm glad you're here.

Happy Reading,
Dennis Maynard
Rancho Mirage, California

IF YOU ENJOY READING THIS BOOK,
PLEASE RECOMMEND IT TO A FRIEND!

"Look at those Christians. Look at how much they love one another."

(Pliny, a pagan Roman Governor
that persecuted Christians in the first century.)

BOOK THREE

CHAPTER 1

Every well-bred southern lady knows that the most important meal of the day is breakfast. If the old axiom "the quickest way to a man's heart is through his stomach" contains any truth at all, that pathway is opened first thing each morning for the Falls City's elite. Breakfast is routinely received in the little room just off the kitchen, known as the breakfast room. That is, on all days except when *the help* comes to prepare the morning meal for the family. On those days, breakfast is invariably served in the dining room.

When eating in the breakfast room, the everyday china pattern is used. Cloth napkins are still preferred. A tablecloth on the breakfast table is customary, but placemats of a finer quality are acceptable on occasion. When preparing the morning meal for the breakfast room, the menu can be more simple. Fresh brewed coffee, orange or grapefruit juice, granola with fruit and yogurt, sweet rolls, croissants, or toast and jelly.

Sophisticated ladies and gentlemen always dress for the day before presenting themselves for breakfast. It is the responsibility of the lady of the house to insure that the children, if any, are not only dressed for breakfast but for their day's activities as well. It is customary for a small arrangement of fresh flowers to adorn the table. In season, these can come from the family garden. When flowers are not in season, a standing order for fresh cut flowers can be made with Albert Rawlins. Albert Rawlins Florist is located over on First Street. He is the preferred florist by all the finest families in Falls City. No family of distinction would even consider using any other florist for their social affairs. The morning paper is placed next to the plate of the head of the house. A television set is never permitted in the breakfast room.

Saturday mornings are the only reprieve from this routine. Saturday is golf day. Coffee, juice, and sausage biscuits are the customary menu. The children are permitted to have their favorite cereal, Krispy Kreme Doughnuts, or sweet rolls. The biscuits are often prepared by *the help* the day before and placed in the refrigerator overnight. The lady of the house needs only to bake them in the oven before serving. But even on Saturdays, no one in a proper southern home would think of coming to the breakfast table in their bedroom clothes.

On the mornings that *the help* comes, breakfast in the dining room is a more formal affair. This is the custom in the home of Henry and Virginia Mudd. Shady started working for them right after they were married. She had actually been with Virginia's family for several years. Shady's father and mother had worked for Virginia's parents. Virginia could not recall a time when Shady's family had not been a part of her life. Shady's father had been her parents' driver, gardener, bartender at social affairs, and general repair man. Shady's mother had been Virginia's nanny. She also did all the household chores for her mother. Shady was their only child. She and Virginia would occasionally play together when they were children.

"Good Mawnin', Miss Virginia."

Virginia Mudd smiled at Shady as she poured her a glass of juice and handed it to her. "Is everything ready?"

"Yes'm. I have the dining room all set up just the way you like it. The breakfast is in the silver pieces on the servn' buffet."

Virginia walked into the dining room. The table was properly set with the breakfast china. The Mudds owned three sets of china. One set was adorned with bright blue and pink flowers. This particular set had belonged to Henry's mother and his grandmother before her. Henry's mother had given this particular pattern to Virginia when she and Henry had been married for seven years. The gift of the china was the formal, but unspoken, acknowledgement that Virginia had been officially accepted into the Mudd family. Virginia had instructed Shady to use this pattern during the spring and summer.

The second set of breakfast china had green ivy leaves on it with gold edging. Virginia had chosen this china before she was presented to society. Her grandmother gave it to her the afternoon of her Debutante Ball. This was the china that was used for autumn and winter. If the Mudds were hosting a Sunday buffet after church, they would use their wedding china on those occasions. This was the china that she had listed on the gift registry at Brown's Fine Jewelry Store. It was simply designed, but elegantly appointed, with a small pink rose bud and a gold band. She had received all the pieces she needed as wedding gifts and had returned some of the extra pieces to the store for credit. Virginia actually looked forward to the Sunday occasions when she could use her wedding china. Social occasions gave her the opportunity show off her beautiful home and her exquisite taste in furnishings. Most Sundays, however, the Mudd family would go to the Falls City Country Club for brunch following Sunday services.

Shady could fix the best cheese grits Virginia had ever eaten. She lifted the lid on the silver service containing the grits. Shady watched her expectantly. Virginia tasted the grits. "Shady, just what do you do to these grits?"

"Now, Miss Virginia, you know I can't tell you. My momma got her res'ipe from her grandma. She had to promise never to share it. My momma made me promise the same."

"But Shady, we're just like family. I just know that your momma wouldn't mind if you told me. After all, she practically raised me."

"Now, Miss Virginia," Shady giggled.

Virginia continued to examine the morning meal. She lifted the lid on the silver container holding scrambled eggs and country ham. "Where are the tomatoes?"

Shady wiped her hands on her apron. "They still warmn', Miss Virginia. I just fix'n to go get' em." Shady scurried off to the kitchen and returned with the tomatoes on a silver tray. They were lightly sprinkled with melted parmesan cheese. Virginia watched her set them on the buffet. She then lifted the lid on the silver biscuit box and touched one of the biscuits. "Shady, these biscuits are going to be cold by the time the family presents themselves."

"Yes'm, Miss Virginia. I have some more in the oven." Shady sheepishly glanced at Virginia and then carried the silver biscuit box back to the kitchen. Virginia Mudd watched Shady disappear through the swinging door that separated the breakfast room from the dining room. She knew that she and Shady were the same age, but Shady looked so much older. Virginia smiled as she remembered the times they used to play together in her backyard. Shady lived with her parents in a small cottage behind her parents' family home. Even after Shady's mother died and her father couldn't do much, Virginia's parents continued to let Shady and her father live there.

Shady returned with the biscuit box. "You've done a good job, Shady. Everything looks so nice." A large smile crossed Shady's face. "Thank ya, Miss Virginia."

"Good Morning, Darling." Henry Mudd walked into the dining room and kissed his wife on the cheek. Shady nodded at Henry and then quickly exited back into the kitchen. Henry was dressed in a dark blue suit, starched white shirt, and a maroon bow tie with white polka dots on it. He walked over to the captain's chair at the dining room table. He sat down and picked up the morning paper.

"Good Morning, Mommy. Good Morning, Daddy." The two Mudd children ran into the dining room, hugging first one parent and then the other.

"How are the most beautiful girls in the world?" Henry gushed. "I swear, Virginia; these girls just get prettier and prettier." He kissed each of them on the cheek. "Since you girls insist on being so pretty, I'm just going to have to send you off to boarding school. You know the kind. It's going to be one of those schools with a big electric fence all around it. That way we can protect you from all the boys that are going to want to marry you."

The girls giggled and took their places at the table. "Ohh...Daddy, you're so silly."

"Silly or not, I know what I'm going to have to do. So you just prepare yourselves."

The girls continued to giggle as they unfolded their napkins and placed them on their laps.

Virginia interrupted, "Now, now, settle down. Henry, you know better than to get them all excited before they leave for school."

"Excited or not, I know what I'm going to have to do. Just look at how pretty these girls are getting, Virginia. What choice are they leaving me?"

"Oh Henry, stop it." Virginia opened the door leading into the breakfast room and kitchen. "Shady, the family is ready to be served just as soon as we have grace."

Shady came into the dining room carrying a silver coffee pot in one hand and a pitcher of fresh squeezed orange juice in the other. She stood silently by the door as each member of the family folded their hands and bowed their heads. Henry closed his eyes. The two little Mudd girls squeezed their eyes shut and folded their hands just beneath their chins. Virginia Mudd folded her hands in her lap, but she did not close her eyes. She chose rather to watch her two daughters. She loved them so deeply she was almost moved to tears to see the angelic looks on their faces. Henry used his quiet prayer voice as he whispered, "Bless O' Lord this food to our use and us to your service. Keep us ever mindful of the needs of others. Through Jesus Christ our Lord." The family and Shady all joined in the "Amen".

After Shady had finished pouring the beverages for the family, she then went to the buffet and prepared each of the family members a plate, beginning with Henry. When all were served she returned to the kitchen. The family ate in silence. Henry Mudd looked with heartfelt gratitude on the feast spread before him. He had a beautiful wife. His two sweet daughters completed his family portrait. But even beyond these great joys in his life, Henry thought of his success as an attorney. He was well-known and respected in all the right circles in Falls City. They belonged to all the right clubs and societies. He was a Warden at First Church. He had a beautiful home, friends, and health. His eyes grew misty with gratitude. The good Lord had smiled on Henry Mudd and he was ever so thankful. He then folded the newspaper in thirds so that he could read selected articles while he was eating. When he was finished, he stood and kissed each of the girls on the top of the head. "You girls have a wonderful day at school."

Together they smiled, "And you have a wonderful day at the office, Daddy."

Henry walked over to his wife. "And what do you have planned for this beautiful day, Virginia?"

Virginia shrugged. "Oh, I have a list of errands to run."

"Oh, like what? Will you be coming downtown?"

"Henry, I'm not going to bore you with my list of household duties. I don't want you to concern yourself with my routine. Everything I have to do is so trivial that if I tell you, well…it will just make my life appear so uninteresting."

"I just thought if you were going to be downtown, we could meet for lunch. I've got to meet with that poor excuse for a Rector again. I swear, Virginia, that man hasn't got one redeeming quality. I just don't care for him."

Virginia nodded, "I know what you mean, but it just seems like our every effort to get rid of him fails. What do you have to talk to him about now?"

"Oh, I won't bother you with that either. I know I'm going to be wasting my breath, but I am one of the Church Wardens so I have to do it. God, I just wish I could figure out a way to get rid of that son-. . . ."

"Henry!" Virginia interrupted, "the girls."

He nodded. "I'm sorry, girls. Daddy just gets so exercised sometimes."

"Well, don't do it around the children."

"Yes, darling, your point is well taken." He smiled at her and took her hand and kissed it. "Did you tell me you were going to be downtown?"

"No, I won't be downtown. I have so much on my schedule I just hope I can get it all done before you get home this afternoon."

He kissed her on the cheek. "Don't tire yourself. There's always tomorrow." He kissed her lightly on the lips this time. "I love you."

"And I love you too."

Shady came back into the dining room. "Do you need anything else, Miss Virginia?"

"Yes, Shady, I want you to drive the girls to school. I'll also need you to pick them up today."

"Yes'm. Anything else?"

"No, that's it. You know what needs to be done here at the house today."

"Yes' m."

Virginia stood on the back porch and watched Shady drive her car down the driveway with her smiling daughters in the back seat. She waved at the girls and they waved back until the car turned onto the street and was out of sight.

A strange but familiar warming sensation washed over Virginia Mudd. She smiled with both anticipation and excitement. She hurried up the stairs to the master bath. She quickly undressed. Shady had already drawn her bath water. She only needed to add just a bit of hot water to it. She poured some of her most fragrant oils into the tub and lowered herself into the warm water. Today was Monday. It was the best day of the week. She used an expensive perfumed bar of soap that she had bought at the Nieman Marcus in Atlanta to wash herself. After she dried with a thick towel, she reached into the back of her dressing room drawer and brought out a bottle of perfume she used only on these occasions. She sprayed the bouquet on her chest, her wrists, her legs, and very lightly on her upper thighs. She looked up and got a glimpse of her reflection in the mirror. She smiled back at herself. She liked what she saw. The warm feeling of anticipation lodged in her stomach. She saw the red flush on her chest. She stood and leaned toward the mirror so that she could get a better look at herself. She wanted to look perfect. On these days being beautiful was just not enough. No, she wanted to be radiant. She did not put on any undergarments. She simply pulled her dress over her body. She knew he liked her to come to him that way. She giggled, "Virginia, you look ravishing." She knew that before lunch she would be.

CHAPTER 2

A lot of clergy take Monday off. After the long weekend, many priests believe they need to have a day of relaxation away from the parish. The Reverend Steele Austin thought otherwise. He believed it was in the best interest of the parish for him to be in the office on Mondays. He needed to make sure the staff had their week's assignments before them. He wanted to evaluate the Sunday services while they were still fresh in his mind. He wanted to plan his week with his secretary, Crystal. The two of them had agreed soon after he moved her from receptionist to his secretary that they would keep Mondays free of all appointments. That way he could focus on the mail, telephone calls, and the calendar. Of course, there were always exceptions. Occasionally, there would be a funeral or an important pastoral call he needed to make.

The downside of this arrangement was that with Friday being his designated day off, it was often interrupted by other parish events, socials, or wedding rehearsals. He was seldom afforded the luxury of a full, uninterrupted day off. On more than one occasion, he had been slightly envious of the professionals that enjoyed an entire weekend free of work responsibilities. Many often enjoyed extended three day weekends.

Steele opened his office door and walked over to his desk. Through his office windows he could see the front door of First Church. It was surrounded by a beautiful churchyard that was also a historic cemetery. He could see the fresh flowers that family members would place on the graves of departed loved ones each Sunday. He sat down at his desk and picked up his calendar. He turned in his chair to look out at the portrait that nature had painted just outside his office window. It could easily be a picture on a postcard or calendar. His mind drifted.

"Our lives will be all backwards." He explained to Randi after he asked her to marry him. "Most of the population will be taking weekends off and I'll be working. I won't be home. While most folks are enjoying long family holidays I'll be shifting into full mode to do all the extra services. The only thing I can promise you is that I'll try to make the time I have with you quality time. You'll have my full and undivided attention."

"It doesn't matter to me, Steele." She reassured him. "But can't you take two days off a week? I mean, one day out of seven hardly seems fair. Most weeks you might not even get a full day."

He nodded, "I know, but clergy are still on call twenty-four—seven. Most are only granted one day off a week."

She put her arms around his neck. "Steele Austin, I'd rather have one day with you than seven days with any other man on the face of this earth."

"Excuse me, Father. Are you praying?" Steele was jolted out of his thoughts. He turned his chair to face the familiar voice. It was Crystal.

"No, I was just having some pleasant thoughts. He smiled, "I confess that I was thinking about what it would be like to have a full weekend away from this place."

Crystal blushed with embarrassment. "Father Austin, it's a lot easier to come back down here after you've been away for a couple of days. I really don't know how you do it."

"I'm not sure I do either."

"Here's your mail and your telephone messages. I've put the most important ones on the top." She handed Steele the stack of letters and the familiar pink telephone slips. "There really are only a couple of calls that just have to be returned today, the rest could wait until tomorrow if you want. The first call you need to return is to Bishop Petersen, but you can't call him until tomorrow. His secretary said that he's not in the office on Mondays. He wants to work out the details for his visitation next Sunday. You did remember that his parish visitation is next week?"

Steele nodded. A mischievous look crossed his face, "We did tell the sextons to put extra wax on the floors, didn't we?"

Crystal put her hands over her mouth, "Father Austin…"

Steele laughed, "Oh, don't mind me. I'll return all of these calls today. I prefer to touch paper only one time."

"Do you want to go over your calendar now?"

He nodded and for the next half hour they coordinated his work week. He tried to leave some open spots for her to schedule appointments with people that needed them, but he also blocked out time to study, prepare his sermon, and make his hospital calls.

"Father Austin, may I talk to you confidentially about something?"

Steele looked up from his calendar to study the face of his secretary. It was bright red. He could see that she was very nervous. He thought she was on the verge of tears. Steele stood and walked over to his office door and closed it. "Crystal, let's sit over here. He took a seat on one end of the couch and she sat next to him.

"Father Austin, this has to be held in confidence." Her voice was shaking.

"Whatever you have to say will remain in this office."

"Well, you know that I'm loyal to you."

"You've never given me any reason to question your loyalty."

"Father Austin, what I'm going to say to you comes out of that loyalty."

"Go on."

"A very close friend of mine was at a dinner party the other night. She doesn't go to First Church, but one of our staff members and her husband were there."

She paused and took a deep breath. Tears did well up in her eyes and one dropped down her cheek. Steele pulled a tissue from the box on the sofa table and handed it to her.

"This staff member was saying some very unkind things about you to the people at this dinner party. Some of their guests were from First Church."

"Like what?"

"Well, she was saying that you're not a very spiritual person. She accused you of only being concerned about the business affairs of the church. Her husband said you shouldn't even be a priest. She also told everyone that the staff all agrees with her, but they're afraid of you."

"Do you feel that way, Crystal?"

"Father Austin...absolutely not! I haven't heard that from anyone else on this staff. We all value you as a spiritual leader. I'm not an Episcopalian, but I've learned so much from you. I'm always telling the pastor at my church about all the good things you do over here."

"I appreciate your telling me this, Crystal. I won't repeat it. Do you want to tell me who was saying these things?"

Crystal was silent. She wiped the tears from her cheeks. Steele waited patiently. The only sound in the room was the ticking of the old Ball

School Clock that Steele had hanging on his office wall. It had been a gift to him from a Senior Warden in his former parish.

"Father, that's not all that she said."

"You mean...there was more?"

"Father, if what I've been told is true, this woman and her husband are out to get you."

"Then Crystal, I really need to know which staff member you're talking about."

Again Crystal was silent for several minutes. She stared at her hands which she has nervously folded on her lap. Then she looked up in order to look Steele in the eyes. She whispered, "It was Judith Idle and her husband."

Steele was stunned. "Elmer and Judith? They're always so nice to my face." Judith was one of the first program directors that he had hired. She and her family had been members of the parish when he arrived. They seemed so devoted to the church. They were both very active in several of the parish ministries. He had even asked her husband to consider running for the Vestry. "You said that there was more."

Crystal nodded, "Father, she accused you of using your discretionary fund to give money to Gay Rights organizations and to other liberal political groups."

Steele felt the anger well up inside him. "She's entitled to her opinion as to the quality of my spirituality, but those accusations verge on slander."

Crystal's eyes widened. "I trust my friend to be telling me the truth about what Judith and her husband were saying about you, but you can't repeat what I've said. I need this job and I don't want to be caught in the middle of some big church fight. I just want you to be careful."

"Thanks, Crystal. I know that this was difficult for you. I'll consider it a gift from a friend. I'll keep my eye on her."

Crystal wiped her eyes.

"Why don't you step into my private bathroom over there and wash your face before you go back to your desk? Take your time." And with that he hugged her and thanked her again. She hugged him back.

Steele went back to his desk and sorted through his mail. A large white envelope caught his attention. The return address was for a law firm in San Antonio, Texas. He opened it. Inside was a letter from

Charles Gerard, Search Committee Chair for St. Jude's Episcopal Church. The brief note welcomed Steele into their discernment process. It asked him to complete the enclosed questionnaire and return it to them in the accompanying postage-paid envelope as soon as possible.

The questionnaire contained only four questions.

1. *Describe your relationship with Jesus Christ.*
2. *Tell us why you believe God is calling you into the discernment process with St. Jude's Parish.*
3. *How do you think the Church should respond to the contemporary issues of sexuality which are so controversial?*
4. *Have you ever done anything in your life for which you are ashamed? If so, what have you learned from it?*

He was distracted from the paper by Crystal opening the bathroom door and walking back into his office. He had almost forgotten she was in there. "You look much less stressed."

"Thanks, Father Austin." She smiled. "And what we talked about?"

"Crystal, I appreciate everything you told me. No one will ever know that you shared that information with me."

"My friend said she was willing to tell you herself if you needed."

"Thanks. I'll keep that in mind."

Just then his private line rang. He picked it up. There were only a half dozen people that had the number for the direct line into his office.

"Hey, handsome."

"Hey yourself, beautiful lady."

"What are you doing?"

"I was just reading over the questionnaire from San Antonio."

"And what do you think?"

"Actually, I'm quite impressed by their questions, but I'm having second thoughts. I mean, do we really want to move to San Antonio? Randi, I've just gotten some of the outreach projects started here and I want to make sure that they'll be able to sustain themselves. The parish is doing well. And we now have some good friends in this town. I don't know anymore. I mean, Falls City is beginning to feel a little bit like home."

"Listen to me, Cowboy. I'll do whatever you want to do. There are lots of things I like about this place. Travis has his play group and I've got my girlfriends. If you want to stay here for a little longer, then let's just do it. Moving is always risky. You never know what you're going to get. Just remember what my daddy always says."

Steele chuckled, "Oh, which one of his pearls of wisdom would that be?"

"Oh you think you're so funny. You'll recall him pointing his finger at me and saying, 'Remember, not everything that glitters is gold.' "

"Then, you won't mind if I just focus on First Church and forget about San Antonio?"

"As long as I'm with the men I love it doesn't matter to me."

"Men? What men? Is there something you need to tell me?"

"You and Travis, Father Insecurity."

"I've got to go. What time will you be home?"

"Around five, I hope. See you then."

Steele took another look at the welcoming letter and the questionnaire. He placed the letter on the corner of his desk. He planned to hand write a response asking to be removed from the process. He tossed the questionnaire into the trash can next to his desk.

He was just about to return his first telephone call of the morning when Henry Mudd walked into his office. Crystal was close behind him. She asked, "Mister Mudd, do you have an appointment? I try to keep Father Austin's calendar clear on Mondays. Did I forget to write your appointment on his calendar? I'm so sorry if I did."

Henry Mudd stopped and looked back at her. "No, I didn't have an appointment. And as the Junior Warden of this parish I shouldn't need one." Crystal stepped back sheepishly.

Steele stood and motioned to her with his hand. "It's okay, Crystal. I'll make time for the Junior Warden." Crystal walked out of the office, once again on the verge of tears, and shut the door behind her.

"What can I do for you, Henry?"

"I'm going to make this brief, Parson."

"Henry, Parson is a perfectly acceptable word, but I get the feeling that when you use it I'm not being complimented."

Henry sat down opposite Steele's desk. "I'll leave the compliments to your liberal fan club."

"Let's just get this over with. What do you need to say to me?" Steele had developed just about as much distaste for this man as he knew that he had for him.

"It's come to my attention that your staff is afraid of you."

Steele felt the anger well up in his chest, but he bit back a response. Thanks to Crystal, he now knew exactly where those sentiments were coming from.

Henry started pointing his finger at him as though Steele were a hostile witness in one of Henry's trials. "Not only are they afraid of you, but your staff is starving for spiritual guidance. I don't have to tell you, Misturh Austin, that I don't think you're a very spiritual person. I don't even think you should be wearing a collar. You'd be much better off running a dress shop or a bar for your queer friends."

Steele was restraining his anger. "Is that all?"

"No surh, that's not all." Henry stood and was cowering over Steele. "I have it on good authority that you're using church funds to support homosexual organizations and other liberal political groups. You need to know that I plan to ask the Vestry to investigate."

Steele exploded. "Now listen to me, I've already had my funds investigated twice by you guys and the only thing you've been able to come up with is some lame reference to my record keeping and using better judgment. You and I both know that means I've done nothing illegal and that you guys just don't approve of my discretion."

Henry smirked. "Correction, Surh. They're not your funds. They're church funds. You administer them, true. But if I find out that these accusations are true, then you're out of here; there won't be anyone who can help you."

Steele stood to respond. He was furious.

Henry held up his hand. "That's all. I'll let myself out. I'll see you at the next meeting of the Vestry, Misturh Austin. That is, if there is a next Vestry meeting for you." He then spun around and headed for the door. He opened it and then slammed it behind him.

Steele sat back in his chair. Absolutely all of the energy was drained out of him. He just could not figure out why that jerk could get to him the way he did. He then thought about doing battle with that gang yet one more time. Henry, Ned Boone, the Bishop, and the Vestry united in their battle against him for yet another round. He closed his eyes in an effort to pray. No words came to him so he just sat in silence listening to the rhythm of his own breathing. When he opened his eyes, he was staring at the trash can. The questionnaire from San Antonio was the only piece of paper in it. He reached down and retrieved it. He placed it on his desk, picked up his pen and started filling it out.

CHAPTER 3

If Lakeland, Alabama could ever grow up, it would be the sister city to Falls City, Georgia. The little community itself was built around a man made lake. It was composed mainly of blue collar workers who were there to take care of the needs of the weekend and seasonal residents. The financially well-healed from Falls City and a couple of the larger communities on the Florida border own vacation homes in Lakeland. They keep their boats in their private boat houses adjacent to their weekend homes to use for fishing and water skiing. During the week and in the winter, the homes around the lake are for the most part empty.

Virginia Mudd had a girlfriend that owned one such home. She was the only other person in all of Falls City that knew the darker side of Virginia. If push came to shove, Virginia knew she didn't really have much in common with Alicia Thompson. They weren't of the same social class and moved in totally different circles. They met at the home of a mutual acquaintance several years ago. They had enjoyed their conversation with each other that night and agreed to go to lunch the next day. That's when they learned that they had one particular thing in common. They both shared a love of the smoke.

Henry knew that Virginia had experimented with marijuana when she was in college, but he had no idea that she still craved it. He would not approve. She would go over to Alicia's when Henry was out of town. Alicia always had a joint that they could share and then they would laugh through their haze as they cleaned out a box of chocolates or a gallon of ice cream. Alicia was one of the people that she could complain to about Henry.

Alicia had been married twice. Both marriages were brief and ended in nasty divorces when each husband had caught her with other men. Currently she was in a long term relationship with a man who would occasionally sleep over. They could take trips together, but marriage was not an option that either of them wanted to consider. They had a comfortable arrangement. Alicia believed that Henry had been a mistake for Virginia. She knew that Virginia loved him for the good father and provider that he was, but she was not in love with him. For that reason, she could empathize when Virginia would magnify his acts of neglect or questionable comments that he made to her. She could listen to Virginia vent about Henry and understand. She didn't mind covering for Virginia so that she could be with her lover. In some twisted way, Alicia believed that by helping Virginia hide her secret from Henry she was getting even with all the men that had hurt her.

"Henry is good to me most of the time." Virginia would whine. "But he expects me to run the household on a budget. Can you believe that? A budget! I've asked him for a larger clothing allowance, but he refused. It would be nice if he'd just give me ten thousand dollars every now and then to spend any way that I want. He has it. He could do it. I mean, is that asking so much? He could give me ten thousand or even twenty-five thousand a couple of times a year to spend. And he could do it without asking me any questions about how I spend it."

"Well, I wouldn't put up with that." Alicia always told Virginia exactly what she wanted to hear. She never disagreed with Virginia when she critiqued Henry. "Men are such fools. They're so stupid. I just hate it when they think that we're the dumb ones. Why don't you leave him?"

"And go where? He really does take good care of me. It's just there are times I can't even stand to look at him. When he touches me, my skin literally crawls. I make every excuse I can come up with to keep from having sex with him. When I have to do it with him, I try to get it over with as quickly as possible. If he tries to prolong anything I just pull him over on top of me. He thinks that I can't wait for him. If he only knew what I was really thinking. Still, he's a good father. I can't hurt my girls."

Alicia was the only other person in Falls City that knew about her affair with Jacque. She had even brought her lover over to Alicia's house for dinner when Henry was busy or out of town. The three of them would share a joint and a quiet evening of conversation. Alicia would often encourage Virginia and Jacque to take advantage of her guest room before leaving.

As Virginia's car reached the outskirts of Lakeland, she recalled the first time that she met Jacque Chappelle. The Howard Dexters at First Church had invited Henry and her to go to the Magnolia Club for dinner. The Dexters were big supporters of the Falls City Art Museum. Jacque

Chappelle was the new Museum Director. He had just gotten into town and didn't know anyone. They wanted him to meet the Mudds.

When Virginia saw Jacque for the first time she was enamored by his boyish good looks. His French accent only added to his mystique. Virginia was seated next to him at dinner. Jacque stared intently into her eyes when they conversed. A couple of times she actually forgot that there were other people at the table. Halfway through the main course she decided to risk it. She slipped her heel off and with her toes found Jacque's pants cuff. She lifted his cuff with her foot and massaged his ankle with her toes. He met her stare and smiled at her. She then lifted her dress up over her knees. She reached over and took the hand he had resting in his lap on his napkin and placed it on her leg. He caressed her leg ever so gently. She whispered in Jacque's ear, "I don't have any panties on." She looked at the other dinner guests. Henry was engaged in a conversation with their host and hostess. He was not aware of the flirtations going on in his very presence. That excited her all the more.

She pulled into the driveway of Alicia's lake house. Jacque's car was not here yet. The radio was playing, "Lady, oh lady, do you have cheating on your mind?" She leaned her head back against her seat and listened to the lyrics. "A man can always tell when a woman is on the move," the radio blared. She chuckled, "Every man in the world but Henry. God, he's so stupid." Then, there were days when Virginia Mudd thought all men were stupid. On this, she and Alicia were in total agreement.

She turned the rear-view mirror so that she could check her lipstick and mascara. She wanted to look her best for Jacque. She remembered that night after dinner at the Magnolia Club; she hadn't been able to sleep. She asked Henry on the way home what he thought of Jacque. "I like him." Henry had replied. "He seems like a real nice fellow for a Frenchman. I hope he does a good job at the Museum. It does need some help. I do find it strange that such a strapping young man isn't married. Do you think he might be queer, Virginia?"

If there was one thing that Virginia was sure of it was that Jacque was not a queer. He was all man. She called him at the Museum the next morning after Henry had left for work and Shady had taken the girls to school. They had agreed to meet for lunch. He insisted on preparing lunch for her at his apartment. He gave her the address. They never got around to eating. She fell into his arms as soon as he opened the door.

The passion between them ignited a fire deep inside her. It was their first Monday together. That was almost three years ago.

Jacque's car pulled up beside her. When he stepped out, her heart skipped a beat. The very sight of him brought a smile to her face. He was wearing a tight turtleneck sweater that showed off his trim midsection. He came over and opened her car door.

"Hello, beautiful."

"Do you have one?"

He smiled, "I have a couple. I also have a little surprise for you."

She squealed with laughter. "Oh, that's no surprise. I'm quite familiar with that, or have you forgotten since last week?"

"No, my love. Not that. Although, I do plan to give that to you at least twice." He held out his hand. There were a couple of pills in the palm of his hand.

"What are they?"

"Something one of the artists gave me. They will enhance our pleasure."

"Oh, goody, goody." She felt just like a naughty school girl.

She handed him the keys to the lake house. He opened the door. They walked through the living room and directly into the master suite. She went into the bathroom and closed the door. She wanted to make sure she was ready for him. She undressed and then finished her preparations by spraying her abdomen and upper thighs one more time with the perfume that she had in her purse.

When she opened the door he was already naked and sitting on the bed. He was lighting the joint. He stared at her. "God, you're absolutely gorgeous."

The odor from the marijuana cigarette filled the bedroom. She loved that smell. She loved the way he looked at her. She loved the way he made her feel about herself. She couldn't help but contrast his body to Henry's. Jacque was trim. He went to the gym on a regular basis. He didn't have one bit of fat on him. He was not muscular, but slender. His body actually reminded her of an adolescent boy. He had no chest hair. Henry, on the other hand, was soft. The hair on his chest and back was unruly. His idea of exercise was a round of golf with several drinks and a big meal in the clubhouse afterwards. His waist often drooped over his pants. Henry wore ugly boxer shorts. Jacque wore no under shorts at all.

Virginia came out of the bathroom completely naked. She loved getting naked for Jacque. She delighted in the way that he looked at her. It just wasn't the same with Henry. She would come out of her dressing room completely unclothed. Henry would hardly glance up from the legal papers he would routinely bring home with him. Virginia had fantasized about getting naked for other men. Then, she realized she really only wanted to get naked for Jacque. She slid under the sheet next to him. He handed her the joint. She took a long drag on the cigarette and held the smoke in her lungs before exhaling. She coughed a bit while releasing the smoke.

"Did you check to make sure he's where he said he was going to be?" Jacque inquired.

"Yes, my little worry wart. I called the Rector's Office. The Rector's secretary said that he was in a meeting with Father Austin. I then called his office. His secretary said that his ten o'clock appointment was waiting on him. Did you make sure you weren't followed?"

"No one followed me. I'm sure of that."

She placed her hand on his chest and felt its hardness. "Jacque, as long as we have been coming up here no one has ever seen us. The only person that knows about us is Alicia, and I trust her not to tell anyone. She's my friend. As for Henry, well, he's just so pathetic. He's just plain dumb."

He put his hand behind her head and brought her lips to his. She opened her mouth to welcome his tongue. She lay back against the pillow. She put her arm around his waist and pulled him over on her.

They rested for a while. They ate a couple of candy bars that he had brought for them and talked about the Museum and some of the things that he was trying to do with it.

"What about the pills?"

"Oh, I almost forgot them. One of the artists that has some pieces in the current exhibit gave them to me. He said that they will really add to our pleasure. He swallowed one and gave her the other. He got up and filled a glass at the bathroom sink. He handed it to her. She swallowed it and drank the water. He stood beside her. She could not wait for the pill to work. She reached for him and brought him to her.

They showered together and she put on a change of clothes that she brought with her. She did not want to take any chances that Henry would smell him on her. She and Jacque had agreed long ago to always wear companion perfume and cologne when they were together, but still she didn't want to take any chances.

Jacque left first. She gave him a ten minute head start before leaving. It gave her time to think. It was these Mondays with Jacque that made her marriage tolerable. She knew that she wasn't in love with Henry and she wasn't sure if she was in love with Jacque. She just knew that she needed these Mondays with Jacque. She missed him when they couldn't be together. But it wasn't just him. It was having someone to share a joint with. He was someone that made her feel good about herself. Jacque made her feel special. She felt like a woman when she was with him. With Henry, she was simply playing a role. She was a dutiful wife. She was a faithful church member. She was a community volunteer. She was an upstanding and responsible leader in the city. She was one of the finest citizens Falls City had to offer. But, oh God, with Jacque she could be Virginia.

As she drove home, she had the increasingly familiar conversation with herself. Why didn't she feel guilty? Clearly, she was violating her marriage vows. If Henry ever found out what she was doing he would divorce her and take the girls away from her as well. But she was careful. She did everything in her power to make sure that Henry never found out. That was her only real worry. She just needed to make sure that he didn't discover her secret.

As she turned onto the street leading to their house, she turned the rear view mirror to look at herself. She wanted to make sure that there were no signs or smells of Jacque on her. She had just had a wonderful day with a friend. She told herself that she deserved it. She was a good wife to Henry. She took care of his house and his children. She supported him in his career. She was a good person. She did all the things that her church and community asked of her. There was no reason for her to feel guilty. Besides, Henry had hurt her feelings on more than one occasion. He did not always do the things for her that a woman needs to have done for her. Sometimes he was just so moody. He would get in dark spells and not talk to her. No, she wasn't doing anything wrong. After all, she was entitled to have some fun. She and Jacque were consenting adults. She wasn't hurting anyone. What Henry didn't know wouldn't hurt him.

She turned into the driveway leading to the garage in the back of their house. Henry's car was parked in the garage. She pulled up beside it. She froze. The warm glow that she had known all day with Jacque was now replaced with anxiety. Her hands were shaking as she turned off the engine. "What's wrong with you, Virginia?" She uttered. "You haven't done anything wrong. You've simply had a nice day with a friend. Besides, it's your body. You can do whatever you want to with it. You don't have to have some man telling you what you can or cannot do. Now get hold of yourself." Henry came to the back door. "Are you okay?" He called to her. "Do you need me to help you carry anything in out of the car?"

Suddenly, she felt the need to do something nice for him. She knew exactly what she would do. She would have Shady fix him his favorite foods for dinner.

CHAPTER 4

Here are the deposit slips from the money counters." Crystal walked into Steele's office and placed the deposit slips on his desk. There were separate deposits for endowment funds, the operating account, the memorial funds, and the funds administered by the Rector. Steele glanced down at them and frowned.

"Is everything in order, Father Austin?"

"I think so." He picked up the deposit for the operating account and examined it more closely. "Are the money counters still here?"

"No, they all left some time ago. They put these slips in your mailbox as they were leaving."

"Thanks, Crystal. Is Doctor Drummond still here?"

"I think so, I just saw him in the staff break room a few minutes ago."

"Will you please ask him to see me before he leaves for the day?"

"Anything else I can do for you, Father? It's past five o'clock and I really should be getting on home to my husband."

Steele waved at her. "No, that's all I need. You go on home. All of this work will be waiting on us tomorrow. I'll see you in the morning."

Steele reached into the file drawer in his desk. It contained the monthly financial statements the business manager had generated for the Vestry over the last few quarters. He also had the deposit slips from the money counters in it. He had been adding up the deposit slips the past few weeks for the operating account and found that there was a discrepancy between the total amount of the receipts being reported to the Vestry and the amounts recorded on the deposit slips.

"You wanted to see me, boss?" Horace Drummond knocked on Steele's open door and walked into his office. He seated himself in the chair opposite Steele's desk. Horace Drummond was the associate that Steele had called to oversee the various outreach ministries he had started with the income from the Chadsworth Alexander Endowment Funds. Horace's salary and allowances were also being paid out of the endowment. That was the one saving grace that had made his ministry at First Church possible. Not only was Doctor Drummond an African American priest, but within months of his arrival, he fell in love with and married Almeda Alexander, one of the wealthiest white women in Falls City. His call and subsequent marriage had created quite a stir.

Steele was amused to hear Almeda's seduction of Horace described for him by one of the the ladies of the Altar Guild. Her description was succinct. "Father Austin," she said breathlessly. "Almeda Alexander just plucked him like a chicken!"

"How's it going, Horace?" Steele walked across the room and closed his office door. He returned to his seat behind his desk.

"Did I do something that displeased you?"

"No, not at all. Why would you ask that?"

"Well, when the boss asks to see you after office hours and then closes the door to the office when you get there...gosh, Steele, what would you think?"

Steele laughed. "Oh, quite the contrary. I need your counsel." Steele and Horace had become much more than working associates. They had become best friends. They were each other's confidants and confessors. Steele loved Horace Drummond as though he were his very own brother.

"What's bothering you?"

"I need to get your take on a couple of staff issues. It goes without saying that this conversation remains between us."

"As always."

"Give me your impression of Judith Idle."

"Well, she is certainly impressed with her own righteousness."

"And as a staff member."

"Frankly, Steele, I know enough to tell you that she is not one your supporters."

"Do you think she's dangerous?"

Horace was silent. He closed his eyes. Steele thought that he was praying. He hated putting him on the spot this way, but he knew that Horace would give him a straight answer. After a couple of minutes, Horace opened his eyes and looked directly at Steele. "You know, friend, when I was ordained thirty years ago, people would stand up when a priest or a bishop entered the room. It's just not that way any more. The bishops were quite literally our fathers in God and priests were respected members of the family. Things have changed. I guess we don't have anyone to blame for a lot of that but ourselves. I do think that there's one thing that must never change."

"What's that?"

"There can only be one Rector in a parish and any staff member that can't be loyal to that Rector needs to be removed."

"And Judith Idle is one of them?"

"If I were sitting in your chair, I would fire her."

"Just like that."

"No, I think you're going to have to figure out a way to make it her idea to resign."

"You think she's really that dangerous?"

"I think she and her husband are venomous. Their self-righteousness gives them the platform they need to work their own agenda in this congregation. A lot of people in this parish and some of the staff are blinded by her pretense of holiness. A lot of folks describe her as sweet. But frankly, Steele, she's just too much sugar for a nickel. Personally, I think the Idles are the most dangerous enemies you have in this place. I don't have to remind you that it was the self-righteous that crucified the Lord."

Steele leaned back in his chair and folded his hands behind his neck. "Wow, I think you're way ahead of me on this one. What's their agenda?"

"Anything that can get folks worked up enough to oppose you." Horace laughed, "Heck, Steele, the woman has to punctuate every other sentence with a *praise Jesus.* Does that sound like the type of spirituality you're teaching at First Church? Frankly, I don't trust anyone who wants to use Jesus to further a vindictive agenda."

Steele knew she had a holier than thou attitude about her, but so did her husband. He had a more difficult time with her husband since he had heard from some pretty reliable sources that he had a girlfriend up in Savannah. He had also been told that he was quite the player when he went on golfing trips with his buddies.

Steele's thoughts were interrupted by the sound of Horace's deep laughter. "Horace, you even laugh like you just swallowed an altar rail. I swear if I had your deep stained glass voice I would rule the world. Now, just what part of my misery right now do you find funny?

"Elmer...that's his name. I mean have you ever thought about his name...Elmer Idle? You realize that one of my hobbies is to match people up with cartoon characters."

"Now that's an interesting pastime for a priest."

"It's one of my sanity exercises. I find it to be quite helpful, especially when I encounter a difficult personality. Let's take Elmer Idle, for example. You know which cartoon character I've associated with him?"

Steele chuckled, "Pray tell and don't hold back."

"Elmer Fudd."

Steele laughed. "Darned if I don't think that's a perfect match."

"Except for the fact that I think I've insulted Elmer Fudd. In my opinion, Elmer Fudd is smarter and better looking."

Steele chuckled. "Remind me to never get on your dark side. I would hate to think about which cartoon character you would choose for me."

"Oh, that's an easy one. It came to me the first time I ever met you. You're faster than a bullet, more powerful than a speeding locomotive, and able to leap tall buildings in a single bound."

With that they both lost themselves in laughter. "And, Judith... which character would you choose for her?"

"Easy one. Miss Piggy."

"Damn, Horace. I never thought about it, but you're absolutely right. But enough of this passive aggressive relief, I've got to decide what to do with her."

Horace leaned forward in his chair. "Steele, she's dangerous. Both of them are. They may be the most dangerous foes you have in this parish. Not only is she on the staff, but he's running for the Vestry. It's like having enemy spies at the campfire."

"Yes, and I invited them to come to the tribal dance." Steele put his finger to his temple and pretended to pull a trigger.

"The thing that I think makes them the most dangerous is that they have convinced most everyone in this parish that they are Super Christians. It's next to impossible to cast ulterior motives on people who would have you think they were the honored guests at the Last Supper."

Steele nodded. "I need to ask you about Ted Holmes."

"What about him?" Horace looked confused. "He appears to work really hard. He's always here. I could be wrong, but I think he's the first one here in the morning and the last one to leave at night. He's even here on Sunday mornings. I don't know much more to say about him than that. Does he ever take a day off?"

"I know that he's taken a few three day weekends since I've been here, but you're right. He appears to be very diligent."

"Hasn't he been here longer than any other staff person?"

"I think that's right. I believe I saw in his personnel file that he had been here almost fifteen years when I came. They promoted him from bookkeeper to business manager. I could be wrong, but I'm not sure he's ever taken a vacation."

"Like I said, he certainly gives the impression of being a hard worker. He's never uttered a single word to me about you. But then, if he didn't like you, he would know better than to say anything to me. Why are you asking about him?"

Steele opened the folder that was on his desk. He showed Horace the discrepancy between the deposit slip totals he was getting from the money counters and the amounts reported on the Vestry financial statements over the past few months. Horace whistled, "Have you asked him about them?"

"Not just yet. I wanted to see if there was a pattern."

"You realize that there could be a perfectly sound explanation for all this. I have to admit that accounting is not my long suit."

Steele nodded. "I know. I just wanted to run this past someone. You're the first person I've shared my suspicions with."

"I guess I would hope for the best and see if he can't give you a reasonable explanation. The accounting types all speak their own language when it comes to financial statements."

"I hope you're right. I guess I should give him the benefit of the doubt. He's always been very cooperative and he's worked well with me on most everything I've asked him to do."

"Anything else on your mind, boss?"

"No, that's enough."

"I'd better get home to Almeda. She's made her favorite thing for dinner tonight."

"Oh, what's that?"

"Reservations."

"Sounds like you're adapting to married life."

"My friend, I couldn't be happier. She's a wonderful woman. I never dreamed that I would have these feelings at my age. Steele, I feel just like a young man in love. I am absolutely smitten by the woman."

"You give us all hope. I'm really happy for both of you. Now go on home before you get us both in trouble with her."

After Horace left, Steele studied the deposit slips and the totals some more. He looked at the financial statements. He was just about ready to close the folder and go home himself when his eye fell on the balance sheet for the last month. He compared the balance sheet to the budget statement. His heart skipped a beat. His instincts were telling him that the numbers were just not adding up.

CHAPTER 5

Almeda Alexander Drummond was one of the happiest women on the face of the earth. She simply could not stop smiling. She went to sleep each night nestled in the arms of the man she loved. No, she not only loved him, but she was in love with him. The feelings running through her since Horace Drummond entered her life were like none she had ever known. She was now able to compare the love that she held for her departed Chadsworth with the love she had longed for in her life. Horace had filled the emptiness that had haunted her first marriage.

Almeda pulled her car into the First Church parking lot. A few years ago she had appointed herself the custodian of the church grounds. Steele Austin confirmed her appointment with the Vestry not long after he arrived. She shuddered as she recalled the cruel reception that she had given Steele and his sweet wife Randi. She regretted every ill thought and betrayal. Steele and Randi were now her closest friends. She had asked both of them to forgive her.

She walked through the churchyard past Chadsworth's grave. She stopped for just a moment. She used to bring fresh flowers to put on his grave each week, but since her marriage to Horace she had ceased that practice. She had discussed the matter with Horace. While he had no objection to her continuing to do so on a weekly basis, she had given considerable thought to the matter. She concluded that it would be best if she resorted to the socially acceptable practice of honoring his burial place only at Easter and Christmas.

Her eye was drawn to Willie's grave. Willie had been the janitor at the church for years. That alone was enough reason for him not to be buried in the exclusive First Church Cemetery, but he was also a neg... Almeda caught herself and grimaced. She strained to get a closer look at Willie's grave. It had a big wreath of plastic flowers on it. She felt herself bristle. On this one, she and Steele had not been able to agree. In spite of the Vestry resolution to the contrary, Willie's family continued to put plastic flowers on his grave. Most of the respectable people in the parish still had not gotten over the fact that Steele had buried the black sexton in the churchyard…and then it hit her. Where would she and Horace be buried? She felt ill. She would need to discuss this with Horace. Had she not married again she would have been buried in the Alexander family plot next to her husband. Horace's first wife was buried in Washington D.C. Perhaps he would want to be buried next to her. No! She stomped her foot. No, Horace was her husband. She loved him as she had never loved Chadsworth. She wanted to be buried next to Horace. "Oh, I'll just think about that tomorrow." She uttered out loud. "But, Horace and I will have to sort this out."

Spring in south Georgia is particularly beautiful. Spring in the yard of First Church is magnificent. The wisteria was in full bloom. The purple blossoms wrapped through some of the live oaks and dropped carelessly through the branches. The Spanish moss hanging from the branches of the magnolias only added to the floral tribute. The azaleas and dogwoods had been strategically placed by professional landscapers long ago. Now, in their maturity, the churchyard became a portrait. It was not at all unusual to see local and visiting artists sitting in the churchyard in front of easels with paintbrushes in hand.

Almeda continued her inspection of the church grounds. Everything appeared to be in order. There really wasn't much for her to do. It was still a bit early to plant the summer annuals. She took a seat on one of the benches near the fountain next to the gate leading into the cemetery. Once again her eyes fell on Chadsworth's grave. She had tricked him into marrying her. They conceived two children together, but she had even timed those very rare seductions in their marriage as to best insure their success. She had multiple lovers throughout their life together. It was only after his death that she learned his secret. She had been married to a gay man for the greater portion of her life.

A tear dropped down her cheek. She reached into her jacket sleeve and brought out the silk hankie she had hidden there earlier. She dabbed her eyes. She and Chadsworth had only been playing at marriage. They were pretending. All those years they had been living a lie. Chadsworth had not been true to himself. She had been playing a role. And their marriage had been a farce. Love him? Of course she did. She loved him as a friend and a companion. She loved him for providing for her. And she loved him for the person that he was. He was kind and generous.

Just then she saw Horace walking from the church over to the office building. He did not see her, but just the sight of him brought a smile to her face. She had never planned on feeling the way she did about him. In truth, she had never known the kind of love that she had for him. She didn't even know that such a love existed except in romance novels. Long ago she had dismissed those as feminine fantasies. Now she knew her feelings to be true.

She loved the way Horace made her feel about herself. He really did bring out the best in her. She felt beautiful when he looked at her. His touch made her feel wanted and desired. And she felt so secure in his arms when he held her.

A passing car honked at her and the driver waved. She turned to see that it was Mary Alice Smythe. She waved back. Mary Alice was pulling into the church driveway. Mary Alice had been the Altar Guild Directress at First Church for as long as Almeda could remember. She parked her car next to the sacristy in the parking spaces reserved for the ladies who had altar duty.

Almeda turned back to her thoughts. She had not intended to fall in love with a black man. There were two black men among her many lovers during her marriage to Chadswoth, but if truth be told, she held some deep prejudices against them. Both of them had been quite handsome and very muscular. She knew that she had bedded them in an effort to hurt Chadsworth. But how had she hurt Chadsworth? He never knew about them, or did he? She shook her head. Before Horace she would have been among the first to repeat all the negative stereotypes about black men. Horace had changed all that.

She caught herself smiling once again. She stood and decided to continue her inspection of the grounds. This morning she had put on a hat with a full brim around it. Horace liked her in hats. He encouraged her to wear them. The sun felt good on her cheeks. She removed the hat so that she could enjoy the sun's warmth all the more. Her walk brought her to the large magnolia tree standing in front of First Church. It was a magnificent specimen. She noted that there was quite a mess underneath it. She leaned down for a closer look. It appeared that someone had actually been sleeping underneath the tree. She put her hands on her hips. "Well, this will have to be corrected."

Almeda stood back so that she could better study the situation. She cupped the elbow of her right arm in her left hand. Then she thumped her fingers on her cheek. "What to do, what to do?" She rehearsed in her mind the various solutions to the problem of the magnolia tree. Through the decades the tree branches had been left to grow from the ground level up. She approached the tree and lifted one of the branches. All the dead leaves and blossoms from the past several years lay in a big mess at the base of the tree. She stood back so she could study it further. Then an idea came to her. She knew exactly what needed to be done. She would have all the branches trimmed up the tree trunk for the first four or five feet. By doing that, the area underneath could be kept clean. It would be a different look for the tree, but it was her decision that the pruning was necessary. It would be easier for the yardmen to clean underneath it. Yes, it would be a different look, but the pruning would produce a cleaner look for the entrance to the church. She would stop by the office and inform the Rector that, as chair of the garden committee, she had made this decision.

She seated herself once again on the park bench near the magnolia tree. She turned her face to the sun. She closed her eyes. Her face soaked in the warmth. Not everyone had accepted her marriage to Horace. They had hosted a party on New Year's Eve. She was pleased that absolutely everyone on the list that she'd invited had at least made a brief appearance. She was careful not to invite anyone that she didn't expect to attend. She also knew that several came out of social courtesy mixed with a large dose of curiosity.

The first social rejection she'd received after her marriage to Horace was from the governing board of The Magnolia Club. The letter was brief and to the point. It simply reminded her that The Magnolia Club is a men's club and that wives of members enjoy limited privileges in the club through their husband's membership. Since her husband was now departed and she had remarried a man who was not a member of the club, her privileges were revoked.

She did not show the letter to Horace. She reasoned that it was not a big loss since women were afforded such limited access to the club anyway. She was unsure just how they would respond to invitations to be dinner guests at the club. The same would be true if they were asked to attend a wedding reception. So far, that had not been a problem. Absolutely no one had invited them to have dinner with them at the club. By the same token, Horace had not been asked to do any weddings that would require their presence. She frowned. It came to her that Horace had not been asked to do any weddings at First Church. She so wanted him to be accepted. She did not want him to be hurt. She would have to have a word with the Rector on that matter as well.

The second letter came with a check for fifty thousand dollars. It was from the manager of the Falls City Country Club. The letter was equally clear and to the point. The board of the club had amended its by-laws. When a member's spouse died or there was a divorce the board would refund the couple's initiation fee. The surviving member or members would then need to reapply to the club for membership. The letter concluded with a reminder that the club has very strict membership standards. She had not shown Horace this letter either.

She had not heard from the Women's Club, the Cotillion or the Debutante Society. She had not been asked to be the one of the spring trainers for the Junior League. This disappointed her since she had been a trainer for the Junior League for most of her adult life in Falls City. Mary Alice Smythe did offer to step aside and name her as President of the Altar Guild. She thought that would make a statement to the Falls City society. Horace, however, advised her against it. He didn't think it wise for the spouse of one of the priests to serve in that capacity.

There didn't appear to be anything that required her attention in the churchyard. She would stop by the office and advise Steele of the problem underneath the magnolia tree. She stood and started walking toward her car. As she did she saw Virginia Mudd pull into one of the spaces reserved for the Altar Guild. Almeda hurried her pace toward the office building. If there was one person in all of Falls City that she could not tolerate, it was Virginia Mudd. She believed with every fiber of her being that she was a complete phony. She had heard that the Mudds were having a large dinner party for the Bishop when he visits on Sunday. She knew that she and Horace would not be invited. She was actually relieved. She didn't like the Mudds and she liked that pompous little Bishop even less.

As she was walking toward the parish house she recalled a statement that Abraham Lincoln had made about his future wife's last name. The then future President had mused as to why the Todds needed two d's at the end of their name when God was satisfied with one. She chuckled. "Do the Mudds really believe they are superior to the Lord?"

Her path took her past Chadsworth's grave one more time. She stopped and stared down at what would have been her future resting place. She had always wanted to be buried in this cemetery next to Chadsworth beneath the steeple of the church she had so loved. It was part of the reason that she was so devoted to the gardens. She knew that one day her remains would also rest in the warmth of this south Georgia soil.

It was the Alexander Family Plot and because of her marriage to Chadsworth she was entitled to a burial spot next to him. Suddenly her eyes widened and the smile that had become the essence of her daily attire since marrying Horace returned to her face. Chadsworth's ashes were buried directly in the ground beneath his headstone. The place that his body would have been buried was unused. Horace could be buried in that spot. She could now be buried in the cemetery of her choice next to Horace and near Chadsworth. Her heart sang. It was the perfect solution to her dilemma. Now, she only needed to convince Horace. As she climbed the steps leading to the parish house, the plan unfolded in her mind. She knew exactly when she would convince him. The when was also the how.

CHAPTER 6

The Side Street Market is located on one of the feeder streets leading into the most exclusive section of the town. It's the dream of every little girl in Falls City that one day she will live in one of the beautiful houses on River Street. To do so means that she will have to marry locally and she will have to marry well. Most of the homes are passed from generation to generation. The remainder are sold quietly to a local citizen of the seller's choice and without benefit of a realtor.

The Side Street Market itself is not pretentious at all. It's actually a medium sized house that had been converted into a grocery. There are only enough parking spaces around the store for ten or twelve cars at a time. While the appearance of the market is not impressive, the customer base is represented by Falls City's finest. It's one of the places to see and be seen. Those who want to be accepted into society will often frequent the market in hope of that very thing.

The prices at The Market, as most of the patrons call it, are more than one would pay at one of the chain grocery stores. *The help* are never sent to The Market to shop for the family. They are, however, often brought along as a decorative item. They also push the shopping cart. Larger shopping trips are done by the family employee, shopping list in hand, at one of the supermarkets. Shopping at The Market is primarily a social exercise.

The Market does have some of the finest cuts of meat in the city and correspondingly some of the most expensive. One of the conveniences offered is the ability to ask the cashier to "put it behind the counter." Simply put, this means that you can charge your groceries and receive a statement in the mail on a monthly basis. Only the finest families are extended this courtesy. If you can go to The Market and have your request to "put it behind the counter" honored, then you know that you've arrived.

The Market will deliver your groceries, if asked, but then that defeats the purpose of going. Some of the finer citizens do both. They go to The Market, do their shopping and socializing, and then have their groceries delivered. Those who request home delivery primarily live in homes on River Street that have a sign on their front gate that reads, "Deliveries in the Back." For these residences, home delivery is an agreeable arrangement.

Virginia Mudd pulled her new black Mercedes SUV into the parking lot at The Market. It pleased her to park in one of the only two remaining spaces left. That meant that The Market would be full of customers. She regretted the fact that Tuesday was Shady's day off. She preferred to have Shady accompany her when she came here. On those days, she would also insist that Shady wear her uniform. She really didn't need anything. Shady had done all the shopping yesterday when she was at…just the thought of it made her tremble with joy. The thought of him—"ohh"—she caught herself and looked around to see if anyone had heard her. Oh well, she'd find something to buy.

When she walked through the door she was greeted with a chorus of, "Good Morning, Mrs. Mudd." She smiled at each of the cashiers as they greeted her. The store manager came out from behind his counter, "Mrs. Mudd, so nice to see you. How's your husband?"

"Thanks so much for asking. He just works himself to the bone. Poor dear, I do worry about him."

"And those beautiful daughters of yours?"

"Honor Roll at First Church School," she beamed.

"I just know that you and Mister Mudd are so proud of them. Are you looking for anything special, Mrs. Mudd?"

"No, I just need a couple of items." Then she remembered that the girls had asked her to pick up some things for the food drive the school was having for the poor.

"First Church School is having a food drive for the poor. I really don't know what the poor eat." Her eyes fell on a basket of artichokes. She picked one up. "Would some of these be good? Do you know if the poor eat artichokes?"

The manager appeared embarrassed. "Mrs. Mudd, I would think that maybe you should stay with some canned goods for the food drive."

"Oh, very well, if you say so, but the poor just don't know what they're missing. A nice artichoke with some fresh drawn butter and brie cheese is just delicious."

"Yes, M'am. Do you want me to have one of my boys put together some canned goods for you?"

"Oh, I guess so. Do you have anything that I might care for?"

He leaned toward her ear and spoke in a hushed voice, but only after he had looked around to insure that no one else could hear. "If you're interested, we just got in some fresh gulf shrimp. They're in the back. I'm only telling my very best customers about them."

She smiled. "Then tell them to put a couple of dozen together for me. My Henry does love shrimp and I'll have them prepared for his dinner tonight. I'll pick them up at the meat counter when I get to the back of the store. Tell me, do you think the poor eat shrimp?"

"Yes, Mrs. Mudd, I'm sure they do, but I don't think that shrimp would be a very good item for a food drive."

"Oh, very well then."

"Thank you, Mrs. Mudd. I'll go back there and get those shrimp ready for you myself."

Shrimp, she thought to herself. I don't want to boil and peel shrimp tonight. I'll save them and let Shady do it tomorrow. Or maybe I'll just give them to the girls to take to the school for the food drive anyway.

She pushed her basket down the center aisle hoping to see someone she could visit with when her heart skipped. She stopped. Jacque was standing with Mrs. Howard Dexter. They were engaged in a very intense conversation. Martha Dexter appeared to be visibly upset. Jacque was standing in a defensive pose. He was definitely being cross examined. Virginia was on the verge of panic. Oh my God, she thought. She knows. She knows about Jacque and me. Virginia didn't know whether to turn and run out of the store as fast as she could or to try to help Jacque convince her that whatever her suspicions they were wrong. She could do neither. She just stood frozen. She could not get her feet to move.

"Virginia," Martha Dexter called to her. "Come down here and help me talk some sense into this boy."

"What....?" She tried to speak, but the words caught in her throat. She cleared her throat and moved toward them. Her voice was shaky, "What do you need me to help you with?"

"Oh, that exhibit he has over at the Museum right now."

Relief washed through Virginia. She extended her hand to Jacque. "Bonjour, Monsieur Chappelle."

"Bonjour, Madame Mudd." Jacque maintained a non-descriptive look on his face.

"Why, I didn't know that you spoke French, Virginia."

"I don't, Martha." Virginia took her hand back from Jacque and extended it to Martha. "I just know a few phrases from last summer when we took the girls to Paris. Now, just what is this about an exhibit at the Museum?"

"Well, you just have to go see it for yourself. I think it's terribly inappropriate. I was trying to get Misturh Chappelle here to take it down."

Jacque did not respond. "I've not seen the exhibit so I really can't speak on the subject."

"Well, believe me, after you see it you'll agree with me. It's profane."

"Please, Mrs. Dexter." Jacque pleaded. "It's art. It needs to be appreciated for exactly what it is and no more."

Virginia found herself growing uncomfortable. "Listen, I don't think I can help the two of you settle this, so I'm going to continue my shopping."

"Misturh Chappelle, are you going to be at Virginia's dinner party on Sunday?"

Virginia felt her anxiety return. "Oh, Martha, the luncheon on Sunday is primarily for the people at the church. I don't believe you even attend First Church, do you, Mister Chappelle?"

"Nonsense," Martha interrupted. "I insist that you invite him, Virginia. That way we can continue this conversation. I hope you will go by the Museum and see the exhibit for yourself before then, Virginia, so that you can help me convince him that it's utter nonsense."

Virginia's mind was racing for a way to get Jacque and herself out of this dilemma when Martha asked, "Twelve thirty is the time it all begins, correct, Virginia?"

She nodded.

Martha continued, "We'll see you at twelve thirty on Sunday, Misturh Chappelle. Is that acceptable, Virginia?"

Once again she could not find any words and simply nodded her head.

"Good," Martha smiled. "Then it's settled."

Jacque turned and walked away. "Until Sunday, ladies."

Martha smiled. Virginia's gaze fell to Martha Dexter's overbite. She had the worst overbite she had ever seen in her life. Her front teeth were covered with lipstick. "He's a rather handsome man, don't you think, Virginia?"

Her question was followed by a long stare. "I really hadn't noticed, Martha. I guess he's sort of cute if you like that type."

Martha chuckled, "Oh, and if he's not your type just what type would you prefer?"

Virginia regained her composure, "Why Martha Dexter, I'm absolutely shocked by your behavior. Henry is my type. I'm a happily married woman and I don't have any interest in any other man."

Martha continued to chuckle as she walked away, "If you say so, Virginia, if you say so. But then doesn't your generation believe that what their husbands don't know won't hurt them?"

Virginia found the entire experience so unnerving that she forgot to pick up the shrimp she had ordered at the meat counter. She didn't buy anything. She walked away from her empty shopping cart and out to her car. As she passed the cashiers she was once again greeted by a chorus of, "Have a nice day, Mrs. Mudd."

The drive from The Market to her driveway was but a few short blocks. She looked at her hands on the steering wheel and realized that they were shaking. Her insides were trembling. What on earth did Martha mean by those last few comments? I think she suspects something. She believed that she and Jacque had handled the situation with discretion. "Oh, you're just getting paranoid," she whispered. Then again, Martha Dexter is no one's fool. She is also one of the biggest gossips in Falls City. Not only does she give it out, but she also receives gossip on a regular basis. Then she remembered that Martha was a volunteer of some sort at the Museum. She could have seen her at Jacque's office. She had met Jacque at the Museum several times. Martha could have been lurking in the shadows and seen the two of them together. She tried to recall if she'd ever seen Martha there, but then, Martha could have seen her without her knowing it.

As she pulled into the driveway, her anxiety increased even more when she saw that Henry's car was parked in the garage. Terrified, she ran into the house. He was sitting at the breakfast room table eating a sandwich. "What are you doing home?"

"It's lunch time and I was hungry." He wiped his mouth with his napkin. "I didn't want to go to the club for lunch so I came home and made myself a sandwich."

She felt herself relax once again. "We need to add one more for our party on Sunday."

"Oh?"

"I ran into Martha Dexter down at The Market. She was arguing with Jacque Chappelle. You remember? He's the Museum director."

"Yes, I remember him."

"Well, Martha took it upon herself to invite him to our party on Sunday. I had no recourse but to go along with her."

Henry walked over to the refrigerator and put some more ice in his Coca-Cola. "I can't think of any reason that he wouldn't be welcome here, but I think it's going to be pretty boring for him. Most of the conversation is going to be about church."

She nodded, "I agree, but she didn't give me much of a choice."

Henry put his plate and glass in the dishwasher. "You need me to help you bring in the groceries?"

"Groceries?" She was puzzled.

"Didn't you say you went to The Market? You did buy some groceries while you were there, didn't you? Are they in the car?" He started walking toward the back door.

"Delivery—no—no—delivery. They're going to deliver them."

He walked toward her and stared into her eyes. "Are you ill? You look white as a sheet. Are you coming down with something?"

"I am feeling a little tired. I think I'll have a little nap before time to pick up the girls from school."

He kissed her on the lips and brought her close to him in a warm embrace. "I'll see you this evening. I've got to get back to work. I hope you get to feeling better. I love you."

She stood in the kitchen until she heard his car go past the house and down the driveway. A cold sweat broke out on her face and spread over her entire body. She climbed the stairs to the master bedroom and lay down on the bed. She wasn't there for very long. She sat up and then ran into the bathroom. She made it just in time.

CHAPTER 7

Randi had morning sickness. Or to hear her tell it, "My morning sickness has morning sickness." Steele felt so helpless listening to her through the closed bathroom door. He couldn't help it, but he also felt guilty. When she was back on the bed, he got up and went into the bathroom to run cold water over a wash cloth. He brought the cloth back into the bedroom and placed it on her forehead. "Gosh babe, I just don't remember you being this sick with Travis."

She was barely able to manage a nod. Steele kissed her on the cheek. He couldn't keep the words back. "I'm so sorry, honey."

Randi punched him on the arm with her fist. "You oughta' be. It's all your fault."

"Ouch!" He protested. "That hurt."

"Good."

Steele had called Crystal to let her know that Randi wasn't feeling well and that he would be late coming to the office. She reminded him that the only thing on his calendar was the staff meeting. "Ask Doctor Drummond to preside at the staff meeting."

Steele went into the nursery. Travis had dressed himself for pre-school. "Hey buddy, let's have another look at your outfit."

"I dressed all by myself, Daddy."

Steele chuckled, "I see you did. I think maybe you might want to put on something different."

"Why, Daddy? This is my favorite shirt and these are my favorite pants."

Steele walked over to the closet and took out a different shirt. "I know they are, but they really don't go together very well. Arms up." He pulled the shirt Travis had chosen back over his head and helped him put on the one Steele had picked out for him. "You can wear your favorite pants, but the shirt and pants need to match. Now, let me re-tie your shoes for you." He tied Travis's shoestrings and then ran a brush through his blonde hair. He then stood back to have another look at his son.

"You look mighty handsome, young man. Let's go give mommy a kiss goodbye." He picked Travis up and carried him into the master bedroom to check on Randi before leaving. "Feeling better?"

She nodded. "Give mommy a hug and a kiss, Travis. Tell her to have a nice day." Steele leaned over so that Travis could kiss his mother. He did the same. Just then the telephone rang. "Hello."

"Father Austin, this is Crystal."

"Yes."

"I just wanted you to know that we just came out of staff meeting."

"Yes."

"Father, Doctor Drummond gave a very pointed lecture to the staff on being loyal to the Rector and supporting you in your vision for the parish."

"I didn't ask him to do that."

"Does he know that I talked to you?"

"Crystal, I would never betray a confidence, even to Doctor Drummond. He knows nothing about our conversation. I did find out that he's way ahead of me on Judith Idle."

"I'm relieved. Thank you. But Father Austin, I think most all of the staff has been ahead of you on Judith for some time."

"I'll be at the office in about an hour. I've got to take Travis over to pre-school and he's late already. See you soon."

Randi sat up in the bed. "Is something wrong?"

He kissed her again. "You don't worry about anything."

"Travis, tell mommy you love her."

"I love you, mommy."

"Call me if you need me."

When Steele got to the office he went into the break room and poured himself a cup of coffee. He then walked into Crystal's office. She handed him his telephone messages. "Bishop Petersen is at the top of the stack."

He nodded. "Where's the mail?"

"Mister Holmes is not here yet."

"So? I just saw the mail truck leave the parking lot."

"Yes sir, but Mister Holmes is picking up his car at the dealership. He was having it serviced."

Steele was really confused. "Crystal, what does that have to do with the mail?"

"Father Austin, Mister Holmes insists on going through the mail before it's put in the staff boxes. It's been that way for as long as I've been here."

Steele felt a knot in his stomach. "And what happens to the mail until he gets here?"

"One of the bookkeepers locks it up in a cabinet."

Steele thanked her and walked down the hall to the finance office. "Good morning, ladies. Which one of you has the mail?"

The bookkeepers looked sheepishly at each other. The Administrator's secretary, Rebecca, responded. "Father Austin, I have the mail locked up until Mister Holmes has an opportunity to go through it."

"Will you please get it for me?"

"I'm sorry, Father. I can't do that."

"What do you mean you can't do that? Have you lost the key?"

"No sir. It's just that Mister Holmes told me that if I ever turned the mail over to anyone before he had a chance to go through it, he will fire me."

Steele motioned for her to follow him into the hallway. He closed the door to the finance office. The hall was empty. He whispered, "Rebecca, let me put it to you this way. If you don't get the mail for me, I'm going to fire you. If you do get the mail and hand it to me right now, I'll guarantee you that neither Mister Holmes or anyone else is going to fire you."

She nodded and opened the door to her office. She went to her desk and took a key from a drawer. She walked over to a row of cabinets. She opened one of the cabinets and took out the mail. It was in a small plastic postal box. "He's not going to like this."

"Let me worry about that."

Steele carried the mail back to his office. He placed the box on his desk and began thumbing through it. He came across a piece of mail that caught his attention. He then found another and then another. He opened them. A sick feeling washed over him. He was now more sure than ever that something was just not right in the finance office. He just didn't know what.

Crystal came into his office. "Mister Holmes is back and he's furious. He's really letting his secretary and the bookkeepers have it."

Steele stood and walked down the hall to the finance office. He could hear Ted yelling through the closed door. He opened it to see that the finance secretary and the bookkeepers were all in tears. "Ted, my office...now!"

Steele turned and walked back into his office. He knew that Ted was following close behind. Steele waited for him to enter and then shut the door. He walked behind his desk and motioned for Ted to take a seat.

"First, I never want to hear you verbally abusing anyone in these offices again. Do I make myself clear on that one?" He nodded sheepishly. "Second, I am issuing instructions that the mail is to be delivered to my secretary each day. She will be putting it on my desk for me to thumb through. After I've done so, I will ask her to give it to the parish secretary to put in the staff mail boxes."

"Now Father Austin, you don't need to do that," he blurted. "I sorted the mail for Doctor Stuart and I don't mind doing it for you. You're a busy man. You don't need to concern yourself with anything so trivial as the morning mail."

"Ted, it's done. You will no longer be sorting the mail."

Ted slumped in his chair.

Steele studied him for a couple of minutes. He could tell that he'd hit a nerve. Ted did not look back at him but sat looking at the floor. Steele shoved the envelopes and statements that he had opened across the desk toward Ted. "Now, can you tell me about these?"

"I don't understand. What is it you want me to see?"

"Ted, let's stop playing games. Can you tell me why the financial statements for these parish accounts are addressed to you personally?"

Ted sat upright in his chair. "They're not addressed to me. They're addressed to my attention."

"No, Ted they are addressed to you at this address."

Steele thought he saw tears welling up in Ted's eyes. "No, Father, you misunderstand. Once again, I was just trying to save you and Doctor Stuart clerical work. I asked them to be addressed to me so that you wouldn't be bothered."

"Ted, I'm going to have Crystal type out a resolution that I will sign and then have each of the Wardens and the Treasurer sign it as well. It will instruct the financial institutions to remove your name from the parish statements and instruct that from this day forward they are to be addressed to the Rector, Wardens, and Vestry of First Church. Do you understand?"

He nodded.

"I was surprised by a couple of these statements. I didn't realize that we even had accounts in these banks. I think this will also come as a surprise to the Vestry." Steele shoved a legal pad and a pen across the desk. "Write down the name of every bank or financial institution that is currently holding funds on behalf of First Church."

Ted started writing.

"I caution you not to leave out a single account. If I find out that you have left out so much as a ten dollar savings account, I promise you that the next telephone call I make will be to Chief Sparks and the Office of the District Attorney."

Ted stuttered. "I'll have to go to my office to get the account numbers."

"That's fine, but you will have them back to me within the hour."

"Is that all?"

Steele was doing everything in his power to keep his anger under control. He had really liked this guy. He had even thought of him as a friend. He was having a hard time keeping his feelings of personal betrayal separate from his responsibilities as Rector. He knew that he didn't have any evidence of wrongdoing, but suspicions were flowing through his every fiber. "Can you explain this to me?" He took a manila folder from his desk drawer and walked around the desk to stand next to where Ted was sitting. He opened the folder and placed it on the desk in front of him. "These are the total of the deposits according to the money counters. These are the totals for these same Sundays that you reported to me and the Vestry in the financial statements. You will notice they do not agree."

"Father Austin, the average age of our money counters is eighty-four. They make mistakes. I've not bothered you with it because I considered it to be my job. I simply correct the deposits before putting them in the bank. It's really not a problem for me and it gives the older people in our parish something to do."

Steele didn't believe him. "Okay, I'll accept that explanation for now, but you need to know that I plan to talk to the money counters. Now explain these to me." Once again, Steele placed some statements before him. "These statements are all marked past due, but you show them as paid in these financial statements. Now, Ted, how can that be?

"Father Austin, are you familiar with accrual accounting?"

"Yes, Ted, I am. I actually do know the difference between accrual accounting and cash accounting.'

"Well, Father, I don't pretend to be a CPA, but the way I've been doing the books is called accrual accounting. As I understand it, you carry liabilities forward and show them in the financial statement as paid, even if they've not yet been paid."

Steele suspicions were now verified even further. "Oh, I think you're quite the accountant, Ted."

"Anything else?"

Steele studied the financial statements for just a minute. "No, but I will have some more questions a little later. Don't forget to bring me the names, addresses, and account numbers of every financial institution holding funds for First Church. You now have twenty minutes to get them to me."

"Yes sir," Ted stood and walked to the door. He turned back and looked at Steele. "Father Austin, all of this can easily be explained. I was just trying to help you out by doing my job."

Steele looked back at him. He had lost every confidence in the man. "Let's just hope so for your sake, Ted."

Ted Holmes walked into the finance offices. He was visibly shaken. He walked past the wide-eyed bookkeepers and his secretary. He shut the door to his office. He was filled with fear. He had to do something and he had to do something quick. And then it came to him. He picked up the telephone and dialed a number. "Mister Mudd, please. Tell him it's Ted Holmes over at First Church. Tell him it's urgent."

"One minute, please." The telephone was filled with the sounds of elevator music.

"Ted, it's Henry Mudd. What can I do for you, buddy?"

"Henry, this is a difficult telephone call for me to make, but I just have to tell someone."

"Go on."

"Henry, you and I have known each other for a long time. I've been here at First Church for almost fifteen years. Heck, Henry, I can remember when you were an acolyte. I even remember working behind the scenes at your wedding. I came to your daughter's baptisms. You and I have always worked well together."

"I know all that, Ted. You're doing a great service for our church and I, for one, really appreciate it."

"I know that you do, Henry. I've always thought that our relationship was closer than church employee and parishioner. I mean, I have always considered you to be a friend."

"We are friends, Ted. Now what can I do for you?"

"It's about the Rector."

"Let's hear it. What's that sorry son of a—oh, what's he done now?"

"Henry, I have some information on the Rector's Funds that I think you had better see. I don't think you all looked deep enough last time."

Henry was exuberant. "I knew it. Get it all together. I'm going to nail that sorry excuse for a priest and this time I'm going to nail him good. Nothing would make me happier than to send him a Christmas card to his new address in care of The Federal Penitentiary at Leavenworth."

"I have some things I think you need to look at right now. I also think they will make more sense if you can get access to his personal funds as well. I would start by asking to see his bank account and his credit card statements."

"That's a good idea. Why didn't I think of that? Bring what you have over to my office right away."

"No problem. I'll see you in a few minutes."

"Thank you, Ted. You're a good man. We'll want to work closely with you on this."

"You can count on me, Henry. We've known each other a long time and we both have the best interest of the church at heart."

When Ted placed the telephone back on its receiver, he leaned back in his chair and smiled. "Gotcha, Misturh Austin. I'll teach you to mess with me."

Ted opened the door and walked through the finance office. "Are you leaving, Mister Holmes?" his secretary asked. 'Yes, I'll be gone for the rest of the day."

Steele waited the twenty minutes. Ted Holmes did not return to his office. He once again walked down the hall into the finance offices. "Is Mister Holmes here?"

"No sir, he just left for the rest of the day."

"He did what?"

"He said he was leaving for the rest of the day. Is there something I can do for you, Father?"

"Do you have a list of all the financial institutions holding funds for First Church?"

"Just those that the auditors list in their annual report."

"That's not good enough. I have financial statements on my desk for financial institutions that are not listed by the auditors."

"I don't know anything about that, Father Austin. I don't think I can help you."

Steele returned to his office. He picked up the telephone and dialed the direct line for Bishop Petersen.

"I've been waiting on your telephone call, Father Austin."

"Yes, Bishop. I apologize. I'd intended to telephone you earlier in the day. There have been some developments in the parish that I really need to discuss with you."

"Let's just do that on Sunday."

"Bishop, one of the things I wanted to ask you about was whether or not you wanted Randi and me to take you to lunch after services on Sunday."

"I already have luncheon plans. The Mudds are having a brunch in my honor at their home. I don't guess that you're invited."

"No, I don't think that we are, but Bishop, I really need to talk with you at some length."

"Have Drummond do the early service. I'll be at your office around 7:30. Have a fresh pot of coffee made."

"That'll work for me."

"Of course it will. It's what your Bishop has told you to do. Now, you can do something for me."

"Yes?"

"Would you please tell me why First Church has not paid its diocesan assessment for three months?"

Steele grabbed the financial statements that were still on his desk. He quickly glanced at each of them.

"Austin, are you there?" The Bishop sounded angry.

"Yes Bishop, I'm here. I'm also looking at the financial statements for the past three months. They indicate that we have sent the money to the Diocese."

'Well, you haven't and I'm tired of running interference for you with the rest of the clergy in this Diocese."

"Bishop, that's part of what I want to talk to you about. I think when you hear what I have to say you'll begin to understand. In the meantime I'll make sure that the checks are mailed to the Diocese.'

"Well, I hope so. The mission clergy are dependent on your support. I have to go, Father Austin. I have another call waiting on me. I'll see you on Sunday."

Steele's line went dead. The Bishop received the call that had been holding for him. "Bishop, this is Henry Mudd. I have Ted Holmes, the Business Administrator at First Church sitting in my office. We need to talk with you."

CHAPTER 8

Steele spent the rest of the week organizing the financial information he wanted to go over with the Bishop. He organized each aspect of what he wanted to show him in separate manila folders. In one folder he put the page from the annual audit listing the accounts in the financial institutions that were the subject of the audit itself. In that same folder he placed the financial statements that he had discovered for church funds which were not a part of the audit.

In yet a separate folder, he put the financial statements that Ted Holmes had prepared for the Vestry meetings. He prepared a chart showing the weekly deposits reported by the money counters and the actual amounts that were deposited in the bank. He and Crystal had called all their creditors and made a list of accounts that were past due or not yet paid. He included in that folder additional copies of the financial statements generated by Ted Holmes indicating that these accounts and the diocesan assessment had been paid.

He felt like he was ready for the Bishop and mentally rehearsed his presentation several times. He did not discuss any of this with Randi. He didn't want her to worry about anything. Her morning sickness was turning into a nausea that continued through the day. She was sleeping more than usual. Steele hired a sitter to come in and take care of Travis when he got out of pre-school at noon. The sitter stayed until he got home around five o'clock. Most days Randi slept until he did get home. She would wake for a light dinner which she often had difficulty holding down. She then went back to bed and slept through the night until her nausea would wake her in the morning.

Steele called the obstetrician to talk to him about her. He comforted Steele with the knowledge that physically Randi and the baby were fine. He told him that this phase would pass in a short time. For Randi's sake, Steele hoped that he was correct.

Steele got to the office early Sunday morning to prepare for his meeting with Bishop Petersen. He made sure that there was a carafe of hot coffee waiting in his office. He had also stopped at Krispy Kreme to pick up some fresh doughnuts. He was sitting at his desk when the Bishop entered.

He stood and walked to the door to greet the Bishop. The Bishop shook his hand and then walked behind Steele's desk and seated himself in the Rector's chair.

"Coffee, Bishop?"

"No, I stopped for a cup of coffee on the road. I don't think I need any more right now."

"Then, how about a Krispy Kreme?"

"Well, I guess I could do with one of those."

Steele held the box for him. The Bishop chose three doughnuts. "Now what is it that you need to talk to me about?"

"Bishop, I have reason to believe that our Business Manager may be handling the church finances in an unethical fashion. Now mind you, I'm not accusing anyone of anything, but I need you to look at what I've prepared. I need your counsel and guidance."

"Have you discussed your suspicions with any one else?"

"Yes. I discussed them with Doctor Drummond, but I did not show him the things I need to show you."

Steele couldn't tell if the Bishop was impatient or disgusted with him. "Just what are these things?"

"Bishop, if I could show you the contents of these folders that I've prepared for you." Steele opened the first folder with the audit statement and the bank statements in it.

"I'm not an accountant. I don't understand numbers. It won't do you any good to show me this stuff. I don't even balance my own checkbook. My wife does all that for me."

"But Bishop, let me just walk you through a couple of these items."

The Bishop reached for the doughnut box and brought out two more Krispy Kremes. "Austin, I only want one thing from you. Do you have my assessment checks?"

"I haven't been able to ask the Business Manager about them because he took the past week off."

"Good," the Bishop smiled. "He's a hard worker and deserves some time off. I want those checks mailed to me first thing tomorrow."

"Bishop, that's what I wanted to talk to you about." Steele opened another folder. "See, these statements show that we are current with our assessment.

The Bishop didn't even look at the folder Steele had placed in front of him. Instead, he closed the folder. "Father Austin, you're wasting my time."

Steele was perplexed. He was trying to figure out how to get the Bishop to listen to him.

"Father Austin, there is one checkbook that I do want to examine. Bring me your Discretionary Fund checkbook."

Steele was caught off guard. "I don't have it, Bishop. My checkbook is kept in the finance office. They issue checks for me when I submit a check request. I don't even sign them. The bookkeepers use my signature stamp and that of the Administrator's to sign the checks."

"Do you know where they keep it?"

"Of course."

"Then go get it."

Steele took the keys to the finance office out of his desk drawer. He went into the finance office and opened the parish safe. He removed the checkbook to his Discretionary Fund and to the other funds he administered. He returned to his office. "Bishop, I brought my Discretionary Fund checkbook and the checkbook for all the funds in my charge."

"What's the difference?"

"Well, as you know, Discretionary Funds are given for me to use at my discretion for parish purposes. The other funds are directed funds that that donors want me to expend for particular ministries."

The Bishop took the checkbooks and thumbed through them. "Are these your balances?"

The Bishop had an index finger on the balances noted in each ledger. "Yes, Bishop, those are the respective balances in each fund."

The Bishop let out a low whistle. "Do you realize that the combined balances of these funds are larger than the salaries of some the mission priests in this Diocese?"

"I hadn't thought of it like that, Bishop."

"Everything appears to be in order in these particular checkbooks, but then again I'm not an accountant. Have you promised any of these Discretionary Funds to anyone?"

"No, why do you ask?"

"I have a need that you can help me meet. I want you to write me a check out of your Discretionary Fund."

"How much do you need, Bishop?"

"Make a check for five thousand dollars payable to my Discretionary Fund. I will use it to help pay for some of my expenses to attend the next meeting of the House of Bishops and my trip to England for Lambeth Conference."

Steele shrugged. He really didn't feel like he had any choice except to honor the request. "Now, back to the folders, I really need to get your guidance on how to proceed."

"I don't have the time or expertise to help you with that sort of thing." The Bishop stood and put the check Steele had given him in his wallet. "Let's get on over to the sacristy. How many confirmands do you have ready for me?"

"Sixty-three."

"I guess you have just about saturated the liberal population here in Falls City. Wasn't your last class well over one hundred?

"That's correct. I'll have another class ready for you in September."

"I guess there are more liberals in Falls City than I realized."

Steele chose not to respond. "Bishop, you're leaving me in limbo here. I don't know how you want me to proceed."

"With what?"

Steele wrinkled his forehead. "How do you want me to proceed with an investigation of these financial inconsistencies?"

"Father Austin, Ted Holmes has been the Business Manager at this parish for as long as I can remember. No one has ever questioned his ability or his integrity. He is a fine servant of the Lord. He works hard for this parish. Beyond all that, I consider him to be a friend and I don't like what you're suggesting about him. Now why don't you just spend your time visiting the sick and let Ted handle the business affairs of the parish. You need to let all this nonsense go and get back to doing whatever it is you plan to do next that will upset the good folks in this parish."

"I'm not sure I can do that, Bishop."

"Upset folks?" Rufus chuckled. "I think you're quite good at that."

"No." Steele felt his face flush. "About these financial records."

"Leave them alone, Austin. Now, have you told your organist that I want a quiet interlude for the procession?"

"Yes sir, he understands."

Rufus Petersen liked being the Bishop. He delighted in all the pageantry that went with the office. When he was ordering his Episcopal vestments, he made sure that his Bishop's staff was made of metal with a heavy metal tip. A lot of Bishops had Episcopal staffs that were made of wood. He wanted nothing to do with that. He wanted his shepherd's staff to be heard when he walked down the aisle. He always insisted on carrying it himself when he made his Episcopal visitations. Only he didn't carry it. He walked with it. He took delight in hearing the metal crosier tap against the stone floors of his churches as he walked down the aisle. He wanted them to know that the Bishop was coming. For that reason he instructed the organists to hold the opening hymn until he was at the Bishop's chair. They were to play quietly during the procession so as to insure that the tap—tap—tap of the Bishop's staff could be heard on the pavement as he walked down the aisle.

The visitation of the Bishop was something that many congregants avoided. Rufus Petersen was not known for his preaching ability. When his considerable deficit in this area was coupled with a prolonged Service of Confirmation, most worshippers opted for the early service or simply chose not to attend church on that particular Sunday. The people at First Church were no different. Had it not been for the members of the Vestry, the confirmands, their families and visitors, there would be a surplus of empty pews.

Rufus Petersen expected all the fanfare when he made his visitations. A Bishop's candle was to be placed on the altar. This was a small candle placed next to the chalice symbolizing the presence of one of the successors to St. Peter was present. He traveled with a banner that had the Seal of the Diocese on it. This banner was always processed and then stood on one side of the altar. There was a second banner that he also took on each of his visitations. This banner had a statement attributed to one of the early church fathers on it. It read, "Where the Bishop is, there also is the Church." This banner was also processed and placed opposite the diocesan banner at the altar. The Bishop would remove the Bishop's hat, known as a mitre, when he arrived at the altar. He would place it on the altar itself. There it would reside for the course of the service. He put it on his head only for the absolution, blessing, and again at the recessional.

"Beloved in Christ." The Bishop stood in the pulpit. Since he was small in stature he also traveled with a wood box that he would stand on to preach. "As your Bishop, it is my great joy to be with you this Lord's Day. I fear that I must begin by correcting the Rector on one thing." There were a few uncomfortable chuckles in the congregation. Steele felt the embarrassment wash over his face. He didn't have a clue as to what needed to be corrected.

The Bishop swelled his chest and played with his pectoral cross as he continued. "The Rector was most gracious in his introduction. He also welcomed me to First Church. It pains me to have to remind the Rector that the Bishop does not need to be welcomed to that which is already his. The Bishop is the chief pastor of this Diocese. The Rector serves at my pleasure. This parish and its property belong to this Diocese. As the Bishop, that means they belong to me. Thank you, Father Austin, for your good intentions, but I suggest that you read again the Constitution and Canons of the Episcopal Church." Once again there were some uncomfortable chuckles. Steele managed a polite smile.

"My Beloved, as your Bishop..." Steele observed that Bishop Petersen did not even attempt to tone down the pompous nature of his presentation. Clearly the man was enjoying his moment in the sun. His sole purpose in this visitation was to remind the congregation that he was the Bishop.

"You are a valuable part of this Diocese. This Diocese needs you and you need the Diocese. The ministry of Jesus Christ is not limited to Falls City. Those who need to receive the message of the Gospel extend far beyond these parish boundaries. You are needed. I call upon you to recommit yourself to bringing the Gospel of Jesus Christ to every man, woman and child in this Diocese. You cannot do it alone, and I cannot do it without you. We are in this together. Bishop and congregations. Congregations and Bishop. This is the combination that insures our faithfulness to the Great Commission."

Steele was sitting next to Horace. He couldn't contain himself. He whispered, "What the hell is he talking about?"

Horace whispered back. "Brother, I think only he and the Almighty know for sure." They both chuckled.

"The resources of the Church are vast, but they are precious. There are those who would squander that which God has entrusted to us. It is your responsibility and my responsibility to make sure they not do that. We cannot let the various pet projects of parish leaders, be they ordained or lay, divert precious funds from the primary ministry of our Lord. The Great Commission is very specific. We are called to preach, teach, and baptize. Every thing else is secondary. I call upon you to recommit yourselves this day to that ministry."

The Bishop leaned on the pulpit toward the congregation. He held up the hand on which he was wearing the ring he was given when he was ordained a Bishop. With the fingers of his other hand he pointed to his ring. "In my office, I have a chart that traces my apostolic succession. At the top of the chart is Jesus Christ and the Apostle Peter. Then the names of every Pope and Archbishop of Canterbury through the centuries are listed in chronological order right down to the three Bishops that consecrated me. Then comes my name. That chart reminds me every day that I am a true successor to the apostles. Those sacred twelve were specifically chosen by our Lord. As a successor to St. Peter, only the Bishop can speak with clarity and authority on matters of faith. It is with that authority today that I plead with this great congregation. You are the largest parish in my Diocese. As the largest, you are the star in my Diocesan Crown. I plead with you to be a guiding star. Do not allow the various pet projects of the liberal minority deplete the precious treasury of our Lord. I call upon you to focus once again on the work of bringing the lost into a saving relationship with Jesus Christ. No, as your Bishop I do not ask it. I demand it! This is my godly admonition to each of you on this Lord's Day. Receive it as such in the Name of the Father, the Son, and the Holy Ghost."

"Well, Steele, what did you think of that? Horace whispered.

"So much for feeding the hungry, clothing the naked, and caring for the widow and orphan. I don't think they were a part of the godly admonition." Steele looked over at Horace. They both rolled their eyes as the Bishop paraded back to his throne.

Horace could not contain himself. He whispered in Steele's ear. "Brother, I think we were just taken out behind the barn."

Steele smiled, "That explains the pain I feel in my lower posterior."

They both chuckled. The Bishop caught their eyes and gave them a most unholy look.

CHAPTER 9

Virginia Mudd had learned at an early age the proper way to entertain a large group of people. She had benefited from her mother's training and the classes taught by a woman who preferred to be called Miss Manners. Then, of course, there was the training she had received in the Junior League. As would be customary, she had sent engraved invitations to each of her twenty-four invited guests. A reply card and a stamped return envelope were enclosed in each invitation. Each card had been returned with a positive response.

She now had to make provision for a twenty-fifth guest since Martha Dexter had taken it upon herself to include Jacque Chappelle. Socially, what Martha had done was most unacceptable. Virginia had been suffering with a nervous stomach since her encounter with Martha and Jacque at The Market. She couldn't stop thinking about Martha's attitude. She feared that Martha had uncovered the secret she and Jacque shared. Still, she had to focus on her dinner party.

Virginia employed the chef at The Magnolia Club to prepare the meal. Since The Magnolia Club was closed on Sundays, this would be no problem for him. The chef was routinely asked by club members to assist them with their dinner parties. The meal would be served buffet style. The food would be displayed on her dining room buffet. The guests would pick up the plates at the end of the buffet and serve themselves. They would then go to one of the three tables she had prepared. Place cards were at each seat. She had placed a seating chart near the front door. It indicated in which of the three rooms the individual guests would be dining. The dining room itself was reserved for the Bishop, Mr. and Mrs. Ned Boone, Henry, Mr. and Mrs. Ted Holmes, and Mr. and Mrs. Elmer Idle.

She would sit with the guests dining in the living room. She thought long and hard about putting Jacque at her table. The temptation to be able to sit next to him was most appealing. But with Martha Dexter in the next room she just didn't think it wise, so she decided that it would be best if she and Jacque were at separate tables in separate rooms. She put his place card in the great room where the third dining table was located.

When the guests arrived, they would have valet parking available to them. She had made arrangements with the valet service at The Magnolia Club to be available in front of their home. She had also contracted with two of the club bartenders. There would be one bar in the living room. A second bar would be in the great room. Shady would move about the rooms with silver trays of hors d'oeuvres. She had also employed her neighbor's maid to assist Shady.

As the time for the guests to arrive drew near, Henry and Virginia along with their two daughters stationed themselves just inside the front door. In Falls City, when an invitation indicated that an affair was to begin at twelve thirty, then it meant twelve thirty. Only the rudest of guests would not be punctual. Their daughters knew to assist them in greeting their guests and then within minutes of all arriving, they would retire to the playroom upstairs. Virginia had employed a sitter to take care of their every need during the party.

The Bishop was the first to arrive. Henry motioned for the living room bartender to come over. "What can we get you to drink, Bishop?"

"I think I'll have a bourbon and branch. Make it long on the bourbon and just a splash of branch."

"Yes surh, Bishop." The bartender nodded. "I'll be right back."

The other guests continued to arrive in an orderly fashion and soon the house was filled with the noise of conversation. Virginia nervously awaited the arrival of Jacque. Howard and Martha Dexter arrived. Martha looked directly at Virginia and smiled a knowing smile. "Where is Misturh Chappelle?"

"Why, Martha, I don't believe he has arrived yet." Virginia took Henry's arm. "Darling, has Mister Chappelle arrived yet? I don't believe I've seen him."

Henry looked back at his wife and gave her a puzzled look. "Virginia, you've greeted every person that I have. He hasn't arrived."

Virginia felt like Martha was watching her every expression. "That's too bad. I was anxious to finish my conversation with him. You'll make sure he finds me when he arrives, won't you Virginia? You need to be a part of our conversation."

Virginia nodded and tried to conceal the knot that was in her stomach. "I'll make sure he finds you, Martha."

The Dexters had just moved over to the bar when Jacque did arrive. Virginia's heart skipped. He was wearing a long dark overcoat with a red cashmere scarf around his neck. His black hair was shining in the sun. He slipped the overcoat off as he entered the house. His slender body looked magnificent in the dark suit he was wearing. Virginia thought she was going to faint. Here was her lover in her house shaking hands with her husband. Virginia presented her hand for Jacque to shake. "Welcome, Mister Chappelle, we are so pleased that you could join us." Virginia looked toward the bar and realized that Martha Dexter was watching the two of them. She had that same knowing smile on her face.

Virginia was quite careful not to find herself alone with Jacque, even in conversation in the crowded room. He caught her eye several times and gave her that devilish smile that had melted her on more than one occasion. She was actually relieved when the chef came out and whispered to her that all was in readiness. Virginia rang the small silver bell that Shady brought to her. It got everyone's attention.

Henry welcomed their guests, "My Lord Bishop, ladies and gentlemen, Mrs. Mudd and I are so grateful to you that you've taken the time on this Lord's Day to share in our hospitality."

There were several murmurs of appreciation in the room. "We are especially pleased to have in our home on this day The Right Reverend Rufus Petersen, who is the Bishop of our Diocese. Before I ask the Bishop to bless our food, I would like to take this opportunity to thank him for the wonderful sermon that he delivered this morning. Right Reverend Sir, everyone in this room can only hope that your wise words of admonition and counsel did not fall on deaf ears."

This was followed by a volley of "hear—hear" around the room. Henry continued, "Ladies and gentlemen I beseech you to lift your glasses in a toast to one of the greatest Bishops in the Episcopal Church today. Bishop, we appreciate you." This was followed by the tinkling of glasses and another volley of "hear—hear."

The conversation at each of the tables fluctuated from local gossip to sports to politics to some good natured kidding about golf and tennis games. The conversation in the dining room, however, focused on the group's favorite subject—The Reverend Steele Austin. Henry began, "Bishop, we have two members of the First Church staff sitting at this table. You have already heard what Ted here has to tell you. Judith, perhaps you could give us some insight as to just what is going on down at the church."

"Well, Bishop, I certainly appreciate the opportunity to speak with you. This is a real honor. Elmer and I are some of your most devoted admirers. We really appreciate your leadership. We just lift you up in our prayers at every meal. We thank Jesus every day that you are our Bishop."

Rufus Petersen pretended to be embarrassed. "You are much too kind, young lady, but I do appreciate all prayers on my behalf. Now, what is it that you need to tell your Bishop?"

"Oh, praise Jesus. You're everything that I had hoped you would be. Bishop, you just need to know that the staff is dying spiritually. Isn't that right, Ted?"

Ted nodded. "Don't be afraid to tell it like it is, Judith. I think everyone at this table has the best interest of the church at heart. We all want to do what is best for First Church."

"Yes, Jesus thank you. Can't you just feel the Lord's presence at this table?" Judith smiled and her husband put his arm around her and smiled as well. "It's just that the Rector is not a very spiritual person. He's just much more concerned about the finances and the business affairs of the church than he is in the spiritual needs of the staff and the congregation."

The Bishop nodded, "You're only confirming what I'd already suspected. I've thought from the beginning that Steele Austin was only interested in his own self-aggrandizement."

Judith folded her hands and closed her eyes, "Oh, thank you Lord for giving us such an insightful Bishop to lead us."

Elmer rubbed his wife's shoulders. "As you can tell, Bishop, this has been at the heart of our prayers for months now. We just believe something has to be done about this man. We need a spiritual Rector. And if I could be frank..."

The Bishop motioned his encouragement with his hand. "Continue."

"Bishop, I just don't know what the search committee was thinking when they found this man. I don't hear any good things from his former parish. I've made some discreet phone calls and well, let's just say my worst fears have been confirmed."

"Yes, I'm aware of some of that of which you speak." Rufus encouraged him to continue. "Please speak your mind."

"Thank you, Bishop. I appreciate that. I have a letter here in my coat pocket I want to show you later. It's from someone I knew at Episcopal High School in Virginia. He's now a member of the clergy. In this letter he states that he knows that Austin was a womanizer in his last parish." Elmer slapped his hands down on the dining room table, shaking the china and silver. "Bishop, we've really scraped the bottom of the barrel to find this Rector."

"I couldn't agree with you more." Henry nodded. "My guess is that you're only echoing the opinion of everyone at this table, if not in this house. Bishop, you said that the Rector wanted to meet with you this morning. Are you free to tell us what he wanted?"

"I don't mind at all." The Bishop motioned for Shady to fill his wine glass. "Thanks to the telephone call that you and Ted here made to me last week, I was ready for him. It seems he wanted me to join him in investigating your books, Ted."

Ted chuckled. "Well, then, I'm glad that we called you. What's the old expression? 'The best defense is a good offense.' "

"Exactly." Henry Mudd exploded. "I can guarantee you that there's going to be an investigation, Bishop, but it's not going to be Ted's books. No, we're going to go back to the beginning and we're going to look at every check Steele Austin has ever authorized."

Ted joined in, "I think you'd better get copies of his personal financial statements, including his credit card statements."

"We're going to x-ray his x-rays. You can count on that." Henry was getting visibly angry. "What did you tell Austin, Bishop?"

"I handled him the same way I suggest that you do. I simply ignored the files he had put together on Ted. I could see right through what he was trying to do. He's simply trying to divert attention from his own financial mismanagement. I agree with you. It's not Ted's books that need to be investigated, it's the Rector."

The Bishop took another sip of his wine and then sat back in his chair. He studied Ted Holmes for a couple of minutes. "Mister Holmes, I do have one question for you."

Ted felt himself growing uncomfortable under the Bishop's gaze. He shifted in his seat. "Ask me anything you want, Bishop." He reached for his glass of water to quench his dry mouth.

"Can you tell me why First Church has not paid its diocesan asking for three months now?"

Ted looked around the table. Everyone present was staring at him in surprise. He thought quickly. Then, he leaned back in his chair in order to mirror the Bishop's posture. He nodded, "I must apologize for that, Bishop. The checks are in my desk drawer. They're signed, stamped and ready to be mailed."

"Then why haven't you mailed them?"

Ted shook his head and wiped his eyes with his hands. "Bishop, the Rector won't let me mail the checks. He has threatened to fire me if I mail the checks to you. He says that he has his reasons. Frankly, Bishop, I don't think Steele Austin shares our appreciation for you and your ministry."

This time it was Rufus Petersen that slapped his hand down on the dining room table, literally shaking the silver and china. "That's exactly what I thought was going on."

Ned Boone had been silent throughout the entire exchange. "Gentlemen…and ladies, I don't want to throw cold water on your enthusiasm, but haven't we been here before? This guy is just like quicksilver. Just as soon as you get him in your hand and squeeze, he gets away. Just what makes any of us think that we will be able to get the goods on him this time?"

The Bishop nodded, "Ned, I agree with you that he's one slippery character. This time, however, we're several steps ahead of him."

"Oh?"

"This time, Ned, we're going to beat him at his own game. He made the mistake of showing me his hand. He wants to put the spotlight on Ted. Well, it's not going to work. Agreed?"

The entire table echoed, "Agreed."

"Has anyone ever questioned your bookkeeping, Ted?"

"Let me answer that, Bishop." Henry Mudd volunteered. "There has never been a single member of the parish, no warden, no Vestryman, no treasurer, no auditor even so much as suggest that we correct even the smallest detail of Ted's work. I know that for a fact, because I've served in most every one of those offices over the past fifteen years myself. Ted here is like member of our family. He has the complete trust of this parish. Hell, I sure trust him a lot more than I do that Okie."

Ted smiled, "Thanks, Henry. Thanks to each of you. My wife and I really appreciate the confidence that you place in us. I've just tried to do my job the best way I know how."

Judith Idle gushed, "Praise Jesus, you know that we're all grateful for you, Ted."

Ted smiled, "But Henry, how are you going to be able to keep the focus on Father Austin? What's going to keep the Vestry from letting his diversion tactics work? If I become the focus of their attention, then the Rector is going to get away with his wrongdoing."

"That's just not going to happen." Henry was even more emphatic than before. "Bishop, we're going to need your help with this. We've just got to keep him from implementing his plan."

"You'll have my full cooperation. Consider it done." The Bishop looked at Shady. "Now, little lady, I'll bet you have some dessert and coffee ready, don't you?"

Shady smiled, "Yes surh, Bishop. I'll be bringing it right now."

"Good." The Bishop drank the last of the wine in his glass. "Now, let's talk about something else. I'm tired of Steele Austin ruining my meals."

After dessert and coffee was served, the guests returned to the living room for after dinner drinks. The bartenders carried silver trays with small glasses of sherry and drambuie on them. Shady offered each of the gentlemen a cigar from a beautiful wood humidor. On cue, at exactly 3:00 p.m., the guests began to leave. The two maids and the bartenders stood near the front door with all the guest's coats so that they could assist them as they were leaving. One by one they would approach Henry and Virginia and thank them for their hospitality. Jacque Chappelle shook Henry's hand and thanked him for including him in such a beautiful occasion. He told him he had a lovely home. Henry thanked him for coming and told him that it pleased him that he'd had a nice time.

Henry continued to receive each of his guest's farewells and then something caught his attention. He was standing in the middle of the living room facing the front door. He was talking to Martha Dexter. He looked past her to see that his wife was talking with Jacque Chapelle. She then walked with him out onto the front porch and they shut the door. Henry excused himself and walked to the front hallway. There was clear decorative glass on either side of the door. He could see them facing each other. They were continuing to talk. There was something about their familiarity with each other. Henry thought that they seemed awfully comfortable together. And then he saw his wife reach up and straighten the hair that was on Jacque's forehead. It wasn't just that gesture. It was the way they were looking at each other. Henry Mudd felt the blood drain from his face.

CHAPTER 10

Virginia Mudd did not sleep very well that night. She could not erase the image of Martha Dexter staring at her and Jacque. It seemed that every time she and Jacque even passed each other Martha was watching them. She had that knowing smile on her face. Virginia was certain; Martha Dexter knew her secret.

Should she meet Jacque at the lake house tomorrow? They had met there most every Monday for the past three years. She needed to be with him. She needed to talk to him. She needed to talk to him about Martha Dexter. She needed him. She longed to feel his arms around her. She wanted to hear him assure her that everything would work out. She could not sleep. She was restless. Virginia was aware that her husband was not sleeping very well either. "Henry, can't you sleep?"

He was silent for a long time. He did not respond. She thought perhaps she had been mistaken. Maybe he was sleeping. She sat up so that she could look at him. In the moonlit room she could see that his eyes were open. He was staring at the ceiling. "Henry, is something wrong?"

He did not speak. Henry could not get the picture out of his mind of his wife lifting Jacque's hair off his forehead. His blood boiled as he replayed the scene of the way they were looking at each other. She was just too damned comfortable with him. They were familiar with each other. The only thing he needed to know now was just how well they knew each other.

"Henry," she shook him. "Talk to me. Did I do something?"

He looked at her. "I just have a lot on my mind."

"Anything I can help you with?"

"No."

There were a thousand questions going through his mind. He tried to remember if he had ever seen Virginia and Jacque together. He remembered all the times that he accused Virginia of being a flirt. Her response was classic. "Don't be crazy. I was just talking to that guy. I was just being friendly."

He couldn't get the images out of his mind. He had seen her giving the singles bar stare to more than one man, but he'd just looked away. God, he was such a fool not to call her on it. But when he did ask her about her flirtations, she made him feel like a jealous adolescent. He'd always respected her privacy. He'd never snooped on her or even yielded to his suspicions when he'd had them.

"Henry, don't you feel good?"

"I guess not. Maybe I'm just tired." He looked at her. Her face was strained. He wondered. Does she look guilty, anxious, or both?

"It's that Steele Austin, isn't it? We're just going to have to get rid of him once and for all."

"Go to sleep, Virginia."

"I don't think I can."

Henry sat up in the bed. "I'm going to the guest room. I think I'll be more comfortable in there."

"Really, Henry?" Virginia whined. She felt like he was angry with her but wasn't telling her. "Henry, darling, I wish you would talk to me."

"I've got to get some sleep. I'll see you in the morning." Henry needed to ask his wife one question and one question only. Her answer would determine his next course of action. He stopped at their bedroom door. "Virginia, what do you have planned for tomorrow?"

Her heart skipped a beat. "Oh, I don't know, Henry. I have my list. I'll just do the things that are on my list."

Henry looked back at her through the darkness. "Your list… anything in particular?"

"Oh, you know, stuff. Just stuff."

Henry had the answer he had anticipated. He now knew exactly what he needed to do when he got to the office.

Virginia was sleeping when she heard Henry's car drive down the driveway past the master bedroom window. She heard her daughters talking to Shady. They too were on their way out. Shady was taking them to school. Virginia looked at the clock on her bedside table. She had overslept. She was even more concerned that Henry had not bothered to wake her. Then she remembered that she was going to spend the day with Jacque. Martha Dexter and her knowing gaze passed in front of her. She didn't care. She needed Jacque. She needed to talk to him. She needed to be with him. And no one was going to stop her.

"I want you to put a LoJack on her car. It's in our garage right now. Send one of your boys over there and get it attached. She won't be leaving for another hour or so. Then I want you to put at least three cars on her. Don't let her know that she's being followed. Find out where she goes today and then call me when she gets back to our house. If she gets suspicious, send in a couple of decoys, perhaps a man and a woman. Let her think that she's lost them if you need to. I'll meet you here for a report about 5:00 o'clock." Henry had a great deal of confidence in the investigator. His law firm had used him on multiple occasions through the years. He just never thought that he would be using him for this purpose.

When the investigator left his office to get his team in place, Henry opened his card file. He now needed to call every member of the Vestry of First Church. Henry was tired of people trying to make a fool out of him. He was going to put an end to all of it.

Steele Austin asked Crystal to tell the money counters that he wanted to meet with them as soon as possible. "First, let me tell you just how much I appreciate all that you do."

"It's our privilege to be able to serve in this way." Carl Levitz was the chief money counter. "You realize that all of us have experience as cashiers in a bank? We like being able to serve the church in this fashion."

"Again, I appreciate the fact that you give up your every Monday morning to do this for the church. I am interested in your procedure. Can you tell me what happens to the money after the ushers receive it on Sunday?"

Carl responded. "There's a drop safe in the floor of the sacristy. The ushers drop the collection in bank bags and put them in the drop safe."

"Does it always require two ushers to do this?"

"No, I don't guess so. I guess one usher could take the plates and put the offerings in the bags. I've never seen anything that says two ushers have to do it."

"Go on. What's next?"

"Well, I guess the money stays there overnight until one of us retrieves the bags on Monday morning."

"Can any one of you do that or do you always do it with another money counter?"

"Oh, Father Austin, whoever gets here first gets the money bags. All of us know the combination to the drop safe."

Steele could see dozens of red flags waving in front of his face. "Do you then wait on another person to arrive before opening the bags?"

Carl chuckled. "Father Austin, it sometimes takes us all morning and right through lunch to count the money, make copies of the checks on the copy machine, and then put it all together to give to Mister Holmes to take over to the bank to deposit. We can't afford the luxury of waiting on each other. Whoever gets here first starts right to work."

Steele saw breeches in the internal controls that you could literally drive a semi-truck through. "Who counts the offerings from the daily services? And, what happens to all the checks that come in the mail?"

Carl shrugged. "I guess Mister Holmes counts those and puts them in the bank."

"Do you get a copy of the deposit slips after Mister Holmes has put them in the bank?"

"Heck no, once we've finished on Monday we consider our job to be done."

"Carl, I think I'm going to make some changes in the procedure."

"Now, Father Austin, don't you have more important things to do? Why on earth would you want to fix something that's not broken? We've been doing it this way for years and it works just fine. Isn't there some spiritual work you need to be doing? You shouldn't waste your time on the business affairs of the church."

"I understand your concern. I don't think you'll find the new procedure very difficult."

"What do you suggest?"

"Generally, I just don't think it's a good idea ever to have the tithes and offerings left with a single individual. I think that there should always be at least two people present."

"Don't you trust us?"

"I trust you. But if I were you, I would insist on having another person present with me to protect myself."

Carl nodded, "I see your point. I just never thought of it like that."

"I also think that the people who count the money and make out the deposit should take it to the bank."

"Is there some problem with Mister Holmes taking it to the bank?"

"I didn't say that. Again, it's for your protection. You counted it. You prepared the deposit slip. To protect yourselves, two of you should take it to the bank."

Again, Carl nodded.

"I'm going to suggest that the Altar Guild drop the weekly offerings in the drop safe and I'm going to instruct my secretary to do the same with all the checks that come in the mail in the course of the week. They will remain unopened and will still be in their mailing envelopes. I want there to be only one deposit a week. I want you folks to count it and take it to the bank, but never alone. I always want two signatures on every count and every deposit."

"I understand." Carl stood, "You know, it's so strange, Father Austin. What you've suggested would be standard procedure in every bank and financial institution. I just never thought of needing to do it in a church."

"We need to do it to protect you, Carl, and all the other money counters."

Carl extended his hand. "You can count on us."

When Carl had left his office Steele picked up the telephone and called the office of the parish auditors. He asked to speak with the head of the firm. "This is Father Austin over at First Church."

"Yes, Father, what can I do for you?"

"I have a couple of questions about the audit that you do for First Church."

"Yes?"

"How long have you been doing our audit?"

"Oh gosh, Father, I guess for fifteen years or so, maybe longer."

"I've discovered that First Church has funds in a couple of different banks that were not included in our last couple of audits."

"Father, if you will look at the audit report you will note that we specifically list the funds that we've been asked to audit. We also issue a disclaimer that we make no attempt to discover other funds. The subject of our audit is the funds that we are asked to review. In your case, I believe these are restricted to the operating account, the clergy discretionary funds, the funds administered by the Rector, and the parish endowment funds."

"So, what you're telling me is that we could have a dozen other funds, but they would not be the subject of your audit?"

"That's correct. In fact, you and I both know that you do have other funds that are not presented to us for audit."

Steele frowned. "What funds?"

"We don't audit the Altar Guild fund, the flower fund, the memorial fund, your bookstore fund, the cemetery fund; these are just a few of the ones that I'm aware that exist at First Church, but they are not the subject of our audit."

"One more question."

"Sure. It's your dime."

"I saw the auditors that you sent over here last spring. I promise you that I don't think the guys had gone through puberty yet."

Steele could tell that he'd hit a nerve. There was an icy silence at the other end of the phone line. Then he got a response. "Listen, Father Austin, my firm does not charge First Church our full fee to do your audit. We almost do it pro bono. We use our new hires and our interns to do your work, but I personally review their work myself. We are giving you a deal."

Steele felt the need to smooth things over. "I don't mean to appear ungrateful. I'm just trying to understand our procedures."

"Now, can I ask you something?"

Steele couldn't imagine what that would be. "I got a telephone call from Henry Mudd just before you called. He wants me to send one of my auditors over there to go through your discretionary fund and all the funds that you administer. He wants him to make a list of every check and a copy of all back up documentation for the checks. I don't understand why this needs to be done. We do a spot check of those funds each time we've done your audit. I just finished reviewing the last two audits and I saw no irregularities. Why do you folks need such a detailed analysis?"

Steele was perplexed. "I really don't know what to tell you. This is the first I'm hearing about this."

"Well, I have a faxed copy of a resolution that Mister Mudd says the Vestry has passed authorizing this additional audit. He wants us to start with the day you arrived as Rector. The Vestry is authorizing up to five thousand dollars for this exercise. It would help us if you could give us some idea as to what they want."

Steele was getting angry. "Again, this is the first I've heard of this. I really don't know what to tell you."

"Well, I have one of my guys on their way over there right now."

"That's fine. All the records are in the finance office." Steele's mind was racing. "Thanks for your help. I need to make another call."

As soon as the line went dead, Steele dialed Chief Spark's office. "Chief, did you get a call from Henry Mudd this morning?"

"Hell yes, what's that idiot up to now? I told him I was sick and tired of this nonsense and I wasn't voting to authorize any more scavenger hunts."

"I appreciate that, Chief. I do need you to come by the office so that I can show you some stuff, or if you want I'll come over to the station."

"I'll swing by on my way home. Let's say around four-thirty?"

"That sounds good. Are you the only one that voted against spending five thousand dollars to audit my funds?"

"No, I understand Howard Dexter voted against it as well, but I don't think it was out of any loyalty to you. We both know he just doesn't like to spend money. You'll survive this one too, Padre. I'll see you later this afternoon."

+

"This is what I want you to do." Henry Mudd's insides were in turmoil. His hands were shaking. He was on the verge of tears. His heart was breaking. His entire body was in pain. "He looked at the photos one more time. And then, he turned to the television behind his desk and turned off the video that the detective had brought him. "I want you to get in that lake house and put hidden cameras in every room. I want you to put a hidden camera in the master bedroom of my house as well."

"Do you want me to put a wire tap on your telephone at home?"

Henry thought for a moment and then nodded. "And keep the LoJack on her car. I don't want there to be any room for doubt. I want irrefutable evidence. For the next two weeks I want you to document her every move. Put your very best people on this. Understood?

"You're the boss."

CHAPTER 11

"Father Austin, this is Charles Gerard calling from beautiful San Antonio, Texas."

Steele's heart skipped a beat. He had butterflies in his stomach. The telephone call had caught him completely off guard. He had given Mister Gerard the direct line into his office, but he had not expected a telephone call so soon. "Mister Gerard…"

"Please call me Charles," he interrupted.

"Yes, of course, thank you. And I would prefer that you call me Steele."

"Well, that could be difficult since most of our clergy prefer to be called Father, but if you like."

"Now Steele, please let me get straight to the point. Our search committee has spent the last couple of weeks reviewing all our candidate's questionnaires and running the first round of references. I have to tell you that we were most impressed by your answers to our questions."

Steele felt himself relax. "Thank you, Charles. It pleases me to hear that."

"We really don't want a long drawn out search process, Father, uhr, I mean Steele. We have a vibrant congregation that is growing and alive. We're looking for a dynamic leader to be our Rector and we want to take our conversation with you to the next level."

"Charles, if you don't mind my asking, how long has your Interim Rector been with you?"

"We don't have an Interim."

"Really?"

"No, our Bishop didn't think we needed an Interim. Our assisting clergy and the staff are running the parish. He appointed the senior assistant as priest-in-charge."

Steele was cautious. "I have to tell you that surprises me. I would think that after your Rector has been there as long as he has, you would need a period of time to grieve over his leaving."

Charles chuckled, "Grieve? No, Steele, everyone is happy for him. He's done a heck of a job for us and now he's retired. He and his wife have a long list of things that they want to do and trips they want to take. We're excited for them that they're finally going to be able to do some things for themselves. Now, don't get me wrong, we're going to miss him. But as I said, the parish is ready to move forward with new leadership. We don't need to take a break. In fact, that might be the worst thing that we could do."

"That's interesting since so many Dioceses routinely do long interim periods between Rectors."

"Our Bishop talked to us about it and actually gave us a choice, but he's not sold on the idea that an Interim Rector is absolutely necessary. He even talked to us about some parishes that went into a decline that couldn't be reversed during the interim period. We have a growing operation and we don't want to lose our momentum by taking a recess. Now, Steele, we're anxious to move forward."

"Do you need additional information from me?"

Charles chuckled again, "No, Steele we want to come visit you there in Falls City."

Steele felt his stomach flip. "Oh, I don't..."

"You're still interested in talking with us, aren't you?"

"Yes, of course." Steele swallowed. "It's just...I mean...I didn't expect your process to move this quickly."

"As I said, Steele, we are a parish on the move. We want to keep growing and developing. We need a Rector to lead us."

"When did you want to come?"

"Would the Sunday after next work for you?"

Steele was really getting anxious. "Charles, it's just that no one here knows anything about this. And quite frankly, I don't want anyone to know about it at least until we're a little further along."

"Steele, we can't go any further unless we have a chance to come there and see you in action. We want to see you celebrate and hear you preach. We need to be able to watch just how you interact with your congregation. We're impressed enough by what we have read and the couple of references that you allowed us to run on you in your last parish, but that's not enough."

"Of course it isn't." Steele thought for a minute. "Is there any way that you can come in and visit but be very discreet?"

"What did you have in mind?"

"Could you just not look like a search committee? I mean...could you arrive separately and not sit together? Could you just pretend to be visitors?"

Charles chuckled again. "Now, Steele, let me share a little Texas wisdom with you. A search committee trying to be incognito is just about like trying to hide a bottle of whiskey in a brown paper bag. It still looks like a bottle of whiskey."

That struck Steele as funny and he let out his anxiety in his laughter. "I know that you're right, but do you think you could give it a try?"

"Yes, of course, but we're going to want to spend some time with you and your wife."

"That's fine. We'll have you all come to the Rectory for dinner on Saturday night. Would that work for you?"

"We'd be happy to take you out for dinner."

"No, Falls City is a small town. I don't think that would be wise."

"Understood."

"Yes, but can we meet with you again after services on Sunday?"

"I suppose so. Let's plan on getting together at the Rectory again on Sunday."

"Then it's all set. We'll see you in two weeks. We'll do our best not to look like we're wearing a brown paper bag."

"Thanks, Charles. At this point in your process that's really important to me."

Steele sat back in his chair. He was torn between excitement and anxiety. He turned to look out his office window. He gazed up at the First Church bell tower and the cross on top of it. He felt himself growing sad at the thought of leaving First Church. He picked up his telephone and called Randi. "Hey honey, how are you feeling?"

"Living on saltine crackers and Seven-Up."

"I'm sorry. I love you for going through all this for our baby."

"I know you do."

"I have something I need to tell you."

"That they've found a cure for morning sickness. The liars. It lasts all day."

"I wish. No, guess who called?"

"Steele, I really don't feel like playing guessing games."

"Of course you don't. I'm sorry."

"Quit saying I'm sorry and tell me who called."

"Charles Gerard from San Antonio. They want to come for a visit in two weeks."

There was silence on the other end of the telephone. "Randi, honey, are you there?"

"Steele, I just felt the baby kick when you told me that. I think he wants to be a Texan."

"Well, he just may get his chance. We'll talk more when I get home. Feel better. I love you."

Steele walked over to the door leading to Crystal's office. "Chief Sparks was going to drop by on his way home. Send him in when he arrives."

"Yes, Father. I also have a message here from Mister Ned Boone."

"What? What on earth does he want?"

"Father Austin, this is a really strange message. He made me write it down word for word."

"Okay, let me see it." Steele took the message from her.

Mister Austin, I've been asked by the Junior Warden to conduct an audit of the funds that you administer on behalf of First Church. In order to conduct a complete audit, I need you to present me with copies of your personal bank statements and all your credit card statements for the entire period that you have been Rector of First Church. I demand that you have them delivered to my office by messenger in no less than twenty-four hours. If there is any part of this message that you don't understand, then I insist that you telephone me immediately." Signed, Ned Boone

Steele looked back at Crystal. "Do you think this man is serious? He really thinks that I'm going to give him access to my personal financial statements?"

"Father Austin, he's a really mean-spirited man. Everyone in this town knows it. He has a no nonsense reputation. I just don't know how you're going to handle this one."

"Well, clearly I'm not going to do it." Steele returned to his office. Just then there was a knock on his open door.

"Hey, Padre. You ready to go get a beer?"

"Chief, I'm not sure a beer is going to be strong enough. You aren't going to believe the latest demand that Henry Mudd and Ned Boone are putting on me."

"Come on. Let's go over to O'Henry's Tavern. They'll have something stronger. Besides, I promised some of the off-duty officers that hang out there I'd make an appearance."

When they walked into O'Henry's, several officers sitting at the bar began to taunt the Chief. "We didn't think you'd show up. Look guys, he brought his priest with him. Father, you're really going to get a bad reputation in this town if you keep hanging out with that old reprobate."

"Don't pay them any mind. These boys come in here because all the decent doughnut shops have told them not to come back. O'Henry's is about the only place they have left to go."

"Take a look at that belly hanging over his belt, Father. That's beer and doughnuts. Now, you don't want to end up looking like him."

"C'mon Padre, the air will be better back here in one of these booths." After they were seated and had ordered their drinks the Chief looked at Steele, "Let's have it. What are Judas and Pilate cooking up now?"

"Let me first tell you what I've discovered about the parish books." The Chief listened carefully as Steele described for him what he had found out from the money counters, the auditors, and by comparing the financial statements."

"That's all room for suspicion, but there's nothing there that could be described as criminal. He could beg incompetence. The auditors have already established their alibi should they need one. You're going to need more than that."

"I know, but I'm not getting any cooperation from anyone. As you know, Mudd has gotten the Vestry to hire the auditors to investigate me."

"Good God, excuse me Steele, but just how many times are they going to investigate you?"

Steele chuckled, "I think they plan to keep on investigating me until they can plant enough seeds of suspicion in as many minds as is possible. I think their goal is to destroy any credibility I currently have. You and I both know that they're going to keep me under the microscope until that happens. We also know that it doesn't have to be anything major. They can do a lot of damage to my reputation with simple insinuation. They've already found me guilty of poor judgment. Honestly, their investigations don't bother me. What bothers me is my gut feeling that the Business Administrator is orchestrating it all. I think he knows I'm onto him so he's working to keep the Vestry from looking at the parish books by keeping them focused on me. You and I know that wasn't a hard sell for Mudd or Boone. They both are continually looking for some excuse to discredit me. The Bishop will jump on anything they can come up with, true or not."

"What did you ever do to those knuckleheads anyway? I don't think I ever knew."

"Well, nothing intentionally." Steele took a swallow of his scotch. "I just refused to be *their boy,* to use the vernacular. They wanted to control me and I wouldn't play. Of course, politically I am their polar opposite, so that doesn't help."

"Steele, I don't have to tell you that those boys are out to get you and nothing is going to please them more than being able to run you out of town on a rail."

Steele nodded, "I know you're right, but I'm not going to let them bully me." Steele took another swallow of his scotch and let it linger in his mouth. "I tried to show the Bishop all the stuff that I just told you about, but he wouldn't even look at it. I know that the Mudds gave a dinner party in his honor after services last week. The Business Manager and his wife were there, as were Ned Boone and his wife. Naturally, we weren't invited. But guess who I think they had as their main course?"

The Chief smiled a knowing smile. "I think that goes without saying. Have you talked to Stone about your suspicions?"

"Chief, he's in Costa Rica on a fishing trip and won't be back for another week."

The Chief slapped his beer mug down on the table, "That man goes fishing more than Jesus and the Apostles. If he's not fishing, he's out hunting. The man has five children, but I don't know when he was home long enough to get them conceived."

They both laughed knowingly. "Of course, the only reason we're laughing is because we're jealous." Steele handed the message he got from Ned Boone to the Chief to read.

"Does he think he's the Internal Revenue? Just when I think that man has dropped to his lowest point he does something like this to prove that he can dive deeper. You know, you don't have to do this."

"Nor do I intend to. I plan to completely ignore him. In the meantime, it looks like I'm all by myself in trying to see if my suspicions about Ted

Holmes are correct. I can't count on either of the Wardens, the treasurer, or the Bishop. But Chief, everything in me tells me that I'm right. If Ted is, in fact, running a diversion on me to slow my investigation of him down…then I know that I'm right."

"If you're right, then Holmes is going to be feeding Mudd, Boone, the auditors, the Bishop and anyone he can get involved to keep you so busy defending yourself that you're not going to have time to investigate his books."

"I know that you're right. Do you have any ideas?"

"Yeah, go to the source?"

"What do you mean?"

"Go directly to the bank. Get the bank to start watching the parish accounts. See if they will help you."

"That's a great idea, Chief. I've got a couple of problems, however. Ted is bosom buddies with the account executive at one of the investment firms the parish uses. He's also a member of the parish. Needless to say, he's not a member of my fan club either. It's a given that he won't cooperate with me. The other problem is that I'm still discovering all the places that he has parish accounts. They're all over town. I've asked him for a list, but he hasn't given it to me."

The Chief whistled. "Just wait 'til Howard Dexter finds out that First Church has money in banks other than his. He will not be happy about that."

"Even with that information, I don't think Howard will help me either. He and Ted have been friends for years."

"Then ride the horse you have."

"There is one bank where I've heard Ted refer to the bank manager as *The Nazi.* I think that manager must have questioned him about some of the things he has wanted to do in the past. That's the only reason I can think of that he would have given him such a horrible nickname."

"It sounds to me like you've found your man."

"Thanks, Chief. I knew you would have some good ideas on how I could proceed."

"I think as soon as Stone gets back into town we'd better catch him up as well. You realize that I'm the first telephone call that you're to make if you get any proof that your suspicions are true?"

Steele lifted his glass for a toast. "I have your telephone numbers memorized, Chief." They tapped their glasses together. "Have I told you lately, Chief, that you're a great friend?"

"Right back at you, Padre...right back at you."

CHAPTER 12

"What's the matter with you, Henry?" Ned Boone removed his reading glasses that were sitting halfway down his nose so that he could get a better look at Henry Mudd's face. "You look like you could use a drink."

Henry pulled his chair out and took a seat at the table. He was joining Ned and the Business Manager from the church, Ted Holmes, for lunch. Just off the large dining room at The Magnolia Club were a series of private dining rooms. Henry had reserved the smallest of the rooms for their meeting. It was a beautiful room with pecan wormwood paneling. There were heavy green drapes over the windows imprinted with pink magnolia blossoms. A small unlit fireplace was in the corner. Above the fireplace was an original oil painting by a Georgia artist of a plantation house with a large field of cotton on each side. Black slaves were picking the cotton in the painting. A brass plaque on the frame under the painting listed the name of the artist and the name of the painting, *Southern Comfort.*

"Oh, I just have a lot on my mind."

Ted Holmes looked up from his menu. "Mister Mudd, I agree with Mister Boone here. Are you sure you're not coming down with something?"

"Don't worry about me, boys. I've just bitten off more than I can chew at work. I have a big case coming up."

"You sure it's not woman trouble?" Ned Boone chuckled.

Henry's stomach did a flip. "No, it's work." Just then a black waiter entered the room. He took Henry's napkin from the plate in front of him, shook it open and handed it to Henry to place on his lap. He did the same with each of the other two men. "Misturh Mudd, Misturh Boone, I jus' wanna tell you and yor' guest here that the kitchen got in some fresh gulf shrimp and they servin' it over rice and beans. It's real good. Now, what can I git you all to drink?"

"I think you should get Mister Mudd a stiff drink." Ned Boone volunteered.

"No, just bring me a sweet tea. I think the sugar in it might give me some energy."

"Well, Henry, the way you look, you need something." Ned nodded.

"You gentlemen knows whut you want to eat?" The waiter asked.

"I'll have the shrimp." Ned closed his menu.

"Me too." Ted followed suit.

"Oh, just make it shrimp all the way around." Henry handed the waiter his menu. When the door was closed Henry continued. "Give me an update, Ned. How's your audit going?"

"Well, Ted here has been a big help. He's certainly pointing me in all the right places to look."

"Are you finding anything?"

"Nothing so far, but I'm just getting started."

Henry shook his head, "Nothing?"

"No, nothing that will really help us build our case. Ted did point out a couple of checks that have been issued without receipts."

Henry pushed his chair back. "But that's not the Rector's fault, Ted. If you issued checks without receipts, that falls on you and the bookkeepers, not him."

Ted turned red. "Well, what am I supposed to do? If the Rector asks for a reimbursement check, I feel like I have to give it to him. It's not my fault. He's my boss."

Henry was disgusted. "Guys, we're going to have to do better than this."

"Don't get discouraged, Henry." Ned Boone interrupted. "Ted here has told me that we need to get copies of Austin's bank statements and his credit card statements. He advises me that once we get our hands on those, we'll find what we're looking for."

"So?" Henry used his fork to fish the slice of lemon and the sprig of mint out of the iced tea that the waiter had just placed before him.

"So, I called Austin's office and told him that we needed him to turn over all his bank statements and all his credit card statements beginning with the day that he became Rector of First Church. I also sent him a registered letter demanding the same."

"Have you gotten a response?"

Ned shook his head, "No, I've not heard anything from him. He just responds with silence."

"Then he's guilty." Henry smiled. "If he refuses to be forthcoming with the information that could prove him innocent, then he's guilty. We've got him, boys. It's just a matter of getting our hands on those statements."

"Now, Henry..." Ned was playing with the silverware around his plate. "I don't have to tell you...I mean, you're the attorney. He doesn't have to turn those statements over to us. I mean, legally he doesn't."

Henry chuckled, "And you think that sanctimonious little priest knows that? Let's just put the fear of God in him and he'll turn them over to us."

The waiter entered carrying a tray with three plates on it. He placed them before each of the luncheon guests. "You gentlemen need anythin' else?" They all shook their heads.

"Ned, why don't you bless this food?" Henry asked.

They all bowed their heads. Ned Boone prayed, "Dear Lord, bless the work that we do at this table. You know better than any of us that what we are doing is the best thing for our church and for your kingdom here on earth. Now bless this food and make us ever mindful of and responsive to the needs of the less fortunate."

There was a respectful, but audible "Amen" from each man present.

"I did call the Bishop." Ned stopped to take a bite of his lunch. He continued to chew and swallowed. "The Bishop said that he could not force Austin to turn over his bank and credit card statements, but he would call him and tell him to cooperate fully with our investigation." Ned took one of the flour biscuits from the basket in the middle of the table. He spread butter on it. "The Bishop didn't have much hope that the Rector would turn them over though."

"And if he doesn't?" Henry responded.

"Then we're going to depend on Ted here to keep pointing us in the right direction. But I agree with you, Henry. If the Rector is not forthcoming, then that's only further evidence that he's guilty of wrongdoing."

Ted Holmes had been silent up to this point. Then he reached into the briefcase sitting at his feet and brought out a manila folder. "I do have these." He handed the two men three copy pages stapled at the top left hand corner. "These are copies of checks that have all been made out to the same man since Steele Austin has been Rector. You'll notice that each one is for a considerable amount of money."

"Who the hell is Nelson Humphrey?" Ned whined.

"He's a bail bondsman. We established that the first time we audited Austin's funds." Henry nodded.

"Boys," Ned pushed his chair back from the table and threw his napkin onto his plate. "This Rector spends more money bailing deadbeats out of jail than any man I've ever met in my life."

"I agree," Henry did not attempt to hide his disgust. "I think it's time we find out just who he's bailing out. I think if we do that we'll also find the money trail that we're looking for." Henry was silent for a minute and then his eyes lit up. "Just who would you say is one of Steele Austin's biggest supporters on the Vestry?"

"Chief Sparks!" Ned exploded. Then a big smile crossed his face. "Oh, I see where you're going with this, Henry. We may be on to something that's bigger than Austin. The Chief may be in on this too. The two of them are in cahoots. The Chief is getting kickbacks from Austin."

Ted Holmes was pleased with the tone of the conversation. "I think you gentlemen have just found the string that will lead us to the real crooks at First Church. I am so grateful to the two of you. Since the Rector started targeting me, I've really been anxious for my job."

"You don't need to worry about your job, Ted." Ned Boone consoled him. "I could see right through his tactics from the moment that sorry excuse for a Rector started questioning your bookkeeping."

"Me too." Henry joined in. "The guilty dog always barks first. Austin is the one that's guilty of wrongdoing here, Ted, not you. You have been our Administrator far too long for any of us to question your honesty. No one has ever questioned so much as one line item on one of your financial statements until this Okie showed up. It's a smokescreen and everyone at this table knows it. But guys, with or without his bank statements, I think we've got him."

The waiter brought him the check on a small silver tray. He signed it. Then he stood, "Gentlemen, this has been a very productive meeting. Ned, are you going to pursue those checks to the bail bondsman?"

Ned and Ted both stood and shook hands with Henry. "Ted and I are going over to his office right now."

"Great." Henry smiled. He patted Ted on the back. "Relax, my friend, you have nothing to worry about. We know who the crook is in this congregation and it's not you."

CHAPTER 13

Steele, you and Randi simply must come for dinner. Horace and I long to have an evening with you. We just have so much to discuss. Now, you will come this Thursday evening. Cocktails will be at 6:30 sharp. Horace has been after me for weeks now to do a rib roast. It's his favorite, you know. We'll see you on Thursday. Bye-bye, now."

"You know, Randi," Steele glanced over at his wife as they were driving toward Horace and Almeda's house. "It's like I've known two totally different Almedas. There was the Almeda that was married to Chadsworth, who quite frankly, was a pain in my sitting place. She was so full of herself. In fact, she was impressed enough with herself for all of us. Arrogant, critical, judgmental..." Steele turned the car onto River Street.

"I know what you mean, Honey. I always felt creepy in her presence. It was as though she were passing judgment on every fiber of my being. I knew that I was just as good as she was, but she...well, she just made me feel like there was something wrong with me."

"She was in an unhappy marriage, we now know that. So, I guess we should have cut her more slack at the time. I felt like I really tried to be her friend, but she just wouldn't have it. Maybe I was too quick to dismiss her. But Randi...a snob is hard enough to deal with, but a rich snob is doubly difficult."

"But Steele, just look at her now." Randi reached over and took Steele's free hand in hers. "You're right. She's a totally different person. Since Horace came into her life she's just so happy."

"Not only is she happy, but she's so much fun to be around. I really do have a good time when we're with her. She's an absolute delight." Steele grew silent as they passed the first of the mansions on River Street. He thought of Chadsworth. He remembered the first time that he ever met him and thought that he should have been a model in a men's fashion magazine. And then he became the keeper of Chadsworth's secret. Deep down, Almeda must have known that she was married to a man that did not want her the way she needed. Maybe some of her behavior was a compensation for her own unmet needs.

Steele pulled the car into the circular driveway in front of Almeda and Horace's house. He stopped and turned off the engine. His gaze fell on the front door and the white columns shining in the moonlight. His mind raced back to that fateful day when he and Chief Sparks had rung the doorbell to tell Almeda that her husband was no more. Chadsworth had taken his own life in an Atlanta hotel. "Is there something wrong, Steele?" Randi touched his arm.

He nodded. "I was just remembering." He got out of the car and went around the front to open Randi's door for her. "I wonder?"

Randi was struggling a bit to get out of the car. Her stomach was now really beginning to get in her way. The morning sickness had passed and been replaced by lower back pain and swollen ankles. Steele extended his hand to help pull her out of the car. She stood face to face with her husband. "You wonder what?"

"Oh, I just wonder how you can be so pregnant and so beautiful at the same time."

"And you, Steele Austin, are lying to me. That's not what you were thinking at all." Then she reached up and pulled his lips to hers.

Steele did wonder just how much of Chadsworth's secret life Almeda knew. She had told him when he interred Chadsworth's ashes that she knew he knew her husband's secret, but just how much of his secret did she know? The priestly seal kept him from asking her and the priestly seal would most likely keep him from ever knowing the answer to his own question.

"Good evening, Father and Mrs. Austin. Doctor and Mrs. Drummond are waiting for you in the library." Steele did not recognize the young Asian man that answered the door. He was dressed in black pants, a white waiter's jacket, and a black bowtie. He led them into the library.

"Steele, Randi," Almeda rose from her chair next the fireplace in the library and walked with open arms to embrace Randi first and then she hugged Steele and kissed him on the cheek.

Horace was behind her. He embraced Randi and then put his arms around Steele. "Welcome, brother. Almeda has been fussing all day trying to make sure that everything is going to be perfect for tonight." Then he whispered in Steele's ear, "The only thing that I care about is the rib roast. The woman has that one down good. You're in for a real treat."

Another couple was standing near the fireplace. Steele recognized the man as the African American preacher that had done his sexton's funeral with him. "Steele, do you remember The Reverend and Mrs. Josiah Williams?"

"Yes, I do. We did Willie's funeral together."

They shook hands. "You have a good memory, Father Austin."

"Please call me Steele. And this is my wife, Randi."

"And this is my wife, Rubidoux."

Steele studied the woman standing before him. She was dressed in a low-cut black dress that exposed the tops of her ample bosom. He quickly diverted his eyes to look at her hat. It was adorned with colorful flowers. She had a bright red boa over her shoulders and arms. Steele's eyes glanced downward so as to take in the entire picture. He was surprised to see that she had on red mesh nylon stockings. Once again he found himself needing to divert his eyes. He looked back at her face. The woman gave Steele and Randi a bright smile. Her teeth were cloud white through her dark red lips. She extended a gloved hand to each of them. "You can call me Rubi. Practically everyone calls me Rubi."

Steele glanced at Randi. She was wide-eyed. He would never stop loving that wide-eyed look she got when she was amazed by something or someone. "You have an interesting accent, Rubi. You're not from around here."

Josiah let out a deep baritone laugh. "Oh, you noticed. The woman has lived in south Georgia for nearly two decades and she still sounds like a foreigner."

"Now, Josiah, you just stop that. I sound just like all the rest of you."

That brought chuckles from everyone in the room. "I went down to New Orleans twenty-one years ago next month. One of my aunts had passed. So, of course, I went to her funeral. I was sitting there in the pew paying my respects when I noticed this ravishing beauty sitting up in the choir. She was smiling at me."

"Oh, you wish." Rubi put her hand on Josiah's arm. "I was just up there singing praises to the Lord. I can't be responsible for what you were thinking."

Josiah reached for her hand and took it in his. "Now, Rubi—Darling, I've told you a thousand times what I was thinking. I was thinking that the Lord and my dear auntie brought me to that church so that I could fall in love with the woman of my dreams." Rubi's smile grew even brighter. Josiah looked into her eyes and squeezed her hand. "I know you folks are going to have a hard time believing this, but right then and there in that church, I fell in love with this beautiful woman. Before the choir had sung the last *Amen* to close the service I knew that I was looking at the woman God intended me to marry. I fell in love with Rubi right there on the spot and I've been in love with her ever since."

Rubi stared back at her husband. He lifted her gloved hand to his lips and kissed it. They were lost in the moment before they remembered that they were being watched. Rubi appeared flustered as she glanced at her fellow dinner guests. "Oh, now you can see just why I stay with this man. He treats me like a queen."

"You are a queen. You're my queen."

"Enough of this. I want to talk with these good people. Father Austin, I have to tell you that I've really been looking forward to having a chance to visit with you. You've really made your mark on Falls City. My husband talks about you all the time. He says that Jesus could use a dozen more just like you."

Steele laughed. "You're quite kind to say that, but I fear you and my wife both hold the minority opinion on that one."

She smiled, "Well, just the same." She then looked over at Randi. "Now, Mrs. Austin."

"Please call me Randi," she interrupted.

She smiled again, "Yes of course. Now, Randi, if I could be so bold? When is your baby due?"

Randi instinctively put a hand on her stomach. "We have four months to go, but just look at me. I'm already as big as a parade float."

Rubi touched Randi's arm. "You look radiant. Josiah here always told me that I was my most beautiful when I was pregnant." She glanced at her husband and smiled. "My man made sure that I was beautiful five times." The room roared with laughter.

"Father and Mrs. Austin, what can I get you to drink?" It was the young man in the white waiter's coat.

"I'll have a ginger ale." Randi smiled.

"Scotch neat." Steele responded. He took the young man's arm and in a hushed voice loud enough for all to hear, "Bring me the good stuff that Horace keeps hidden under the bar." Steele then winked at Horace and smiled. The young man returned quickly with their drinks on a silver tray.

"Please, let's all be seated." Horace motioned for everyone to take a seat.

Once they were all seated, Rubi asked, "Randi, I just have to ask you how the congregation has received your pregnancy?" Horace, Steele, Randi, and Almeda broke out with laughter.

Rubi touched her hand to her heart. "Oh, I'm so sorry; I didn't mean to pry or to offend."

Steele composed himself. "No offense taken, Rubi. It's just that last Sunday this very proper little woman approached me after services during the coffee hour. Her exact words were, 'Father Austin, it's just a bit disconcerting to learn that your wife is with child.' "

Steele tried to keep from laughing. "I asked her what she found so disturbing. And honest to God, she looked up at me and asked if we had given any consideration to adopting. I told her no, but why was she asking. And without taking a breath she replied, 'Adoption is such a nice way for a minister to have children!' " Again, the room filled with laughter.

"Well, I have to tell you folks that until I married Horace here, I had no idea that you men of the cloth could be so passionate." Almeda then put her hand over her mouth and blushed a bright red. The room exploded once again with laughter.

"Personally, Almeda," Rubi interjected, "I'd like to hear more about that passion." That comment brought more laughter to the room. Rubi put her own hand over her mouth. "I just keep embarrassing myself. Perhaps I could blame it on this glass of wine."

"Mrs. Drummond, dinner is served." The young man in the white coat was standing at the library door.

"Saved by the bell." Horace whistled.

"Please let's all go to the dining room now." Almeda took charge. "Horace and I will sit at the end of the table, but then let's have husband and wife sit opposite each other so that we can be boy-girl, girl-boy."

When all were seated and Horace had said the blessing, Steele asked. "I know that this is not my house, but could I be so bold as to offer a toast?"

Almeda gushed, "Oh you darling man. Of course you can."

"Very well then, I want to toast friends old and friends new, but most of all I want to toast our host Horace and his gracious bride, Almeda. You both are gifts from God and we love you for it." Steele was about to lift his glass when Horace put his hand over his mouth and coughed two words. Steele heard them, "Oh, and of course, we must toast Horace's favorite food. Ladies and Gentlemen, let us also toast the rib roast." All chuckled and they clinked their glasses one with the other.

"Josiah, can you tell me how Willie's wife is doing?"

"She's a real trooper. She is one of our prayer warriors. I do believe the woman has a direct line with the Father in Heaven. And do you know that at her age she continues to have the young people in our parish come to her house for a weekly Bible Study. She is absolutely remarkable."

Steele nodded, "And her grandsons? I remember two really fine young men who stood guard one night in front of our house when the Klan was threatening us."

"Chief Sparks has employed both of them. They are now officers in the Falls City Police Department. Their grandmother is so proud of them."

There was silence as the waiter brought the plates prepared with the evening meal from the kitchen. Horace's eyes grew wide at the sight of the slice of rib roast on his plate. "I do hope you have more of this in the kitchen?" Horace asked the waiter.

"Now Horace," Almeda scolded. "You know what the doctor said about your cholesterol."

"Oh, Almeda." "Horace whined. "Let me just enjoy my favorite meal every now and then without listening to that quack's ominous predictions. I tell you folks, Almeda will do whatever it takes to keep me from dying."

Almeda brightened, "You better believe it. I've waited far too long for you to find me not to get every day out of you that I can, plus a bonus."

"Now, can I just eat in peace?"

"Yes, darling, it's better to eat in peace than rest in peace." She smiled at him. "I fixed this especially for you, so you enjoy every bite."

"Thank you. And have I thanked you today for loving me?"

"Yes, don't you remember this morning in the shower..." Almeda blushed.

Steele made the time-out motion with his hands, "Too much information, guys…too much information." Almeda and Horace snickered with embarrassment.

Rubi brightened. "Now I'd like to hear more about what happened in the shower this morning."

"Rubi!" Josiah interrupted. "Do not let her have any more wine."

"Okay then." Rubi turned her attention back to Almeda. "Almeda, if you don't mind my asking, how has it been for you to be married to Horace? I don't want to appear to be nosy, but a white woman of means married to a black man in Falls City. I know that Horace is a priest and all that, but it just can't have been that easy."

Almeda put her knife and fork down. "No, it hasn't. I see the people point at me and whisper behind my back. We've gone out in public a few times, but I have to confess that it's pretty uncomfortable. Now when we go up to Atlanta we don't seem to draw as much attention. We draw even fewer stares when we go to visit Horace's daughter up in Washington, D.C. Here in Falls City, however, we just can't keep from becoming a spectacle."

"And your friends?" Rubi persisted.

Almeda took a sip of her wine. "My true friends have stayed with me. The others I've learned to live without." She emptied her wine glass and nodded at the young waiter standing by the buffet. He refilled her glass. She took another sip. "It goes without saying that both The Magnolia Club and The Country Club found a way to remove me from membership."

"Oh, I'm so sorry." Rubi put her hand over her heart.

"It's a small price to pay for the love of my life. I would give it all up; I would give everything I've ever had up if I could've found my handsome husband fifty years ago."

Horace sympathized. "It's not been easy for Almeda. We've talked about leaving Falls City and going to a community that is more accepting of interracial marriage, but so far she doesn't want to leave her friends and family here."

"You can't leave me, Horace." Steele shot back. "I need you, the parish needs you."

Horace smiled a knowing smile. "Oh, my dear Father, you'll be leaving us long before we leave you. Do you really think that you're going to be in Falls City forever? There's a great big church out there someplace just waiting on you. Who knows, maybe there's a purple shirt in your future."

Steele smirked, "Oh, God reserves that ministry for those who need to be punished for their many sins."

The waiter began clearing the plates. "May I serve dessert now, Mrs. Drummond?"

"Yes, with the dessert wine and coffee for those who desire it."

Josiah asked, "Steele, could I ask a favor of you?"

"Certainly, is there something that First Church can do to help your congregation?"

"Well, I hope so."

"Go on."

"I've got a couple of men in my congregation that work as custodians at your school. They tell me that the gym at the school is not being used most evenings and that it just sits there empty."

"I suppose that's true. I've never really checked on it."

"Well, we have a group of young men in our church that would like to organize some intramural basketball games among the black churches, but they don't have any regulation courts to practice on, or for that matter, play games on. I was just wondering if we could use your gym at the school. We would only want to utilize it when it's not being used for any other purpose. Do you think that would be a problem?"

"Let me check with the Headmaster, but personally I can't see a problem. If it's not being used, it only makes sense to make it available. I'll check in the morning and give you a call."

"That would just be wonderful. Thanks so much. You'll make a lot of young men very happy. I'll personally guarantee that your property will be left safe and secure."

As they were driving home Randi reached over and touched Steele's arm. "Honey, I'm afraid that you made a promise tonight that you might not be able to keep."

"Oh?"

"Steele, I just don't think the people at that school are going to want to open their gym to black basketball players. I mean, Steele, I hope I'm wrong, but most of them send their kids to that school so they don't have to sit next to black students in class."

Steele glanced over at his wife. "You know Randi, sometimes I think I must be one of the most naïve men on the face of the earth. The gym is empty. No one will even be on the property except the security guards, who by the way are black. Now why shouldn't those young men use it?"

She patted his arm. "You know the answer to that as well as I do, Steele. I'm really sorry. I didn't mean to rain on your parade. How are you going to present this idea to the Headmaster?"

Steele clinched his jaw. "I'm going to tell him that we're going to find a way to make it work. The last time I read church law the Rector has full use and authority over church property and that includes the church owned school."

"Oh Steele, I just think you're buying more trouble."

"That may be, but right is right, Randi. I'm not going to back down. Right is right and this is the right thing to do."

"Oh, Honey, I don't know. Maybe we should just give up here and move on to San Antonio if they want us. It just seems like we're always going against the tide."

Steele knew she was right, but he believed he was right as well. He prayed. "Jesus, give me the courage to see this one through. Use me to help Josiah and the young men in his church."

CHAPTER 14

If there is a true patriarch at First Church, it's Stone Clemons. While his family was not one of the founding families of Falls City, their presence is woven into the very fabric of the community. To date, no streets had been named after them, but not a single community project moved forward without his blessing. He was the silent partner in most every new business venture and was a visible but silent guest at virtually every groundbreaking or ribbon cutting.

Stone liked The Reverend Steele Austin. Oh, he didn't like everything that he was doing, but Stone Clemons was a realist. The world was changing. The old South was changing. He had long ago reluctantly accepted the fact that Falls City must change as well. Stone knew that Steele was but the first of many others that would lead the invasion of the future. More than anything else, Stone was committed to justice. He weighed both sides of every argument carefully. His scales always balanced in favor of fair play. Father Austin had not been treated fairly and this caused Stone's blood to boil.

He had done battle with Ned Boone on multiple occasions. When Ned went after the local college president, not once but twice, Stone threw up every legal obstacle the cadre of young attorneys in his law firm could uncover. Precedence upon precedence until Ned finally backed away. Stone helped the man save his job, but it was too little too late. Two weeks after the battle was over, the man's wife found him on the floor of his dressing room. He died from a massive stroke.

Howard Dexter was no stranger to Stone's strong will either. He had challenged him on more than one occasion. He had pretty much dismissed Howard as a greedy little miser. Stone concluded that Howard was more interested in stockpiling money in his little bank than he was in the greater good of the community or the parish. Howard always tried to bridge every argument with Stone by appealing to their family connections. "Your nephew married my second cousin..." In every situation, given a choice between family loyalty and the greater good, Stone always came out fighting for progress.

Stone turned off the engine to his car. He had just pulled into the visitor's parking space. He glanced up at the sign that had been carved in black letters over the white pillared entrance to the red brick building. It read simply—"Law Firm—Henry Mudd and Associates." Henry's firm was not nearly as large or prestigious as Stone's firm, but he did have a couple of law partners and several young attorneys newly admitted to the bar. Henry had earned a reputation as a very aggressive litigator. His firm would take most any case.

He sat quietly in his car, anticipating his confrontation with Henry. Stone thought the Mudds to be a perfect example of resistance to change. They were the poster children for life in Falls City, Georgia. Their ancestral bloodline could be traced all the way back to Jamestown. Both Henry and his wife were educated in the finest Ivy League Schools. They had two picturesque little girls and they were the fourth generation to live in the family home over on River Street. Still, Stone knew that this meeting was necessary.

"What is it that you hope to accomplish?" Stone passed on all the courtesies. He wanted to get right to the point. "Help me understand just what you, Ned Boone, and the others working with you want to achieve."

"The man's a crook, Stone." Henry shot back. "You're an attorney. Trust your instincts. Everything about that sanctimonious little priest points to that fact."

Stone sat silent, trying to absorb Henry's demeanor. Henry was sitting behind his desk but was leaning all the way back in his desk chair. He had opened his bottom desk drawer and had placed one of his feet on it. He portrayed a man who was filled with confidence. But there was something…Stone just couldn't put his finger on it. Somehow Henry Mudd was different. His eyes were bloodshot. He was a bit disheveled. He looked tired.

"Henry, are you getting enough sleep?" Stone asked quietly. "You look tired."

"Oh, I just have this big case that I'm working on." Henry leaned forward and put his arms on his desk. "You know how it is when there's more work than the day provides. I've been burning some late night oil."

"Well, I hope that goes well." Stone studied Henry's face and body language. He had cross examined enough witnesses throughout his own career to know when someone was lying to him. Henry had just lied to him. Every fiber of his being told him that something else was contributing to the lack of sleep in Henry Mudd's life. He just didn't know what.

"The man is acting just like an embezzler." Henry's voice brought Stone back to the moment. "And believe me, Stone, that's my business. I know just what an embezzler looks like and acts like. Steele Austin is displaying all the classic signs of an embezzler."

"What specifically is he doing that would lead you to that conclusion?"

"He's not being forthcoming. We've asked him for copies of his bank statements and his credit card statements and he won't give them to us."

"Hell, Henry. I wouldn't give them to you either. He doesn't have to give you his personal financial information."

"We can't do a complete audit without them." Henry leaned back in his chair and put his hands behind his head. "But it doesn't matter. We're moving forward without them. Ned and I are in the process of verifying every expense he has submitted to the church for reimbursement."

Stone felt his face flush. He was growing angry, but he knew he needed to keep his temper under control. "You're doing what?"

"Well, Stone, I have a receipt right here that I need to ask you about." Henry opened a file folder on his desk. He lifted out a receipt attached to a reimbursement form from First Church. "Austin presented this receipt for reimbursement. He says that he and his wife took your wife and you to dinner. He lists it as a fundraising expenditure. It looks more to me like you all had a nice dinner at the church's expense."

Stone glanced down at the receipt. "Well, Henry, he did take us to dinner. He asked me if we would contribute to a scholarship fund he was setting up for one of the students at the school." Stone picked up the receipt. "Let me see, this dinner check for four people came to eighty-six dollars, including tip. I gave him a check for ten thousand dollars for the church's scholarship fund. Seems like eighty-six dollars well spent."

"Couldn't he have just come by your house and asked you for the money?"

"I suppose he could have, but the boy has class. He knows that if you want to raise large sums for the church, a little wining and dining with the Rector and his wife can go along way to put ink on the check. In our case it was probably not necessary, but you and I both know that a cold call won't work with all the big givers. Father Austin knows what he's doing and we need to support him. The church will be the beneficiary of his efforts."

"That's just my point."

"Again?"

"I don't think the church is the beneficiary of all of Austin's efforts. I think he's lining his own pockets at the church's expense."

"And you have evidence to substantiate that accusation."

"Not yet, but it's coming." Henry opened the file folder and pulled out two sheets of paper with copies of checks on them. "Look at all these checks. They're all made out to the same person."

Stone took the sheets, glanced at them and handed them back to Henry. "I know this guy and so do you. He's a bail bondsman. We've been through this before. The man has a heart for people in trouble. He's posted bail for more than one person. If I remember correctly from the last time that we went through this, most of them have paid his fund back and then some."

"But I want to know who he's bailing out." Henry leaned forward again. He was becoming agitated. "How do we know that he's not laundering church funds through this bail bondsman? He could be writing him checks and they could be dividing the cash."

Stone let out a low whistle. "Henry, have you always been that suspicious? I have to confess that's a stretch even for my investigative training."

"Then you need to wise up, Stone. I'm telling you, the man is a crook and we're going to prove it. I think the trail to his dishonesty just may lead through these checks to this bail bondsman. He's going to tell me who he bailed out of jail or I will be left to conclude only one thing. He's laundering money."

"You know that he doesn't have to tell you who he has bailed out of jail."

Henry slapped his hand down on his desk. "Oh, he's going to tell me!"

Stone chuckled and shook his head. "No, he doesn't have to tell you. The parish by-laws and his own Letter of Agreement protect him from having to disclose the names of the recipients of the discretionary funds. They specifically state that any audit of the discretionary funds cannot reveal the names of the persons who have received assistance through them."

Henry stood and crossed his arms in front of him. "He's going to tell me. Mark my word; he's going to tell me."

Stone stood to match Henry's posture. He studied Henry one more time. "Just between us, Henry, what's really driving you? What is it about Father Austin that you find so distasteful?"

Henry relaxed his arms and walked around his desk to stand next to his office door. "I just don't care for the man. It's as simple as that."

"Can you be a bit more specific?"

Henry put his hand on the door knob and then took it back. He put both of his hands in his pants pockets. "Stone, he doesn't belong here. I mean, look at him. He attended a no-name school. He's an upstart. He has no training in the art of being a gentleman. And he's not a southerner."

Stone was amused. He smiled, "Last time I checked, the endowment at the University of Texas rivals that of either Harvard or Princeton. As for being a Southerner...well, I think most of the graduates of that little four year college think they are."

Henry once again put his hand on the door knob and opened the door for Stone to leave. Stone extended his hand in an invitation to shake Henry's. "You know that I'm going to fight you."

Henry shook his hand. "I'd thought that from the beginning. I wish we could be on the same side, but I figured you would be an advocate for the preacher."

"Henry, this could get real ugly."

He nodded. "Oh, Stone, it's going to be really ugly, but maybe your firm can defend him when the prosecutor files charges against him for embezzlement."

"You're that sure."

"Stone, I'm that sure. The man looks like a crook. He's acting like a crook. Any open-minded person is left with only one conclusion. That priest is a crook and Ned Boone and I are going to prove it beyond a shadow of a doubt."

Stone stood contemplating his statement. "Henry, who gave you all those receipts? Those checks are the property of the church."

"Ted Holmes. Why do you ask?"

"Did you specifically ask him for any of them?"

Henry shook his head. "No, he volunteered to point us toward certain areas that he had questions about himself."

"So Ted is providing you not only with documentation, but he's guiding your investigation."

"I guess you could say that."

Stone stood chewing on that additional information. "And you don't find that suspicious?"

"Why would I find Ted's assistance suspicious?"

Stone shrugged. "Something just doesn't feel right."

Henry extended his hand this time. Stone took it and shook it once more. "Ted's heart is in the right place. He's just trying to help us. He has always worked for the best interest of the church."

Stone wrinkled his brow. "You're sure about that?"

"What?"

"You're sure that Ted is only concerned for the church?"

"I'd trust the man with my life."

"Uhmm." Stone murmured. "I hope that you're right, but something is just not adding up."

"You'll see, Stone. I'm not wasting my time. You'll see that I've been right about that priest all along."

Stone stood in silence staring at Henry. Then he asked the question that he believed he already knew the answer to. "Henry, what are you going to do if you find out that Steele's not done anything wrong? What will you do then?"

Henry shrugged and turned to walk back behind his desk. "He's guilty. I'd stake my life on it."

"Humor me, Henry. What if he's innocent?"

"Then, my friend, we're going to find another way to get rid of him."

"You really feel that strongly about him."

Henry smiled. "I simply don't care for the man. There's nothing about him that I like. This is my church. I've been here my entire life. Stone, mark my words. He's going. I'm staying. I have a burial spot in the First Church Cemetery reserved for me. Steele Austin has no such reservation. There are only two scenarios in his future. One involves an orange prison uniform. If that doesn't work, then the second scenario includes a moving van hauling him back to Oklahoma."

Henry sat down at his desk and started looking through the papers on top of it. "You'll have to excuse me, Stone. I have a lot to do."

Stone stood at the door in silence. He watched Henry. He realized that there was nothing he could say to change his mind. He shook his head, turned, and closed the door behind him.

CHAPTER 15

"Father Austin, we've fallen in love and we want to get married." Steele smiled at Charles Gerard. His deep south Texas accent struck a familiar note in his heart. He had become so used to the south Georgia drawl that he had forgotten the sweet tones of Texas. Not only were Mister Gerard's words encouraging, but his very appearance was making him homesick. Charles Gerard was right about one thing. *A search committee trying to be incognito looks just like a bottle of whiskey in a brown paper bag.* Or at least a search committee from Texas sitting in a downtown south Georgia parish.

Everyone in the place spotted them as soon as they walked in the door. The two men were wearing western boots, hats, and western cut suits with bolo ties. The dresses the women were wearing could have easily been purchased in any dress shop in Falls City, but their turquoise jewelry was a dead giveaway. Steele couldn't help but think about the grief that he had received over his clothing when he first arrived in Falls City. He was made to feel less than presentable because of his western boots and jeans.

"Father Austin, that just may have been the finest sermon that I've ever heard." The other members of the search committee were seated in the Rectory living room. They were all smiling and nodding their heads.

Randi walked into the living room. The two men stood as she entered. She was carrying a silver tray with filled coffee cups and slices of a key lime pie that she had prepared. "If I can't interest you in lunch, at least I can give you some dessert."

"Why thank you ma'am, but we do have to leave for the airport in just a few minutes. We have to turn in the rental car and all." Randi motioned for the two men to be seated. She handed each of their guests a cup of coffee and a dessert plate with the pie on it.

"Tell me, Mrs. Austin, does your husband preach like that every Sunday?"

"He won't admit it, but he does. I've yet to hear him preach a bad sermon."

Mister Gerard took a bite of his pie. "That's mighty fine pie, Mrs. Austin. It's downright delicious." Randi thanked him while he took a sip of his coffee. The others in the room also complimented her on her dessert. "I'm telling you, Father Austin, you're going to be a big hit in San Antonio. That service this morning was absolutely moving. I promise you that your preaching will be a hit with our folks." He chuckled, "Just wait until those snob parishes in downtown San Antonio hear that we've landed a great preacher. They're going to have a hard time living with that one." The other members of the committee murmured in agreement.

"Mister Gerard..."

"Please call me, Charles, Chuck if you want. That's what all my friends call me."

"And please call me Steele. I don't want to get ahead of ourselves. Randi and I agreed to have you visit us, but we really don't know if we want to move to San Antonio."

"Of course...of course." He placed his dessert plate on the coffee table. "We just can't help but be excited. Frankly, Steele, we fell in love with you and Randi over dinner last night. None of us could hardly sleep we were so filled with excitement for our church. We just know that everyone is going to love both of you. You're just perfect for us."

"That's really nice to hear, but we really don't know that much about your parish."

"Oh, we're going to take care of all that. You just need to know that we've visited three other priests so far and you are the first one that every member of this committee has gotten excited about. Shucks, Steele, not only are you going to be a hit, but Randi here is going to be an absolute smash in San Antonio." He smiled at Randi and she blushed. "May I ask you Randi, when is your baby due?"

"Four more months."

"Perfect." He slapped his knee. "We want that baby to be born in Texas. Your baby can be a Texan. That's a proud birthright."

"That's all very nice," Steele interrupted. "We just need a lot more information before we can even begin to think about a move. I've read your profile and I've done some research on your parish. It appears that you are healthy and growing."

"Growing...Steele, our part of San Antonio is growing by leaps and bounds. I promise you that St. Jude's is going to be one of the largest parishes in the entire state of Texas and we want you to be our Rector."

"That all sounds really good, but Randi and I need to pray about all this."

"Of course you do. But we've been talking and we want to give you some more things to consider. The Vestry makes the final decision, but I talked with the two Church Wardens after our dinner last night and they've authorized me to assure you that your financial compensation at St. Jude's will be at least this amount." He reached into his inside coat pocket and brought out a sheet of hotel stationary. He handed it to Steele to read.

Steele glanced at it and then handed it over to Randi. She squealed and put her hands up over her mouth. Tears welled up in her eyes. "Steele, they want to help us buy our own house. Oh God, Steele, I miss having our own home."

"You'll also notice that the parish will provide for your children's schooling, right through any four-year university of their choosing."

Randi handed the paper back to Steele. "This is a very generous offer."

"Oh, Steele, that's not an offer."

"It's not? I don't understand."

"Heck no, that's just a guarantee of our minimum offer. If the Vestry ends up feeling as strongly about you as we do, your final offer will exceed what's written on this sheet of paper."

Steele looked over at Randi. She was looking down and smiling. She had placed one of her hands on her stomach. He figured the baby had just kicked. He could tell that in her mind she had already moved to San Antonio and was in the process of decorating a nursery in her new house. "What else do you need from me to discuss with the Vestry?"

"Father...I know, Steele, but for right now just let me call you Father. Father, we already know that you're the right person for us. We now want you and Randi to come to San Antonio so that you can see for yourselves that we are the right parish for you."

"When?"

"Spring is a beautiful time in South Texas. The bluebonnets should be in full bloom in just about two weeks."

Chuck turned his gaze onto Randi. He caught her eye and she looked back and smiled. "Randi, have you ever seen a Texas hillside covered with bluebonnets?"

Randi shook her head.

"Ma'am, it's as pretty a sight as the good Lord has ever painted. Just as far as the eye can see there's a carpet of blue. There'll be some spots of Indian paintbrush with bright orange, red, and yellow. And occasionally, if the timing is just right, the prickly pear cacti are in bloom as well. It is as though the angels themselves have spread great brightly colored oriental rugs over the entire land. I don't think there is a prettier sight on earth than the fields of Texas covered with bluebonnets."

"It sounds absolutely beautiful, Chuck."

"And little lady, if you don't mind my civic pride, the River Walk in San Antonio is a mecca of shops and some of the finest dining the world has to offer. We want you all to come to Texas. We're going to keep you on the River Walk in the Hyatt Regency Hotel. We want you to have the entire San Antonio experience. We're hoping that you'll stay at least a week with us."

Steele smiled at Randi. Her eyes were not pleading with him to accept, but they were certainly communicating her desire to go for the visit. "That's very generous of you, Chuck. I don't know if we can stay for a week. I mean, I do have a parish here that I must continue to run, but we'll come for a visit. I will try to work it out so that we can be there over the weekend. I would like to attend services at St. Jude's. But like you, I want to be incognito. I don't want anyone but those who absolutely have to know that we're there to be aware of us."

"Agreed, but as I've said before..."

"I know—I know...a bottle of whiskey in a brown paper bag."

Steele looked around the room at the other three members of the Search Committee. "All of you have been awfully quiet. Do you have any questions for either Randi or me?"

The other man spoke. "Chuck here is our spokesmen. We agree with everything that he has said. We want you to be the next Rector of St. Jude's." The ladies all smiled and nodded.

"Before we go, Steele, I do need to let you know that I think we were spotted."

"Oh?"

"A couple of your parishioners asked us what we were doing there. One little lady actually came up to our car as we were getting in it and shook her fist at us. She shouted, 'You're not getting our Rector so just go home.' "

Steele looked over at Randi, "Oh, boy."

Chuck winked at the others in his group and they all chuckled. "You also need to know that one man came up to me and stated that if we wanted you it would please him to be able to come and help you pack."

"I'm sorry about that. I should have warned you that there are more than just a handful that have been planning my farewell party from the day that I arrived."

They all chuckled, "You know what, Father Austin? I think we might just be able to help them do that very thing. They can throw you a bon voyage Texas style." They all laughed some more. "So it's settled. The next time we meet we'll all be in the great state of Texas."

CHAPTER 16

Father Austin, the Chairman of the School Board is on the telephone. He says he needs to talk with you right now." Crystal lowered her voice to a whisper. "Father, he sounds absolutely furious."

"Give me just a minute, Crystal." Steele had been dreading his initial confrontation with the new School Board Chairman. He recalled his first exchange with him. It was just before he was to preside at the funeral for a little girl in the parish that had died. It was Mandy Weller's funeral. Tom and Sara Barnhardt had stormed into his office and demanded that he overturn a decision made by a cheerleader selection committee at the school. They demanded that he, as Rector of the school, appoint their daughter to the cheerleading squad. When he refused, they threatened to remain in his office until he relented. It was not until his secretary came to the door with one of the officers scheduled to escort the funeral procession that they agreed to leave. They had a few choice words for Steele on the way out the door.

"This is Steele Austin."

"And this is Tom Barnhardt. In the future, Mister Austin, I will expect you to take my calls immediately. You have left me sitting here holding this receiver in my ear for ninety-six seconds. Don't ever let that happen again."

"What can I do for you, Mister Barnhardt?"

'Oh, you're not going to be that dismissive of me, *Reverend.* Did I make myself clear about the promptness with which you're to receive my telephone calls?"

Steele felt his anger beginning to rise. He was tempted simply to hang up on this narcissist but resisted the desire. "Mister Barnhartdt, yours is not the only telephone call that I receive in a given day."

Tom Barnhardt began shouting through the telephone. "I'm the g-damn school board chairman. The school operations which are currently owned by your parish have a budget that is four times as large as that of your little church. That makes me the most important person that will ever be calling you for any reason. Now are we clear?"

Steele was really ready to disconnect the call, but knew he could not let those last comments go unchallenged. "Mister Barnhardt, I take all telephone calls and refuse none. I take the calls as they come and change that pattern only in case of a pastoral emergency. Do you have a pastoral emergency?"

Laughter roared out of Tom Barnhardt. "What in the name of everything that is logical would constitute a pastoral emergency? I've never heard of such nonsense. Now listen to me, Austin, and you listen good. Unless you want more trouble than you'll ever be able to handle you take my calls and you take them immediately. Do not subject me to that annoying religious music you play for those who have to wait while you take care of your emergencies." Again, he chuckled. "What utter nonsense. My time is valuable and I'll not have it wasted while you run a Bible School for the neurotic."

Steele was furious. "You've told me just how valuable your time is, so don't you think you should get to the point? Just what can I do for you?"

"You're a real piece of work, Reverend."

"Please call me Steele."

"Oh whatever...You would never make it in the business world, Preacher. You had better stick to hand holding and passing out bread crumbs to that pathetic crowd that throw their money at you on Sunday mornings."

Once again, Steele could see himself hanging up the telephone, but he didn't. "Now that you've made it clear just what you think of the Church, the people who attend Church, me and my ministry, I'm even more confused as to just why you would be calling such a useless incompetent."

"Because the current by-laws make you the CEO of the school, but I'm going to change that. The school needs to be independent of the church. You and your parish are holding the school back. I'm going to put an end to that."

"Is that what you called to tell me?"

Tom Barnhardt let out another roar of laughter. "No, you can just consider that a fair warning. I'm organizing the troops to separate the school from the church. We're going to be coming at you with everything we've got."

Steele was fed up. "Well, thanks for the warning. Now if you don't mind, I need to go downstairs and count the crayons for the Sunday School children."

"Very funny."

"Thanks again for your call, but I really must go now."

"Don't you dare hang up on me, Austin!" Tom Barnhardt shouted. "I have one more ultimatum."

"Yes."

"The headmaster tells me that you want to let a bunch of..."

"Stop, right now!" This time it was Steele that was yelling. "I have no patience for vulgarity or racial insults. Choose your words carefully."

"So you do plan to..."

"Yes, I have given permission to the intramural basketball teams from the African American congregations to use the school gyms for practices and games when they're not being used by the school."

"And I'm here to tell you that's not going to happen."

"Just how do you plan to stop me, Mister Barnhardt?"

"As Chairman of the School Board I will instruct the Headmaster and the staff not to let them in."

"Read those by-laws again, Mister Barnhardt. And while you're at it, read the Church Canons. The Headmaster and the staff work for the Rector, not the School Board. And as for the use of church owned property, that's invested in the Rector and not the School Board."

"Well, that's what we're going to change. And we're going to start at the next meeting of the Vestry."

"That meeting is in two weeks. Do you want me to put you on the agenda?"

"I'll be there along with the entire School Board."

"Then I'll put you first on the agenda."

"It's not going to be a pleasant meeting, Reverend."

This time it was Steele who chuckled. "That's the only kind that the First Church Vestry knows how to have. See you then." Steele was anxious to hang up the receiver before Tom Barnhardt had a chance to respond. So he did.

CHAPTER 17

Steele turned his chair so that he could stare out his office window. The telephone call from Tom Barnhardt was upsetting. His attitude was so reminiscent of the arrogant wall that he had encountered in Falls City from the day of his arrival. Randi and he had concluded after their first few months that this community was filled with a lot of very important people and most all of them were associated in one way or another with First Church.

Steele was well aware of the tension between the parish and the school. He had talked to enough other clergy friends that were Rectors of parish schools to know that having a school was a mixed blessing. A parish school could be a good evangelism opportunity for the parish. Close to half of the students recorded no church affiliation at all on their enrollment forms. Steele saw the school as a fertile mission field for the unchurched and those that were dissatisfied with their current church. The number of school families that would routinely show up in membership classes was proof enough that he was correct in his assumptions.

The parish started the school when the order came down from the Supreme Court that the public schools had to be integrated. This was an undeniable fact. The parish had purchased the land for the school, built the buildings, and underwritten the operations of the school when tuition did not cover expenses. Now the school was financially stable. The budget of the parish was but a fraction of the school budget. The school had outgrown its financial dependence on the parish and now there were those like Tom Barnhardt that wanted to cut the formal ties with the parish.

The parish members that had sacrificed time and money for the school through the years saw those demanding independence for the school as being ungrateful. For them, their arguments for separation were without merit. Those wanting separation only wanted control. Their argument was all about governance and had nothing to do with the quality of education for the children. They wanted to rid the school of the church's influence.

Steele had been subjected to pressure from both camps. He was doing his best not to be caught in the middle. Since coming to First Church Steele had suggested several different plans to the two opposing groups whereby the school board could have more of a role in the governance and the parish could retain control of the Christian Education in the school. Neither side had found his compromise solutions acceptable. It appeared that both were committed to an "all or none" stance. He did not want to be caught in the middle, but that was exactly where he found himself.

"Father Austin, are you there?" It was Crystal on the intercom. He picked up the telephone.

"I'm here."

"Bishop Petersen is on the line. He says he needs to speak to you immediately."

"Oh great, this day just keeps getting better and better."

"He doesn't sound happy."

"Crystal, that man has never sounded happy when he calls me. It's turning out to be one of those days. Which line is he on?"

"66."

"That's just one six short."

"I beg your pardon, Father? I don't understand."

"Never mind, it's just my lame attempt to find comfort in some satanic cynicism."

Steele pushed the button on his desk telephone. "Bishop, what can I do for you?"

"You can send your damn checks, that's what you can do for me! The hardworking people in this Diocese need to be paid their money." The Bishop was yelling. Clearly, he was angry.

"Whoa, Bishop, I don't know what you're talking about. I told the Business Manager to send those checks to you over a month ago."

"Austin, we haven't gotten a check from First Church in three months. Now just what the hell is going on down there? I understand that you're the hold-up. Ted Holmes tells me that the checks are ready to mail, but you won't let him send them."

"Bishop, please, I told the finance office to send those checks just as soon as I learned they hadn't been mailed. Give me just a minute."

"I hope you'll take that minute to put the checks in the mail."

"Bishop, I know that you don't like me to do this, but please let me put you on hold. I need to get a copy of something and then I'll be right back to you."

"A copy of what? Just tell me if you're going to send the checks."

"Bishop, please...bear with me. Just give me a second. I promise I'll be right back." Steele pushed the hold button. He opened the door separating his office from Crystal's. "Crystal, give me a copy of this month's financial statements."

Crystal opened the filing cabinet and handed Steele a folder. Steele opened it and began reviewing the statement as he walked back into his office. He picked up the telephone and pushed the 66 line again. "Bishop..."

"Austin, you need to do something about that music you play when you put a person on hold. It's god-awful. That's the worst choir I've ever heard. What choir is it?"

"It's our choir, Bishop. That's a CD that our choir made. It's been pretty popular with our congregation."

"Well, don't bother to send me a copy. Now...where are my checks?"

"Bishop, I'm looking at the most recent financial statement. It shows that your checks have cleared our balance sheet."

"Well, I'm telling you that they haven't. Now get on top of this, Austin, and get those checks to me. This Diocese needs the funds to operate."

"Yes, Bishop, there must be some confusion. I'll check on it right now." Before Steele could offer the Bishop his concluding thoughts, the line went dead.

Steele pushed the intercom to Crystal's office. "Crystal, ask one of the bookkeepers to come in here."

"Yes, Father."

Steele opened the door to his office. Rebecca, the Administrator's secretary, entered. "Please be seated, Rebecca. I'm hoping that you can help me with something. The financial statements for the past four months show that we are current with our Diocesan payments. I just had a telephone call from the Bishop. He tells me that we are not. I specifically asked you to send those checks over a month ago. Can you help me understand this?"

Rebecca squirmed in her chair. She looked down at the floor. "Father Austin, I don't want to get anyone in trouble."

"Right now, Rebecca, I'm the one that's in trouble with the Bishop. I need to be able to explain to him just why we haven't mailed our share of the Diocesan Budget."

"Well, Mister Holmes told me that you'd changed your mind and that you wanted us to hold the checks a bit longer."

Steele felt his face flush.

"I noticed Mister Holmes did not sign in today. Where is he?"

"He told us that he was going to take a long weekend. I believe that he was going to see his mother in New Jersey."

Steele grimaced. "New Jersey? I thought his mother lived in Birmingham. I'm sure he told me his mother lived in Birmingham. Just where in New Jersey was he going?"

"He didn't say."

Atlantic City, Steele thought. Atlantic City is in New Jersey. "Is his office open?"

"No, it's locked. He's the only one with a key."

"What? You mean no one else in the building has a key to his office?"

"No, Father. Mister Holmes insists on keeping all the original financial records in his office. He says that no one is to have a key to his office but him."

"What about the sextons or the cleaning service?"

"The sextons clean his office, but only when he is there."

"So you wouldn't know if the diocesan checks are still in his desk?"

"No, Father. I wouldn't know for sure, but I asked him about the checks just last week when the parish bookkeeper was reconciling the bank statement. They had not yet cleared the bank. He repeated that you'd told him to hold them."

"Thanks, Rebecca. You've been a big help. Is there anything I can do for you?"

Rebecca looked down at the floor again. She shifted in her chair and then adjusted her dark rimmed glasses. She looked up at Steele. He could tell she was on the verge of tears. "Am I in trouble?"

Steele smiled, "No, Rebecca you're not in trouble. Quite the contrary, you've been a big help."

She managed a nervous smile. "I really like working here. I like my job, but Mister Holmes is my boss. I just hope I haven't done anything to upset you."

"Everything is fine, Rebecca. You don't have anything to worry about. I appreciate all that you do. You are a valuable member of our staff."

Rebecca stood and Steele thanked her again. He gave her a reassuring pat on the back. When she was gone, Steele once again opened the door separating his office from Crystal's. "Crystal, call a locksmith. Tell him I want him over here within the hour."

CHAPTER 18

Jacque, I'm not being paranoid. I swear that someone is following me." It had been difficult for Virginia to give herself completely to Jacque during their lovemaking. She was nervous. She closed her eyes for only an instant. She thought she heard something or someone outside the window. She stared at the bedroom window in the lake house. She watched it as Jacque continued to move over her. He was lost in what he was doing. She was relieved when he finished so that she could talk to him. He gathered her in his arms.

"Are you sure that you're just not suffering with a guilty conscience?"

She looked at his beautiful face. He was almost too handsome to be a man. She thought that he would have made a gorgeous woman. She put her hand on his hard chest and pushed him away. She needed to talk to him. "What are we doing, Jacque?"

"We're making love. We're enjoying each other. I like being with you, Virginia. I look forward to our time together."

She nodded. "I know—me too, but where do we go from here? What's next?"

"What do you mean?"

"How is this going to end, Jacque? How do we end this?"

Jacque sat up in the bed. He reached for his jeans and pulled out a lighter and a pack of cigarettes from one of the pockets. He lit a cigarette and then looked down at her. "Why does it have to end? Don't you enjoy making love with me?"

"Of course I do. I don't know, shouldn't we have a plan for our future?"

Jacque inhaled the smoke deep into his lungs and then blew it out through his nostrils. "I don't understand. Why can't we just keep on doing what we're doing? Why can't that be our plan?"

Virginia sat straight up in the bed. She pulled the sheet up over her chest. "I'm a married woman, Jacque. Have you thought about that?"

"What's to think about? So you're married. I'm not. In my homeland, lots of married women have lovers. The pity goes to the ladies who don't."

Virginia studied his face. For the first time she felt like an object. She wondered if he just looked at her as a conquest. Was she nothing more than his weekly plaything? "Are you just using me?"

"What?"

"It's a simple enough question, Jacque. Are you just using me for your pleasure until someone younger and prettier comes along?"

"Oh, Virginia, please…this is nonsense. I like you. I enjoy being with you."

"I don't want to just be your sexual plaything."

"Virginia—please. Don't think like that."

"Then answer my question. Where do we go from here?"

"Virginia, I'm your lover. You're my lover. That's enough. We don't need any more than that. Let's just continue to enjoy each other."

"For how long?"

"What? I don't know. Months—years, the rest of our lives. I'll be your lover when you're old and gray."

"What if you get married? Do you date? I've never even asked you that. Jacque, do you date other women?"

"Do you really want to ask these questions? Please, let's just relax and enjoy our time together." He tamped his cigarette in the ashtray on the table. He then leaned down and kissed her on the lips. He put his hand under the sheet and began fondling her. She grabbed his hand and pushed it away.

"Talk to me. Do you date?"

Jacque chuckled, "Occasionally. I'm a young man. I have needs. I can't find all my satisfaction just once a week."

Virginia began to feel nauseous. "Are any of these women special?"

"All women are special. Virginia, I'm French. He smiled and tried to kiss her again, but she turned her face."

"What if you were to fall in love with one of these women? What would happen to us if you married her?"

He shook his head. "My Darling, nothing would have to change for us. We would still have the lake house. We would still have each other."

"So, you would cheat on your wife?"

He shrugged his shoulders. "That's such a nasty little word. It would be just like what you've told me about you and Henry. What Henry doesn't know doesn't hurt him. The same would be true for my wife if I were to have one."

Virginia lay in silence trying to absorb what he was saying. Jacque sat up. He once again reached for his jeans. He pulled out a small plastic bag filled with marijuana and a package of wrapping paper. "I know what you need." He rolled the marijuana cigarette and lit it. He inhaled deeply and held the smoke in his lungs. He handed the cigarette to her.

Virginia took it and placed it to her lips. When she had exhaled she looked into his eyes. She wanted a truthful answer. "You can be that cavalier about what we are doing? Wouldn't you worry about hurting your wife?"

"And do you worry about hurting Henry?"

It was as though he had thrown a bucket of ice water on her. "I don't think about it. It's like I got started cheating on him and I just can't seem to stop."

"So I'm an addiction."

"No, I don't mean that."

He took the marijuana cigarette from her and held it in front of her face. "Just like this joint. I'm your addiction. You accuse me of using you. Well, Virginia, why are you using me? Perhaps you want to hurt Henry. Or, could it be that you're just using me to fill some empty hole that you have in your soul?"

Virginia felt the tears well up in her eyes. They streamed down her cheeks.

Jacque placed the cigarette in the ash tray and pulled one of the tissues from the box on the bedside table. He rolled over toward her. He wiped her face. "Oh my Darling, there's no need for tears. The only tears that should cover this beautiful face are tears of pleasure." He wiped her face and then he kissed her gently on the lips. She responded. He probed her lips with his tongue and she opened to receive him. He smothered her face and chest with kisses and gentle nibbles. His hardness pressed against her. She pulled him over onto her.

At her car, she reached up and put both of her arms around his neck. She squeezed him. She did not want to let him go. Then, she thought she heard something. She dropped her arms. "Did you hear that?"

"What? I heard nothing. Virginia, please calm yourself. Will you be here next week?"

She nodded. She got in her car and rolled down her window. She looked up into his eyes. She studied them for an answer to one of her questions. He smiled back at her. She pursed her lips and blew him a kiss.

On the drive home she rehearsed again the questions she had asked him. She heard him answer each of her questions with a question. Then it became clear to her. For now, he had every man's dream. He was having sex with a married woman on a regular basis. There was no risk for him. She was taking all the chances. He didn't have to worry about her making demands on him or his time. It wasn't even costing him any money. They couldn't be seen in public so he didn't have to buy her lunch. He didn't even have to pay for a hotel room. They were using her friend's lake house.

She turned onto River Street. She glanced into her rear view mirror and noticed that the car behind her turned as well. She thought the car didn't belong on River Street. It was an older car. For an instant, she thought she had remembered seeing the car when she left the lake, but she dismissed that thought as quickly as it had entered her mind. Perhaps it belonged to one of the domestics. She slowed to turn into her driveway. The car passed her. It was being driven by a white male. She realized it didn't belong to a domestic.

Virginia sat in her driveway. Jacque had it made. She was nothing more than his plaything. She had no future with him. The only future she had was more of the same. Her future would be filled with rendezvous after rendezvous. There would be more secrets. Her lies to Henry would build on each other. Jacque was right. She was addicted to it all. She was addicted to the lies, the secrets, and the sex. She had started something and now it was as though she couldn't stop. She was nothing more than a prostitute. She laid her head on the steering wheel. Tears rolled down her cheeks. She pounded her fists into her legs. She was a whore. No, whores were smarter than she was. At least they got paid for their services. She was servicing Jacque for free. "Idiot!" she screamed. Then the final piece of the puzzle clicked into place. There would only be one reason that Jacque would ever end their relationship. He would simply tire of her. She knew that when he grew tired of her he would end it. She would be the one that would be hurt. Virginia had never felt so cheap in her entire life.

CHAPTER 19

"Father Austin, I don't mean any disrespect, but should you be doing this?"

Steele was seated behind Ted Holmes' desk. He had the middle drawer open and had retrieved a stack of checks. He found four made out to the Diocese. He found several others made out to various vendors. All of them had been signed by the Wardens. All were dated over the past three months. He looked up at Rebecca standing at the door to the Administrator's office.

"Rebecca, I want all of these checks taken to the post office and mailed today."

"Yes, sir."

"These four checks to the Diocese I want put in overnight mail and sent to the attention of Bishop Petersen."

"Yes, Father; I know that you're the boss, but Mister Holmes left strict instructions that no one was to send out any mail from this office unless he had reviewed it first."

"He also told you to hold these checks until I told him to mail them. He's not here. So I'm telling you to mail them. Rebecca, I'm giving you strict instructions to put these checks in the mail this afternoon."

"Yes Father, you're the Rector. I just hope…"

Steele had opened the file drawer on the Administrator's desk and had retrieved a couple of three-ring notebooks that were stacked at the rear of the drawer. "Rebecca, your job is secure. You have nothing to worry about."

"If you're sure."

"Rebecca, no staff member can be fired without my consent. That includes you. You're safe."

A look of relief washed over her. "Is there anything you want me to help you find?"

Steele placed the notebooks he had just retrieved on top of the desk. He leaned back in the Administrator's chair and studied Rebecca's face. "I'm not even sure that I know what I'm looking for, Rebecca." He thought for a few minutes. "Has there ever been any activity, records, statements or anything that you saw regarding the business of this parish or school that raised a question in your mind?"

Rebecca walked to the front of the desk and sat down in the chair. She was biting her lower lip. Steele watched her. "I just don't want to get..."

He leaned forward across the desk. "Let me tell you something in confidence. You're not in trouble, but I am. There are some powerful people in this parish that want to destroy my priesthood and they want to destroy me. They're insinuating that I've been mismanaging the funds of this parish. I think they've pretty well convinced the Bishop of this Diocese that I'm guilty. Now, if you know anything that might help me clear my name, I need your help. I will be forever grateful to you."

Rebecca had been staring at the notebooks that Steele had removed from the desk. "You may want to spend some time comparing those notebooks. I'm not a CPA, but...well; you'll see what I mean when you study them."

"Thanks. Is there anything else?"

She nodded sheepishly. "You're aware that there is a secret compartment in this office?"

"What kind of compartment? Where is it?"

"One day a few weeks ago, I was bringing the mail in here to put on Mister Holmes' desk. The door was open so I didn't think anything about it, but when I came in he had taken that picture..." She pointed to a large portrait on the wall.

"This one?"

"Yes, if you take it off the wall, you'll see."

Steele removed the portrait to discover that hidden behind it was a metal door with double key locks. He pulled at it with his finger tips, but it was secure. "Call Crystal, and tell her to get that locksmith back over here."

Steele continued to look through the filing cabinets and through boxes that were stacked in the coat closet. When he found a file or envelope that struck him as curious he removed it and placed it on top of the desk. About the time that Steele had exhausted his search, the locksmith returned. Within minutes he had the hidden compartment open. Steele opened it and removed the contents. Inside was a stack of checkbooks and savings account passbooks. He carried them over to the desk. He quickly realized that they were all on different financial institutions in Falls City and surrounding communities.

"Rebecca." He called for her. "Have you ever seen these before?"

"No sir." Her eyes widened.

Just then Steele caught a glimpse of Judith Idle standing in the hallway. She was trying not to be seen, but obviously she was trying to eavesdrop on their conversation. Steele had already learned not to trust her. He had been warned about her by Horace and a couple of other staff members. They told him that she was not his friend or supporter. She took everything she heard in the office and whatever she could contrive herself directly to Henry Mudd and perhaps the Bishop. Steele wanted her to know that he had seen her. He walked out into the hallway and looked directly at her. "May I help you?"

She turned bright red. "I heard there was a commotion down here. I just wanted to see if you needed my help."

Steele glared at her. "Your help is not needed, but thank you so much for asking." Steele then closed the door. He went back to the Administrator's desk and started looking through the various accounts. And then, he chose to simply count them. There were twenty-eight different checkbooks or savings passbooks on twelve different institutions. He went back to reviewing them again. It was then that he realized that they all had one thing in common. Every one of the accounts was in the name of *Ted Holmes—First Church Episcopal—Falls City, Georgia.*

Rebecca had been watching him. "Father Austin, do you plan on taking all of these things with you? If so, I'll go get you an empty banker's box to carry them in."

"Thanks, Rebecca. That would be nice." When she returned with the box, Steele started putting all the things that he had retrieved into it. He started to put the notebooks into the box but decided to open them. He laid them side by side. The first page in each book was identical. One notebook had last year's January financial summary for the parish on it. It looked familiar to him. It had been presented to the Vestry. The other notebook had the same summary on it, but when he compared the two, the second notebook's summary was different. He looked again at the dates. The dates were identical, but the numbers were not. He gave out a low whistle.

Rebecca was watching him. "Did you find something?"

"I'm not sure. Where does he keep the Vestry notebooks from past years?"

"They're downstairs in the storage vault."

"Will you get me the ones for the past five years? I'll be in my office."

Steele carried the box to his office. The locksmith was standing at his door. "You finished with me, Father?"

"Thanks for waiting on me."

"No problem. It's your money. I'm getting paid whether you have me doing anything or not."

"That's fine. What I need you to do is to put a new lock on the Administrator's office and new locks on that wall compartment. I'll need six sets of keys for each. Bring those to me when you're finished."

"You're the boss."

Rebecca entered carrying five notebooks. "These are the ones for the past five years. They also have the auditor's report in each of them."

"Thanks, Rebecca." Steele took the notebook for the year prior to last. He then asked Crystal to bring him his copies of the Vestry notebooks for the previous five years. When she brought them to him he laid the previous year's financial report that he and the Vestry had been given next to the one that Rebecca had brought him. His hunch was correct. The numbers were different. He compared several different statements from the various notebooks. Clearly, Ted Holmes had been giving the auditors one set of books to audit and giving the Rector and Vestry a completely different financial statement.

"Father Austin, are you all right?" It was Crystal. "You're white as a sheet. Do you need to lie down? I'm bringing you a glass of water."

"There's no need, Crystal. I just need some time to sort something out."

"Is there anything you want me to help you with?"

"Not just yet, but I might."

"Did you remember that you have an appointment with the McFaddens?"

"Oh, no, I forgot."

"They're in the waiting room. Do you want me to bring them in?"

"Give me just a couple of minutes. I need to make one telephone call. I'll be quick about it."

Steele shut the door behind Crystal. He took one of the bank statements on his desk and found the telephone number. He punched the numbers into his telephone.

"First Community Bank."

"Yes, this is Father Austin over at First Church. May I speak with your bank manager?"

The line was silent for just a few seconds. "This is Charles Foster. What can I do for you, Father Austin?"

"Mister Foster, I know that you're a busy man, but I need your help with something."

"Yes."

"Mister Foster, don't you have your tellers do spot checks on large deposits and withdrawals each day?"

"Yes, that's our standard practice."

"Could I ask you to add all the First Church accounts to that process?"

"Are you looking for something in particular?"

"No sir, I'm just trying to tighten up our internal controls and I'd really appreciate it if you would do that for us for the next month or so."

"That really won't be a problem. I'll be happy to do it. Father, you realize that one of my tellers had words with your Administrator a couple of weeks ago?"

"Oh?"

"I thought you already knew. He'd tried to cash a check on one of your parish accounts. The check was made out to him and signed by him."

Steele had a sinking feeling. "And?"

"Well, it was a rather large check and the teller refused to cash it based only on his signature. Most all checks of that size on your parish require two signatures."

"Did he use a signature stamp?"

"That's what caught her attention. The check was handwritten and hand signed."

"You said he tried to cash it."

"She brought it to me and I refused the transaction. Father Austin, it was for a very large amount of money."

"Has he attempted anything like that again?"

"No, she keeps an eye on him when he comes in here. Adding this spot check will further safeguard your accounts."

"Mister Foster, why didn't you call me and tell me about this?"

"Father, your name is not on this account. The check was for one of the organizations in your parish. Mister Holmes and one of your church members are the only signatures on that account."

"But it's a church account."

"That may be, but the only signatures on the account are Mister Holmes and your church member. I guess she is the head of the organization."

"I understand. Can I ask you to spot check every account that has First Church on it regardless of who the authorized signatures are?"

"I suppose we could. I'll get my people on it."

"Thanks, I really appreciate it."

Steele put the notebooks back in the box and placed it in his filing closet. He opened his door and Crystal asked Mr. and Mrs. McFadden to enter. They were elderly members of the congregation. They were in attendance most every Sunday and were always seated in the same place. They also attended most all of the parish social events. Steele knew that Mr. McFadden had been a chemist for a large pharmaceutical corporation. He was very precise. Steele's conversations with him had been pretty one-sided. Mr. McFadden liked to dispense his knowledge without emotion and in a monotone voice that could lull most any insomniac into a blissful slumber. Mrs. McFadden had been a homemaker and they had reared four children. All of their children, their spouses, and their grandchildren were active members of First Church. Steele estimated that the McFaddens were in their late seventies or early eighties. Mr. McFadden was dressed in a gray suit with a white shirt and a green bow tie. Mrs. McFadden was wearing a black dress. She was wearing a full bib flowered apron over the dress. Her gray hair was in a tight bun behind her head. She reminded Steele of his grandmother. He invited them to be seated on the couch. "What can I do for you good folks?"

Mr. McFadden looked at his wife. She shot a look at him and then back at Steele. Neither of them spoke. There was an uncomfortable silence in the room.

"I sense that you may be having a disagreement. What can I do to help you?"

Mr. McFadden looked again at his wife. "You're the one that wanted to talk to the Rector. Well, we're here. So talk."

With that, tears began streaming down Mrs. McFadden's face. She reached into her apron pocket and took out a small flowered handkerchief. She dabbed at her eyes. The silence continued.

"Mr. and Mrs. McFadden, it's obvious that there's some tension between the two of you. I want to help, but I can't read minds." Again, there was silence. They both stared stoically into space.

Steele shifted in his chair as he studied the two of them. "Mr. McFadden, your wife is upset. Something has hurt her. At the same time, I sense that you're angry. If I'm to help, you must talk to me."

"Why don't you tell him?" Mr. McFadden hurled the words at his wife. "It was your idea to come down here—so talk."

Her lips trembled and then she buried her face in her hands as she began sobbing. Steele stood and walked over to the couch. He sat down on the arm of the couch and put his hand on her back. "Please, talk to me. You're hurting right now. Tell me what's bothering you." She shook her head.

"Oh, for God's sake!" Mr. McFadden shouted. "She thinks that I don't love her."

"You don't!" She blurted. "You never tell me you love me. I can't remember the last time that you told me that you love me."

"Of course I love you. I take care of you, don't I? Who feeds you? Who clothes you? Who bought you the house that you've lived in for the past forty-five years? Me! That's who. Now just how can you say that I don't love you?"

Once again she buried her face in her hands and sobbed.

"Have you ever seen anything like this, Father Austin? I'd think she's pregnant or going through the change or doing something female if it weren't for the fact that she is eighty-two years old." He shook his head. "I've never done anything in our entire marriage to make you think that I don't love you. I've never betrayed you. I've not so much as looked at another woman."

She lifted her face from her hands and wiped her eyes with her handkerchief. She began twisting it with her fingers.

"Well, you said you wanted to help." He snorted at Steele. "So help."

Mrs. McFadden appeared to be regaining her composure so Steele patted her on the back and squeezed her hands. He walked back to his chair opposite the couch. "Mrs. McFadden, how can we fix this? What is it you want your husband to do that he's not doing? What does he need to do to reassure you that he loves you?"

She nodded and looked over at her husband. "Just tell me that you love me."

Mr. McFadden winced and shifted his position. He crossed his arms in front of his chest. "Listen woman, I told you sixty years ago on the day that I married you that I loved you. If I ever change my mind I'll let you know."

Mrs. McFadden gave Steele a pleading look.

"I think what you asked your wife earlier has a lot of merit. My guess is that she would agree that you've been a great husband, an excellent father, and a fine provider. All of those things are acts of love. I understand exactly what you're feeling."

"He released his arms and put his hands on his knees. Now we're getting someplace. You're a man. You understand these things."

Steele nodded. "Yes sir, I understand, but I also understand your wife's need. You see, it's not enough just to show your wife that you love her. You also need to tell her."

"Why? It's enough for me. She's a wonderful wife. She's a great cook. She keeps a clean house. She's a devoted mother and an even greater grandmother. I couldn't list all the things that she's done to make life good for me through the years."

"She's not asking you to do that."

"What?"

"She's not asking you to list all the things that she has done to show you that she loves you. She's simply asking you to tell her from time to time that you do."

"Do what?"

Steele studied him in disbelief. He wondered if this man was really this dense.

"Tell her that you love her."

"Why? I don't need her to tell me. I know she loves me. She doesn't have to tell me."

Mrs. McFadden shot a sharp look at her husband. "Well, you might just want to ask me. Or would you rather I double starch your underwear? I'd bet you'd ask me if I did that."

Steele chuckled. Both of them chuckled as well. "Before we get out the starch, let's just focus on what's really a simple request. Mr. McFadden, your wife just needs you to tell her from time to time that you love her. That's all. It's really that simple."

"But I don't understand..."

Steele interrupted him. "It's not important that you understand. You need only to accept the fact that your wife needs to hear those words come from your heart. You do all these other things to show her that you love her. She's asking you to just add one more thing to your list. It's a way that you can show her that you love her. Obviously, it means more to her than you'll ever be able to understand."

He looked over at his wife. "Does it really mean that much to you?"

She nodded.

He reached over and took her hand in his. She smiled. "Well, okay then. If it means that much to you, I'll try to remember to do it."

"Why not start now?"

Mr. McFadden gave Steele a puzzled look. "Start what?"

This time Steele winced. He knew the man had a doctorate in chemistry, so he decided to try yet one more time. "Why not tell her that you love her right now?"

"Here? Now?"

"Please, Mr. McFadden, I'm a professional. More risqué words than those have been uttered in this office. Go on. Tell her."

He nodded and smiled at his wife. Her smile had turned into a glow. He moved closer to her on the couch. Once again he took her hand and looked into her eyes. "Margaret Hilda McFadden, I love you." And with that he kissed her. She put her arms around his neck.

Steele cleared his throat. "It appears to me that my work here is done. I'd like to suggest that the two of you go get a room."

They broke off their kiss. Mr. McFadden stood and helped his wife to her feet. "And don't you think for a minute that we don't know what to do in it."

Steele smiled, "Then you give every young man hope."

Mr. McFadden extended his hand for Steele to shake. He smiled, "And you call yourself a professional."

Mrs. McFadden hugged Steele's neck and kissed him on the cheek. He walked them to the door and opened it for them. "And if he forgets to tell you, you just remind him. If that doesn't work, bring him back in here."

"Oh, no you don't." Mr. McFadden smiled. "I've been taken to the woodshed several times in my life. This is the first time that I've ever felt the need to say 'thank you.' But then, Father Austin, I guess that's what makes you the professional."

Steele smiled at them and waved them down the hall. He walked back into his office. There was a box in his file closet that he hoped would help explain the most recent nightmare he had been living at First Church.

CHAPTER 20

Have you shown these checkbooks to Chief Sparks?"

"No, Stone, you are the first person other than Randi that I've shown these things to. I figured that while the Chief is a friend he's a law enforcement officer first. I don't want to call my investigation to a close prematurely. My instincts tell me that there's a lot more to all of this than meets the eye. I don't want to call the Chief until I'm sure that I know all that there is to know. I would really prefer to catch Ted Holmes red-handed."

"Well, Father, I think you have. There's some pretty incriminating evidence here."

Steele nodded. "I know, but I can't help but feel like we don't have the full picture just yet."

Stone picked up the stack of checkbooks and began thumbing through them. "Steele, these checkbooks by themselves are enough to send that thief to jail for several years."

Steele shook his head. "I don't know. I mean, you're the lawyer here, but I think he could try to explain them away."

Stone Clemons laid the checkbooks down and sat back in his chair. He was lost in his thoughts. "How does he carry the church accounts that we know about?"

"You mean the name on the accounts?"

"Yes. I know how they're supposed to be carried, but I'm embarrassed to tell you that I've never checked to find out if they are."

Steele opened a file folder and handed Stone copies of several bank statements. "As you can see, these accounts are all addressed to the *Rector, Wardens, and Vestry of First Church.*"

"And Holmes had these other accounts set up in the name of the church, but he made himself the authorizing agent."

"It appears that way."

"And the financial statements he's been giving to the Vestry?"

"Again Stone, I'm not an accountant but it appears to me that he's been keeping two sets of books. He's been giving one set to the auditors and another to the Vestry."

"But didn't the Finance Committee review the auditor's statements?"

"Stone, I honestly don't think so. I think that everyone has trusted Ted Holmes to a fault. Take a look here at last year's audit statement and then compare it to the statement that was presented at the annual meeting. The numbers aren't the same. The auditors were clearly working from a different statement than the Vestry was given."

Stone shook his head. "Then we're all guilty. The Vestries haven't been doing their job."

"Think about it for a minute, Stone. The annual meeting of the parish is held in January. The year-end statement from the prior year is presented and then the budget for the coming year. People aren't focused on the past year. The new budget is the center of attention. The audit isn't done on the prior year until May or June. The auditors don't give us their report until the fall. Nine months or more pass between the annual meeting and the auditor's report. No one's going to look at the detail. Who would think to go back and compare the statements? It's the perfect scenario for a thief."

Stone nodded. "I just feel like a damn fool. My combined terms on the Vestry add up to over twenty years. Most of those have been with Ted Holmes as the Administrator. When this breaks, you realize that every man that has ever served on the Vestry of First Church is going to run for cover."

Steele smiled. "Yes, and you know who they're going to point the finger at, don't you? It's going to make the job that Mudd and Boone are trying to do on me all that much easier."

"What do you think we should do next?"

"Well, Ted is going to get back from his weekend trip on Monday. He's going to discover that the locks to his office have been changed and that I now have the contents of his little hiding place in my possession."

"That's going to make him real nervous. My hunch is that he'll be sitting on your doorstep when you come to work on Monday. I think you're right. He's going to have an explanation for everything. Or at least he'll have an explanation that Henry, Ned and all his supporters will accept."

"That's the part that bothers me, Stone. I think he's smart enough and persuasive enough to come up with a pretty good story to explain away a lot of this. We need more."

"Then let's get a Forensic Auditor."

"I've thought about that. I don't think the Vestry will authorize it even on the basis of everything lying on my desk. I think the only person that the Vestry can be convinced to audit right now is me. Stone, remember that I'm the one under suspicion. Ted has the Vestry's trust and confidence. He even has the friendship and the support of the Bishop. As the expression goes, I'm up to my eyeballs in alligators and there's not a friendly face in sight."

"I know you're right. Henry Mudd told me just last week that he'd trust the man with his life."

"I know that Ted's going to be nervous. He's probably going to try to cover his tracks, but I just can't help but believe that this is just the tip of the iceberg. I want to give him a little more time to trip up."

Stone stood and began pacing around Steele's office. Steele watched him. He knew that this man's brilliant mind was considering every possibility. After a few minutes he sat down on the edge of Steele's desk. "How do you plan to give him more rope? He's going to be waiting on you when you get to your office on Monday."

Steele chuckled. "Therein is the beauty of it all. I won't be here. Randi and I will be taking a little trip next week. In fact, we're going to be gone through the following Sunday."

Stone raised his eyebrows. "Oh? Pray tell, where are you going?"

Steele shook his head. "I wish you wouldn't ask me that, my friend."

"Well, tell me this. Are you taking Travis with you?"

"No, Randi's parents are arriving this afternoon. They're going to take care of Travis for us while we're gone."

Stone frowned. "Uhmm, so the rumors are true."

"What rumors?"

"I had breakfast this morning in the grill over at the Country Club. A couple of folks asked me if I knew anything about a search committee coming here to look you over."

"I really don't want to discuss it right now."

Stone leaned across the desk and put his hand on Steele's shoulder. "Father, listen to me. I know that some of these bastards have not treated you with the Christian charity they sing about on Sunday mornings, but you don't have to leave here. There are a lot of us that love you. Father, I love you."

"And I love you too, Stone. You're a great friend. I could not have done this job without you."

Stone stood and pointed his finger at Steele. "Now that bothers me."

"I beg your pardon. What bothers you?"

"It bothers me that you just put that statement in the past tense. Have you already made the decision to leave?"

"No, Stone. I haven't made any decisions. I'm just going to go take a look and see if God is calling me to go or is God calling me to stay."

Stone laughed and started pacing the length of Steele's office. "Now let me tell you a story about God's call. It seems that this preacher got a call to a new parish. So on Sunday morning he announced to the congregation that he and his wife would be spending the afternoon in prayer. They wanted to discern if God was calling them to go or if God was calling them to stay."

Stone stopped in front of Steele's desk so he could make eye contact with him. "Well, the church elders decided that they would go over to the preacher's house after services and tell him that they had prayed on the subject and they had concluded that God wanted him to stay. It seems that when they got there they found the preacher's son sitting on the porch steps. They asked if they could speak to the preacher.

The boy told them that this other church had called his daddy to be their preacher. He said that the new church was going to double his daddy's salary. They were going to buy him a new car to drive and set up a trust fund for his children's college education. They were also going to buy the preacher and his wife a new house to live in.

Of course, this all made the elders even more nervous. So they asked if the little boy could go get his daddy. They needed to talk with him as soon as possible. The little boy said that his daddy asked not to be bothered. He was going to be upstairs praying.

The elders grew even more anxious. They asked if they could speak to the little boy's mother. He told them that they wouldn't be able to do that either. She had left instructions not to be disturbed. They asked if she was upstairs praying as well. The little boy replied, 'Shucks no, my mom's upstairs packing! ' "

When Steele had stopped laughing, Stone said, "Father, let me give you and Randi just one little piece of advice."

Steele nodded. "Of course...I value any counsel that you can give me."

"Father, you pass my counsel on to Randi as well. Agreed?"

"Agreed."

"You ready?"

"Yes, I'm ready."

Stone turned and walked to the door of Steele's office. He opened it and then turned to look at Steele. "Father...you listening?"

Steele nodded.

"You sure now? Do I have your full and undivided attention?"

"Yes, Stone let me hear it."

"Now don't forget to tell Randi."

"I won't forget."

"Can you hear me?"

"Yes, Stone, I can hear you."

"Good, because you won't want to ever forget this one."

"I won't forget."

"Think about this on the flight out, but pray about it on the way back."

"Okay, Stone. Speak, your servant heareth."

"Father...Oh Father...You're like a son to me. Think on this and don't forget. Father...everything that glitters is not gold." With that, Stone pulled the door shut behind him.

CHAPTER 21

"We need to talk about godparents for our baby."

The plane had just reached its cruising altitude and Steele was about to reach into his briefcase to pull out the profile on St. Jude's Parish. He wanted to read it one more time. His wife's question redirected him.

"Did you have anyone in particular in mind?"

"Steele, I would like to ask Rob and Melanie."

"But we haven't seen them since their wedding."

"I know, but I talk to Melanie on the telephone all the time and I know that you and Rob e-mail a lot."

"Oh, we just forward each other the latest clergy gossip or joke."

She hit him on the shoulder. "Oh, I'll bet. Listen Cowboy, I've seen a couple of those jokes you guys have exchanged. If Ned Boone or Henry Mudd ever got a look at one of them, they'd hang you out to dry."

Steele chuckled. "Well, just see if I share any more cartoons with you."

"It's not the cartoons that would get you in trouble and you know it."

"Okay, okay. I think Rob and Melanie would be a good choice, but..."

"I know what you're thinking. But you know what, Steele? I don't care. Rob is a decent human being. He's a really good guy. Melanie has turned out to be my best friend. We got really close while she was living with us."

"Randi, I know all that, but I can just hear the First Church gossip now." Steele exaggerated his southern accent, 'Can you all believe it? The Rector and his wife have chosen an accused murderer and an adulteress for their baby's godparents?' "

Randi was resolute. "I don't care. And my response to them will be *'that's nice. That's real nice.'* " With that they both giggled. Randi and Steele had learned that particular expression was a southern way of smiling at an outsider and telling them to go do unseemly things to themselves without them knowing it. "Besides Steele, if things work out here in San Antonio, we won't be baptizing our baby at First Church. We'll be doing the baptism at St. Jude's."

Steele knew that he would respect his wife's choice for godparents. He also knew that if things didn't work out in San Antonio, the tongues would once again wag in Falls City. Randi and he would be the target. Rob and Melanie were good friends. They had been through a lot together. Rob had been accused of his wife's murder. All the evidence pointed to his guilt. He most likely would have been convicted except for a surprise break in the case that cleared his name. As for Rob and Melanie's relationship, well, that was another story. It had started as an adulterous affair but ended on a happy note. Randi, Travis, and Steele had all been a part of their wedding in California.

The plane began its decent into San Antonio. When they arrived at baggage claim Charles Gerard was waiting on them. He was wearing a western hat and holding a sign that he had made on white poster board. It read—*"Next Rector of St. Jude's and His Beautiful Bride."* When they saw it they both smiled. Charles opened his arms to both of them and gave them a warm embrace. "Welcome to Texas. We're so glad that you're here."

Charles went with Steele to the luggage carousel to claim their bags. Randi took a seat nearby to wait on them. When Steele recognized one of their bags he went to the carousel to claim it. When he turned around he saw Charles pointing at his feet. "Where did you get those western boots? You didn't buy them just for this trip, did you?"

Steele laughed, "No, I hate to tell you, but my first pair of hard shoes was a pair of western boots. They're my favorite thing to wear. You can only imagine how they were received in Falls City."

Charles chuckled. "I have an idea. Well, you and your boots will fit right in here in Texas and at St. Jude's. When we get to the car, I have a little welcoming present I want to give you and Randi."

Charles asked them to wait for him on the curb outside baggage claim while he went to get the car. After a short wait, he pulled up in a red Cadillac. He opened the trunk to load their luggage. Steele got in the front seat and Randi got in the back. "Randi, there are two boxes back there next to you. One is for you and one is for Steele. Go ahead and open them."

Randi opened the first box and squealed. "Steele, it's a pink cowboy hat."

"That one's for you, Randi." Charles smiled. "I just don't want there to be any confusion. The gray one is for you, Steele."

"Thank you so much, Charles; you didn't have to buy us a gift."

"I know I didn't, but then, that's what makes it a gift. Besides, I want you all to blend in here in San Antonio. Now go on, put them on; let's see how they fit."

He pulled the car into the circular drive in front of the Hyatt Regency on the River Walk in downtown San Antonio. We decided to keep you here. It's a real nice hotel and close to all the attractions in downtown San Antonio. We want you to spend your first few days just relaxing and enjoying our city." He handed him an envelope. "In here you'll find some tickets for a carriage ride, a riverboat dinner cruise, and several other tourist destinations. You may use them at your leisure."

"Gosh, Charles, I don't know what to say. I mean, when are we going to see the church?"

"Now just settle down. You're in Texas now. You're on Texas time. There's no rush. We're going to do first things first. If you're going to live in San Antonio, then you're going to have to love it as much as we do. So for the next three days we want you to have a little vacation. You keep track of all your expenses. Now, I mean everything. You keep the receipts for all your food, your drinks, and your entertainment. You give them to me before you leave and I'll reimburse you."

Steele shook his head. "No, that's just too much."

"Now listen here, Padre. You don't want to get on my bad side. You save those receipts and you give them to me. It's not polite to turn down a gift. You especially don't want to turn down a Texas-size gift." Charles looked over at Randi. "Now, you see to it that this man of yours does as I've asked him. I think I detect a little stubborn streak in him."

Randi nodded sheepishly and smiled.

"Now, I won't be bothering you for the next few days and neither will anyone else from the church. You just enjoy yourselves. We'll do all that calling committee stuff over the weekend." The bellman had loaded their luggage on the cart. "This man here will take care of you." Charles handed the bellman a twenty dollar bill. "You do whatever Father and Mrs. Austin need you to do to get them settled."

"Yes sir. It will be my pleasure, sir."

Charles reached out and hugged them again. "I'm just so happy that you're here. Now go on and enjoy yourselves. You have my numbers. Call me if you need anything." With that he got back in his car and drove away.

Once they arrived at their room they quickly unpacked and changed into shorts and walking shoes. They were anxious to explore the city. They walked back through the hotel lobby and out onto the River Walk. The River Walk is a paved walkway on either side of the Guadalupe River that winds through the heart of downtown San Antonio. It's lined with shops, restaurants, and hotels. There are small open-air riverboats that pilot tourists along the scenic route. They began their walk trying to the best of their ability to take everything in.

"Isn't this beautiful, Steele?"

"I can't believe we're here. It's so different than what we've grown accustomed to in Falls City."

There were palm trees on the River Walk. Beautiful flowers were everywhere they looked. Some flowers were in planter boxes and others in hanging baskets. Then Steele smelled something he had almost forgotten. It was Texas barbeque. "Randi, do you smell that?"

She squealed, "Barbeque. Steele, we're hungry."

"We?"

"Yes, me and your baby. And we want barbeque."

Once they had found the source of the delicious aroma, a young waiter dressed in jeans, boots, and a white shirt with a western kerchief tied around his neck led them to a table on the patio. Here they could eat and watch the tourists and the riverboats pass by. They each ordered barbequed ribs. Steele ordered a Lone Star Beer. "When in Texas..." he clicked his beer against Randi's iced tea glass." She smiled.

After they had eaten and were fully satisfied, they decided to just sit for a while and take in the scene unfolding around them. Steele reached across the table to hold his wife's hand. She gushed, "Steele, can you believe this? Charles Gerard is so nice and the hotel they're keeping us in is just wonderful. They're giving us a three-day vacation."

A Mariachi band passed by them. They stopped and asked Steele if he had any requests. He smiled and asked them if they knew *De Colores.* They immediately began to sing. When they had finished, he handed them a five dollar bill. The band started playing again and strolled past them on down the River Walk. Just then Randi flinched and grabbed her stomach. She took Steele's hand and placed it in the spot under hers. "Do you feel that?"

Steele smiled. "I think we've just gotten another opinion on Texas."

"And what do you think that might be?"

"I think our baby likes it."

"And what about you, Cowboy, how do you feel? Do you like it?"

Steele turned to watch some of the people passing by. There were plenty of tourists with their cameras, but he also saw some of the locals. The businessmen passing them were wearing their western-cut suits, boots and hats. Some of the women were wearing silver and turquoise belts. He smiled at one young woman that passed them wearing a pair of pink western boots. Just then he spotted a little sign at the café next to them. The sign read *Happy Hour 4-6 P.M. Margaritas.*

"Steele, how do you feel?"

Steele looked into his wife's eyes and squeezed her hand. "Honey, I feel like I've come home."

CHAPTER 22

Henry, this is Judith Idle."

"Good afternoon, Judith. It's so nice to hear from you."

"God bless you, Henry. You know that Elmer and I pray for you every day. We just continually give praise to Jesus that we have faithful men like you on our Vestry."

"Well, Judith, thank you. And how is Elmer? Has his golf game gotten any better?"

She giggled, "You're so kind. Thank you for asking. I'm afraid that his golf game brings a smile to his face on some days and a frown on the others."

Henry chuckled, "I guess as long as the smiles outnumber the frowns he'll just keep right on playing."

She gave a polite laugh. "And your wife, how is your beautiful Virginia? And your lovely daughters—are they doing well? You know that Elmer and I were just saying this morning that Virginia is the very essence of the sacred words in the Book of Proverbs; *a faithful wife is more precious than a jewel of any price.* Do you know that passage, Henry? Isn't it just a perfect description of your Virginia?"

The mention of his wife's name in the context of words from the Bible caused Henry's stomach to do a flip. "My girls just make their Daddy proud every day. They truly are the apple of my eye. I just don't know how I could love them any more than I do. Now, to what do I owe the pleasure of this call?"

"First, I wanted to thank you and Virginia again for including us at the wonderful brunch in your home with the Bishop. Everything was just perfect. But then, with Virginia as the hostess, we would be remiss to expect anything less."

"Yes, yes, we got your very kind thank-you note. You were most gracious with your compliments."

"Words fail to express the joy that we shared in your home that day. I'm afraid that our conversation at the table that day is the reason for my call."

"Go on."

"Henry, you need to know that Elmer and I have prayed about this telephone call all weekend. We fasted all day Saturday. We were steadfast in our study of the scriptures just hoping that God would reveal His will for us through His word."

"Yes."

"Oh, thank you Jesus. I'm so grateful that you understand just how difficult this is for me...and for Elmer as well."

"I sense that you need to tell me something."

"I fear so, Henry. The Lord has not let either Elmer or me rest until we made the decision that I should phone you. Once we made that decision we were at peace."

Henry was growing impatient with her pious babble. "What do you need to tell me, Judith?"

"Henry, I only have the best interest of the church at heart."

"As we all do, but I'm going to have to ask you to get to the point. I have a client waiting for me in the outer office."

"Yes of course, you are a very busy man. God has so blessed you."

"Judith, please."

"Yes, yes, of course. Henry, there's something going on down here at the church offices. I know that the Rector is up to something, but I just don't know what."

"Go on."

"Well, last Thursday, Mister Holmes left town for a long weekend. The man works so hard. He is so devoted to our church. He hardly ever takes a day off and I can't remember him ever taking a vacation, so if anyone deserves a long weekend it's him."

"I agree. He's a very valuable employee."

"Henry, the Rector took advantage of Ted being out of town. He called a locksmith to come down to the church and break into Ted's office."

"He did what?" Henry shouted.

"I don't know everything, but I know that the Rector took a lot of documents out of Mister Holmes' office. I tried to see what he was doing, but he shut the door in my face."

"What kind of documents? What were you able to see?"

"It looked to me like he was taking checkbooks, notebooks, and file folders."

"Well, we'll just see about this. Thanks for calling me, Judith. You did the right thing. I'll take it from here."

"God bless you, Henry. I just know that something is not right. Elmer and I believe that God was telling us to call you. I feel so much better for having done so."

"Thanks again, Judith. I really appreciate your service to our church." On hearing those words, a smile spread across her face.

As soon as he hung up the telephone with Judith, Henry hit the speed dial button he had programmed into his telephone for First Church. He was passed from the receptionist to the Rector's secretary. Crystal answered the phone, "Rector's Office."

"This is Henry Mudd. I want to talk with the Rector, and I want to talk with him right now."

"I'm so sorry, Mister Mudd, but Father Austin is out of the city through next Sunday."

"Where is he? I'm the Junior Warden and I didn't receive any notice that he was going on vacation. Just where is he? I need to talk to him right now!"

"I apologize, Mister Mudd, but Father Austin didn't tell me where he would be going. He did say that he would check back with me about mid-week. He left Doctor Drummond in charge. Would you like to speak to him?"

"No, I don't want to speak to Doctor Drummond. I want to talk to the Rector. When did you say he would be calling you?"

"He didn't say precisely. He just said he would check with me mid-week."

"Well, when he does, you tell him to call me and to do so immediately."

"Yes sir, I'll relay the message. Do you want me to tell him the nature of your call?"

"No I don't." Henry was disgusted. Then he reconsidered. "On second thought, tell him I know exactly what he's up to and he won't be getting by with it. Tell him that by the time he talks to me, I will have talked to the Bishop and every member of the Vestry."

"Is there anything else?"

"No, that should suffice." Henry hung up the telephone. He reached for his palm pilot lying on his desk. He found the number for the private line into Rufus Petersen's office. He dialed it.

"This is the Bishop." The voice answered.

"Bishop, this is Henry Mudd. I hate calling you on your private line, but this is a matter of some urgency. Can you talk?"

"Give me just a second. I was dictating some letters to my secretary." Henry heard the Bishop ask his secretary to leave and to close the door behind her. There was some muted conversation and then silence. "Go on, Henry."

"Bishop, that damn Rector of ours broke into the Administrator's office and stole the church records."

"He's really got a set of brass ones, doesn't he?" The Bishop growled. "We should have anticipated that he would pull something like this."

"Then you're thinking what I'm thinking?"

"It's as plain as the nose on your face." The Bishop snorted. "He found out that your Administrator was helping us investigate him. He got in there and took all of the incriminating evidence. I'll bet he's already destroyed it."

"That's exactly what I was thinking, Bishop." Henry was breathing heavily into the phone.

"Calm down, Henry. You sound like a bull ready to charge a matador."

"If I could get that Rector in my sight right now, he'd be happy to settle for a charging bull."

"Let's just calm down and think this through. We're both smarter than that Okie. That means that the two of us together are four times as smart."

Henry laughed with relief. "I know that you're right. Let's just hope that Ted has made copies of all the records and has them in a safe place."

"Did you ask him?"

"No, he's out of the city for a long weekend. He's not due back until tomorrow."

"That's pretty unusual. Folks tell me he's such a hard worker that he's never gone."

"That's true, Bishop. Ted takes his ministry very seriously. No one will begrudge him having a long weekend to go see his invalid mother."

"Have you confronted the Rector?"

"That's impossible. He's out of town for a week."

"Oh? Where is he? Doesn't his secretary have a way of getting in touch with him?"

"No one seems to know where he went."

"Did he take his wife and child with him?"

"I didn't think to ask, but he never goes anywhere without them."

The Bishop sighed. "It's probably too late to do anything about it, but my hunch is that he's taking another one of his vacations and using church funds to pay for it all."

"You're probably right, but there's another possibility."

"Oh?"

"Yes sir, the rumor mill has it that a search committee was here a few Sundays ago. The talk is that he has gone to look at another job."

The Bishop leaned forward in his chair. "That's the first I'm hearing about it. Do you have any idea where?"

"No one seems to know, but a couple of people talked to someone they suspected of being with the search committee. They said they had a deep southern accent, but it had a Midwestern twang to it. They thought that perhaps they were from somewhere in Louisiana, Texas, or maybe even Oklahoma. They just couldn't be sure."

"Hmmm. I'll tell you what, Henry, let me call a few of those Bishops and see what I can find out. If it's Oklahoma, I doubt if that Bishop will even take my call. He and I don't get along. We're on opposite sides of the aisle on most everything, and that includes Steele Austin."

"And the others?"

"Oh, if he's looking at a job in one of their Dioceses, they're going to want to talk to me before they buy themselves a big package of trouble."

"Bishop, I just don't know what First Church would do without you."

"You're very kind, Henry. We're in this together. We both know what has to be done. Let's just hope that Steele Austin has not outsmarted us on this one."

"I'll find out from Ted first thing in the morning if he has copies of the church records. I'll call you back and let you know."

"Has your investigation uncovered anything so far?"

"Stupidity!" Henry snarled. "I can't see that he's done anything illegal, but he certainly has used poor judgment. If some of this were ever to become public..." Henry stopped and took a deep breath. "You just won't believe some of the things he's supported with the Rector's Funds. No one would ever give another dime to First Church if folks were to find out. Bishop, do you know that poor excuse for a priest has given out over five hundred dollars to a couple of queers so that they could buy medicine for their infections?"

"Stupid is right. It's not illegal, but poor judgment doesn't even describe that. It's just plain dumb. Anything else?"

"There's nothing that you don't already know about. I don't know if we're going to be able to find out just who he's been bailing out of jail. My hunch is that he hasn't been bailing anyone out."

"Oh, then what about the checks to the bondsman?"

"I've had my people do a complete background on that guy. His hands are dirty. He's into everything. He running street drugs, women, gambling, you name it."

"How does he stay in business? Why haven't they arrested him?"

"Bishop, that guy has connections that you and I would envy. Some pretty high-powered politicians in this state use him to secure women to entertain their cronies. He'll never be arrested."

"And that's the type of guy that Steele Austin is giving the hard-earned money of the people of First Church to."

"You got it."

"You think Austin is in business with him?"

"That's my hunch. I just have to prove it. At the very least, I think he's laundering money through that bail bondsman. He's writing the bondsman checks under the auspices of bailing a parishioner out of jail. The bondsman cashes the checks and they split the money. That's how he's paying for his high living."

"That's going to be a tough one to prove."

"If it can be proven, I'm going to prove it. You can count on that."

"Call me after you've talked with the Business Administrator. Also, if you find out just where Austin is, let me know that as well."

"You can count on me, Bishop."

"Give my regards to your beautiful wife. My goodness, Henry, you are one lucky man. I think we're both guilty of marrying above ourselves. I just can't believe how radiant your bride was at the brunch you all held in my honor. Everything was just perfect. She was perfect. I hope that you get down on your knees every night and thank the good Lord for giving you such a beautiful wife."

Henry felt nauseated. A cold sweat broke out on his face. "Yes, Bishop."

"Hug those girls of yours for me. You're a mighty blessed man."

Henry had a difficult time swallowing. "Thanks, Bishop. I'll call you when I know something." Henry hung up the telephone. He reached for a tissue from the box on his credenza so that he could wipe the sweat from his face. And then, without warning, his insides spewed into his mouth.

CHAPTER 23

Ted Holmes took the red-eye from Newark Liberty International Airport to Atlanta. It had been a great weekend. At first, he had lost several hundred dollars at the tables before his luck changed. He ended the weekend a winner on all accounts. He smiled as he recalled the two beautiful women that he had paid to keep him company. They were expensive, but they were well worth it. They just don't make women like that in Falls City, he thought.

He took the parking lot shuttle bus at the Atlanta Airport to his long term parking space. It was still dark. The sun would not be up for a couple more hours. He would get to the office in Falls City before anyone else. He needed to check on things and make sure that all was still in order. He'd had an uneasy feeling about his situation since Steele Austin had started tightening up the internal controls, but he wasn't worried. Henry Mudd, Ned Boone, even the Bishop wanted to get rid of Austin. He was doing some things to help them. They were so anxious for any bit of scandal that they grabbed onto his insinuations like hungry dogs. He didn't even have to accuse the Rector. He only needed to make suggestions. He smiled to himself; as long as they were focused on the Rector's finances, he figured that he was safe. Once Austin was gone he could relax and life would go on as it had for the last decade.

He paid his parking fees and pulled out of the parking lot onto the freeway. He headed south. Until Austin showed up he had things pretty much under control. Old Doctor Stewart left all the financial operations of the parish to him. He never even asked him any questions. If anyone asked a question about the finances at a Vestry meeting, Doctor Stewart's response was always the same. "I'm sure that Ted has looked into that, so we don't have to. I trust him to take good care of the church's money." Ted smiled, remembering that no one ever asked a follow up question.

Doctor Stewart never wanted to be bothered with the business affairs of the parish. He left those to Ted. He didn't even come to the staff meetings. Ted presided at those. All the secretaries, bookkeepers, and janitors reported to Ted. Ted took care of the mail, the bank deposits, the check writing. He worked with the auditors and attended the finance committee meetings. Doctor Stewart preferred to stay focused on the spiritual aspects of the parish.

Things were going pretty well until Austin showed up. That hillbilly just asked too many questions to suit Ted. He was constantly sticking his nose in the business office. Over the past few weeks he had started changing things. He was having the mail sent to his desk. He was working with the money counters on the weekly deposits. That's okay, Ted mused. He simply changed the bank accounts he didn't want anyone to know about to the mail box that he rented. He told each of the banking institutions that the church had asked him to stop having the financial records sent to the church office. They wanted them mailed to a more secure location. No one even questioned his reason for doing so.

The drive to Falls City passed quickly. The sun was now beginning to rise as he drove into the First Church parking lot. He parked in his space. No one else was here yet. He had worked hard for this parish. He had done them a good service, but they had never given him so much as a Christmas bonus to thank him for his sacrifices. He never took a vacation, but did any of them offer to give him additional compensation? Then they went out and brought in that sorry excuse for a priest from Oklahoma. They were paying him twice what they had paid Doctor Stewart. This new Rector was making four times what they were paying him. He resented it. He resented all of it. He wasn't doing anything wrong. He was just collecting what the church owed him.

He took the elevator from the parking lot entrance up to his office. He reached in his pocket for his keys. He slid the key into the dead bolt, but it wouldn't turn. He tried again. Something was wrong. He looked to make sure he was using the right key...nothing. He went over to the finance office door that housed the offices for the bookkeepers and tried to use his key to open that door. Again, it wouldn't open. Something was really wrong. He took a closer look at the locks. They were different. They had been changed. Ted felt sick to his stomach. Anxiety washed over him.

He rushed down the hallway past the receptionist's desk to the staff break room. He slid his key into that lock. It opened. He turned on the light. His hands were shaking. He would have to wait until one of the staff members arrived so that he could find out what had happened. He decided to make a pot of coffee. It was 6:00 a.m. No one would arrive before eight. He sat down to wait. To his surprise he heard someone unlocking their office. He looked up at the clock. It was 6:20 a.m. He walked out into the hallway.

"Oh Ted, you're back. I'm so glad to see you. Elmer and I thought that you might come to work early."

"Judith, what the hell is going on? I can't get into my office."

Judith looked over her shoulder and then behind Ted. She pulled her office door shut. She walked to Ted and put her arms around his neck. She whispered in his ear. "Let's go someplace private. I don't think it's safe to talk in this building. I'll tell you all about it. I'll drive."

Once they were in her car Ted's anxiety was reaching an unbearable level. He was almost hyperventilating. He couldn't stop shaking. "What's going on, Judith?"

She pulled into a parking space in front of a little coffee shop on a side street at the edge of downtown. "Let's go in. It looks like we'll be the only ones in there." Once they were seated in a back booth they ordered a cup of coffee. The cup shook as Ted tried to get it to his lips. "Ted, the Rector raided your office while you were gone."

He did not respond. He just sat the cup of coffee back in his saucer and pushed it away. "I can't drink this."

"I know that you're upset, but I don't think you have anything to worry about."

He didn't find any comfort in her words. "Tell me exactly what he did."

He took a lot of things out of your office. That's really all that I know. I've tried to find out just what he took, but no one is talking. He then changed the locks on your office."

Ted put his hands in his lap. He clasped them in an effort to keep them from shaking. "Then what?"

"That's all I know." She took a sip of her coffee. Then she pushed his cup and saucer toward him. "You really should drink this."

"I don't think I can put anything in my stomach."

"You need to know that I called Henry Mudd. I told him what the Rector had done. He wasn't happy."

Ted felt the pressure he was feeling in his chest lighten just a bit. He didn't know whether it was curiosity or relief. "What did Henry say?"

"Henry is grateful to you for all that you do for First Church. He trusts you completely. He thinks that the Rector wanted to get any records out of your office that would incriminate him."

Ted began to see an opening for himself. He nodded.

"Ted, why didn't you just go ahead and give them to Henry? If you had information he could use against the Rector, why didn't you give it to him?"

In Ted's mind the small opening turned into a large door. "I didn't want to ruin the man. I was just hoping that he would read the handwriting on the wall and leave. I wouldn't want to see a priest go to prison."

"Oh, God bless you, Ted. Elmer and I figured it was something like that. You have such a kind heart. Elmer says that you are the most compassionate man he has ever met in his life. I mean, the way you take care of your invalid mother and all."

"Thanks, Judith. And thank Elmer for me as well. It's great to have good friends like you."

Ted picked up his coffee cup and took a swallow. The warm liquid felt good in his mouth and throat. "What does Henry want to do next?"

"He didn't share that with me. He just knows that you're the key to getting the evidence on the Rector. I know he's going to be anxious to talk to you." Judith put her coffee cup back on its saucer. She then reached across the table and put her hand on Ted's arm. "Ted, I know this is going to be hard for you because you're such a righteous man, but you simply must help us get rid of this Rector. He's not good for our parish. I know that you, more than anyone else, knows the wrong that he's been doing. We need you to tell Henry just what you know. Will you do that?"

Ted nodded. His hands had stopped shaking, but his insides hadn't. Just maybe he could find a way to save himself. He would do whatever he had to do to help them get rid of Austin. Once he was gone everything would be fine. Tears welled up in his eyes and one dropped down his cheek.

"Oh, you dear man. God love you. Jesus bless you. I know this is going to break your heart to have to do this, but Ted, it's for the church. It's what God would want you to do. You'll see. He'll bless you."

When they arrived back at the office, the staff parking lot was full. He walked with Judith up the stairs to the administrative floor. "I wonder who has my keys."

She nodded toward Crystal's office. "I'd start there."

"Good morning, Crystal." Ted tried to gush. "Would you happen to have the new keys to my office?"

Crystal opened her center desk drawer and handed him a key.

"I guess for the sake of security it's a good thing to change the locks on the offices from time to time. Were there any other locks changed that I might need a key for?"

"No, Mister Holmes. I think the finance offices were the only locks that were changed."

"Is the Rector going to be in today?"

"No, he'll be gone for the rest of the week."

"Well, I hope that he's out having a good time. He needs his rest too." Ted held up the key and waved at Crystal. "You have a great day." He walked to his office and slid the key into the lock. It opened immediately. He walked over to his desk and pulled out each drawer. It didn't take him long at all to see what Steele had removed. He rushed over to the coat closet. He opened the first box. A wave of nausea washed over him. He needed to know just what else the Rector had taken. He went back to his desk and pushed the intercom. "Rebecca, are you there?" There was no answer. "Rebecca...Rebecca...are you there?"

"Mister Holmes, this is Sally. Rebecca called in a few minutes ago. She is using some of her compensatory days this week. She won't be in at all. Is there anything I can do to help you?"

"No thanks."

Ted leaned back in his chair. He looked around his office. Then he quickly jumped to his feet. He took the large portrait off his wall. He reached in his pocket for the keys to the wall cabinet. He tried to insert the first and then the second. Neither would go in. He slumped back into his chair. He whispered to himself, "Okay, Father Austin, if that's the way you want to play it, then the gloves are off. You've met your match. I'm going to do whatever it takes to beat you at your own game." He reached into his shirt pocket and brought out a cigarette. He lit it and watched the smoke rise toward the ceiling. He now knew exactly what he had to do next.

CHAPTER 24

The Oaks Club in San Antonio is well-named. It's located in an exclusive residential neighborhood surrounded by large live oak trees. It's actually an old ranch house that had been converted into a private dinner club. The grounds are immaculately landscaped. Clearly, at one time it had been the home for a rancher and his family on a real working Texas ranch. Every effort had been made to maintain the integrity of the house. The large brass plaque that had been placed at the entrance to the club by the Texas Historical Society attested to the authenticity of the architecture. The wide ranch house plank floors were shining underneath the chandeliers. There was a large oak wood bar trimmed with polished brass just off the main entrance. The very predictable horns from a longhorn steer were hanging above the bar. The several rooms throughout the house had been set up for dining. The tables were covered with white linen tablecloths. On each was an arrangement of fresh flowers and a small western style lantern enclosed a burning candle. There were also a couple of private dining rooms. The Vestry of St. Jude's would be meeting with Steele and Randi in one of them.

Charles Gerard and his wife drove Steele and Randi to the club. "Well, Mrs. Austin, what do you think of San Antonio?"

"Please call me Randi."

"And you call me Babs. My name is Barbara, but everyone calls me Babs."

"Well, Babs, I think Steele and I have fallen in love with San Antonio."

"That's so good to hear. You need to know that my husband has fallen in love with the two of you. But now that I see just how beautiful you are, I'm beginning to wonder if it's your husband or you that he's so infatuated with."

"Now Babs, Honey, you know that I only have eyes for you."

She giggled. "Isn't he something? He's been blowing that hot air on me for thirty-four years and I just keep basking in the glow of it all."

She patted her husband on the shoulder. "Yes, Darling...you just keep dishing it out and I'll keep right on swallowing it all—hook, line, and sinker." Then she chuckled some more.

Charles Gerard pulled his Cadillac into the valet parking station in front of the Oaks Club. The valets opened the doors for Babs and Randi. When Charles opened his door he looked down at Steele's feet. "I see you wore your boots, but where's your hat?"

"Well, I didn't know if it would be the thing to wear tonight."

Charles put his hat on his head. "Sir, you're going to be the only man in the room that doesn't have his Stetson on tonight."

Steele was embarrassed. "I'm sorry, I just didn't know."

Charles slapped him on his back. "Partner, I think you've been living around those tight-assed southerners a bit too long. Here in Texas we dress to please ourselves, not others."

The maitre d' was waiting at the door for them. He was dressed in a black tuxedo. Steele leaned over to Randi and whispered, "No hat."

She pinched his tricep. "And you behave yourself tonight, Cowboy." They snickered.

"Mr. and Mrs. Gerard, I've been waiting for you. The rest of your party is all waiting for you in the Longhorn Dining Room. I'm afraid they may be a bit ahead of you with their cocktails."

Charles Gerard put his arm around the maitre d'. "Cecil, I could give those sissies a week's head start and still out drink them." They both laughed.

As they followed behind Charles, Babs, and the maitre d', Steele leaned down and whispered in Randi's ear, "Dorothy, we're not in Kansas anymore."

She smiled up at him. "And I thought I just told you to behave yourself."

"Well, you have to admit that this is not the Magnolia Club. I don't think these people are clones of one another. I think we've come to the land of the living."

"Now, I can spank you."

"Promise?"

There were four long tables set up in a perfect square in the Longhorn Dining Room. When Steele and Randi entered the room, it was filled with the other members of the Vestry and their spouses. They all began applauding when they entered. There were big smiles on every face. When the applause stopped, Charles Gerard took charge. "Now, obviously this is Father and Mrs. Austin. What you don't know, Steele, is that we know more about you than you know about us. We've done our homework. I can even tell you when you lost your baby teeth. Tonight's not about us getting to know you. We already have all the information we need. Tonight, kind sir, we are placing ourselves at your disposal. Tonight, we want you to get to know us."

His comments were followed by more applause. "But enough of this—first things first. Cecil, my priest here will have your best single malt scotch. He drinks his single malts neat. Now, make it a double and tell Ramon not to try to give him any of that stuff on the shelf. I want him to use the bottle that I keep in my private locker. And for his lovely bride, who is with child, I want you to bring her a club soda with a twist of lime."

Cecil smiled, "Yes, sir."

"Charles, how did you know that I like single malts?"

Charles grinned, "I told you. I already know all that I need to know about you."

The first part of the evening was devoted to socializing. Steele and Randi both were amazed that not a single person grilled them on any subject. Rather, each one asked them what they could tell them about St. Jude's, San Antonio, or Texas. They both began to relax and soon felt like they had blended into the group. They were already a part of St. Jude's but they'd never attended a service.

"Dinner tonight will feature some of the finest beef that Texas has to offer. If you have to use your knife to cut your steak, you let me know. We'll send it back to the kitchen. We're going to start with a green salad with blue cheese dressing. There's going to be Texas toast and a Texas-sized baked potato, but you all save some room; dessert is going to be the best pecan pie you've ever eaten in your life." Charles had actually gotten everyone's attention by letting out a shrill whistle. Randi's eyes grew wide when she saw him put his two fingers to his front teeth and blow.

"Now, we're going to be having some good wine from the Texas Hill Country. We're not serving any of that stuff from the land of fruit and nuts out there on the left coast. We're drinking Texas wine!" With that comment the entire room exploded with applause and whistles once again. "Now, you all take your seats. Babs has put place cards at each plate. You can find your own name. That is, all but Billy—hell, we all know that Billy can't read his own name unless it's on a stock certificate. Someone help Billy find his place." That comment was followed by more laughter and a buzz of conversation as people began moving to their places at the table.

"Mrs. Austin, Father Austin, we're just so glad that you're here. Before we say grace I want everyone to lift their glasses." Around the tables glasses were raised. "Ladies and gentlemen, I propose a toast to the next Rector of St. Jude's Parish, his beautiful wife, to all the good folks in this room, to St. Jude's Parish, and last, but by no means least, I propose a toast to Texas!"

All around the table came the shouts, "To Texas."

"Now Father, I don't mean to step on your territory, but at St. Jude's we've been taught that the host at the meal is the priest in charge. Since I'm hosting this little shindig that means that I'm the priest here tonight. So if it's acceptable to you, I'll say the blessing."

Babs interrupted him, "Well, for God's sake Charles, keep it brief. I'm hungry."

"Yes, dear." He smiled. "And I love you too."

"Now all you Texans bow your heads. Tom, shut your eyes. This is not a visual activity." There were more chuckles. "Lord Jesus, you've so blessed our lives together. You've given us a church that is more than a church; it's our home. You've made us brothers and sisters with one another. Now, you've led us to this fine young priest and his wife who will lead us into the future. Bless them, Lord, and bless us as we congregate tonight. And finally, at my wife's request that I be brief, here's the blessing over the food. God is good. God is great. All across the Lone Star State." There were some snickers around the table. "Bless this food and drink. Prosper the laborers who have given us this bread and wine for our communion together. And bless the ranchers that have provided us with tonight's meat."

All at the table responded with an audible, "Amen".

After dinner Charles once again stood and called all to silence. "We now need to give Father and Mrs. Austin the opportunity to ask us some questions. Steele, Randi, we are here to help you feel at home. Ask us anything you want."

Steele and Randi looked at one another. Then Steele stood and spoke. "Charles, members of the Vestry...we want to thank you for the last few days in San Antonio. It's been like a honeymoon for us."

One of the Vestry interrupted him, "It must have been a shotgun wedding." Everyone laughed.

Steele and Randi laughed as well. "I know that this is difficult for you to believe, but we just feel so much at home with you all that I'm at a loss for words."

"Hired!" Shouted one of the Vestry.

"At a loss for words, that's my kind of preacher." There was more laughter.

Steele smiled. "I really don't know what to ask you. We're looking forward to seeing the church and worshipping with you on Sunday. I think that will answer a lot of our questions. Why don't you ask us some questions? We really don't mind. In fact, it will probably help us. Please..." Steele resumed his seat and took Randi's hand in his.

"¿Padre, habla Espanol?"

Steele smiled, "Si, hablo Espanol. Pero, yo neccesito mucho practicar."

"Bueno." The man that asked the question responded. "You don't have to speak Spanish in Texas, but it won't hurt. Some of us think that we should add a Spanish service on Sundays at St. Jude's."

"I actually enjoy learning other languages. I have some knowledge of German from college. In seminary I had to study Greek. I've taken several courses in Spanish. I even know a few words in my family's native language of Cherokee."

"Lord, Chuck, have you brought us an Indian to be our Rector?"

"Don't pay any attention to him. He thinks John Wayne was the only true Native American." There was more laughter.

"Randi," a woman asked. "Will you be comfortable living in Texas after living in Georgia? I don't mean any disrespect, but Texas is not at all like the place you've been living."

Randi smiled, "My home is Oklahoma. From what I've seen so far, I won't have any trouble making the transition."

"Oh hell, leave the little lady alone." A rather large man that had lit a cigar in the far corner of the room spoke. "It's not her fault she's in Georgia. And we all know that Okies are just Texans that couldn't swim well enough to cross the Red River." That was followed by even more laughter.

Steele smiled at Randi. "Do you all laugh like this all the time? I mean, you really seem to enjoy each other's company."

Babs raised her hand. Charles smiled at her. "You want to answer that one, Darling?"

"Steele, Randi, the people at this table are my family. That's what makes our parish so wonderful. There isn't anything that Charles and I wouldn't do for anyone in this room. The apostle Paul was describing St. Jude's when he wrote that when one cries all cry and when one rejoices all rejoice. I may love these people even more than some of my blood relatives. I just can't imagine life without them." Steele looked around the table. Everyone present was smiling and nodding.

"Now that doesn't mean I agree with everyone at this table on all subjects." Babs pointed at one of the men across from her. "Lord, Fred over there is a Republican. Can you believe that? I just can't believe that we actually have a Republican in Texas." Then her smile grew even larger. "While I don't agree with Fred on a lot of things, he's family; he's in my church family. If Fred or anyone else at this table ever needs my help they know that they can call on me." Her words were followed by several verbal "Amens" and loud applause.

Charles stood. "Okay, then. I'm going to ask the members of the Vestry to remain. We have some business to conduct. Babs will be driving the Austins back to their hotel. I guess the rest of you know how you're getting home."

A woman dripping in turquoise jewelry and diamonds responded in a deep South Texas accent. "Home nothing. Some of us will be waiting on you at the bar, so make quick work of your business. I for one don't know what you have to decide. I've seen all that I need to see." Then she smiled directly at Steele and Randi, "Father and Mrs. Austin, welcome to St. Jude's." The room once again exploded in applause.

"Steele," Charles whispered in his ear. "I'd like to meet you at your hotel for breakfast in the morning. Is eight o'clock too early?"

"No, that should be fine. Do you want Randi to be there as well?"

"Does she have a say in whether or not you're going to accept our call?"

Steele smiled, "She even has veto power over the Almighty."

"Then we'll see you both in the main dining room tomorrow morning at eight."

Neither Steele nor Randi could sleep that night. They couldn't stop smiling.

CHAPTER 25

"Henry, this is the Bishop."

"Yes sir, my secretary announced you."

"I'm coming to Falls City. I'll be there about one o'clock. Clear your schedule. I need to meet with you."

"Yes, Bishop. I think I can do that."

"Don't think. Do it."

"Yes, sir."

"I'm bringing a consultant from New York City with me. He does a lot of work for the Church Pension Fund. He's in Atlanta for the next few days doing a workshop with the clergy up there on clergy taxes. He's a highly respected expert in the field."

"Why are you bringing him here?"

"I want him to look at all the evidence that you've gathered against Austin. I got lucky. It just so happens that he has this afternoon free. Gather up all the incriminating financial information you have on Austin."

"I have all the records here in my office."

"That's fine. Get us a room at The Magnolia Club. We'll meet over there for a late lunch."

"You think you'll be here around one o'clock?"

"Yes. That should do. Now get the Business Manager at the church to bring any additional information he's uncovered. Is there anyone else that should meet with us?"

"Ned Boone. Do you remember him?"

"I sure do. He's a good man. We could use his help. Let's get him there as well. What about that gal that's on the staff?"

"You mean Judith Idle?"

"Yeah, her. Let's get her to meet with us too."

"She can't come, Bishop."

"And just why not?"

"Women aren't allowed in the private rooms at the Magnolia Club."

"Yes, of course. Well, what about her husband?"

"Elmer?"

"What a god-awful name. I swear I would have changed my name if my parents had called me Elmer," Rufus Petersen chuckled.

"Do you want him to come?"

"Yes; anyone else you can think of?"

"No, I think those would be the only ones that might have any information that we might need."

"Well, before the meeting why don't you call that Judith Idle and pump her for any information she might have? She's probably told her husband everything she knows, but let's just make sure."

"Consider it done."

"I'll see you at one o'clock at The Magnolia Club."

The Magnolia Club was restricted to male members of Falls City's aristocracy. While women were allowed in the front dining room for lunch, they were prohibited from the other eating areas. The one exception was when the main ballroom was opened for the Cotillion, Debutante Society, or a wedding reception.

"Get me a branch and water." Rufus Petersen instructed the waiter. "What are the rest of you boys going to have?"

The consultant from New York ordered an iced tea—unsweetened. Henry, Elmer, Ned and Ted each ordered a vodka and tonic. "Let's get right down to business, boys. William Watkins here is the foremost authority on clergy taxes. He knows more about Canon Law and how the business affairs of the church should be conducted than any person in all of Christendom. He's written a couple of books on the subject and gets paid huge amounts of money to travel around the country giving seminars. We're fortunate that he can give us a few hours of his valuable time."

William Watkins was quintessential New York. From head to toe he communicated all business and no nonsense. He did not even respond to the Bishop's introduction. When the waiter came to take the order even his luncheon choice communicated discipline. "I'll have the white fish, grilled, no butter. Please bring me the sautéed vegetables and a salad with the dressing on the side."

Rufus Petersen, Ned Boone and Elmer Idle each ordered the crab cakes with low country rice. They would start with the lobster bisque. Henry and Ted, however, were more restrictive. Both confessed stomach problems. They each settled for a bowl of chicken noodle soup."

"Show Mr. Watkins the evidence you have against the Rector." Rufus was buttering a big flour biscuit.

Henry opened a file folder and began by showing Mr. Watkins several checks from the Rector's Discretionary Fund. "You see these are made to a bail bondsman. These two are made out to an individual that we haven't been able to identify. These are made out to a drugstore. These to a medical clinic...and look at these, they are made out to an AIDS organization. Then, this one...this one is made out to a liberal professor at the local college. This guy is very critical of the current administration in the White House. The Rector paid him to give one of his anti-Christian and anti-American seminars at First Church."

William Watkins did not even pick up the checks. He glanced at them over the top of his glasses. "Where did you get these?"

Henry sat back in his seat. "I beg your pardon?"

"I asked—where did you get these checks? These checks have been written on the Rector's Discretionary Fund. As such, they are protected under the rules of confidentiality. Where did you get them?"

That was a response that Henry was not at all prepared for. "Well, uhr...Ted here...he's our Business Administrator...he gave them to me."

William Watkins looked at Ted over the top of his glasses. He sat back, folded his arms across his chest and stared at Ted. He didn't say anything for several minutes. It was as though he was trying to read Ted's mind. "And why did you give these checks to Mr. Mudd?"

Ted was also caught off-guard. "Well, uhr...I thought they were suspicious. I thought someone in authority should check up on them."

William Watkins sat silently looking at the two of them. "Could you help me understand just which checks you found suspicious? Was it this one made payable to a bail bondsman? Or perhaps it was this one made to an AIDS organization? Please tell me the grounds for your suspicion?"

Ted sat straight up in his seat. "All of them. I don't think that the church would approve of any of these checks."

Again, William Watkins was silent. "Which part of the word *discretion* do you not understand?"

Henry Mudd became defensive. He felt like he was on the witness stand being examined by a skilled prosecutor. "The Rector's discretion should comply with the wishes of the parish."

"Which wishes would that be? Does everyone at First Church agree on all things?"

"Of course not. But we think the Rector is using these funds for his own personal gain."

Mr. Watkins leaned back in his chair. He pushed the checks back toward Henry Mudd. "You're an attorney. Is that correct?"

"Yes."

"Do you have evidence to support those accusations?"

"Not yet."

"Okay, let me understand. You have copies of checks from the Rector's Discretionary Fund that have been issued by the business office." William Watkins reached across the table and retrieved one of the checks. "Mr. Holmes, is this your signature stamp on this check?"

"Yes, all checks require two signature stamps. The bookkeepers use my stamp and that of the Rector's."

"I see. So your signature is on these checks. Is that correct?"

"Yes, that's my signature stamp."

"Did you approve these checks?"

"Only because the Rector asked me to."

"I see. And then you gave them to Mr. Mudd because you think the Rector is misappropriating church funds."

Ted swallowed hard. "I thought someone should look at them."

William Watkins handed the check back to Henry. "Have you found any evidence that the Rector was making checks out to himself?"

"No sir, but we think he is laundering money through the bail bondsman."

"Why do you think that?"

"Because he won't tell us who he bailed out of jail."

William looked over at Bishop Petersen. "Bishop, what is your diocesan policy on auditing these funds?"

"It has to be done annually."

"By whom?"

"The parish auditors."

"Do you protect the identity of the persons receiving assistance?"

"Yes."

"So the Rector is following your stated policy in refusing to identify the people that he gives assistance to?"

"You're missing the point, William. We know for a fact that this man is a crook."

William sat looking at each man at the table. He made eye contact with them one by one. He spent some time looking at Elmer. "And you sir, what is your interest in all of this?"

"My wife is on the staff. She has shared with me her suspicions about Steele Austin's behavior. She does not see him as a spiritual person. She thinks he's just in it for himself. She has no respect for him as a man or a priest."

"Then why doesn't she resign?"

"I beg your pardon?"

"If she doesn't respect the Rector and she can't follow his leadership, then why doesn't she resign?"

"Because she loves this church and she wants to do what is best for it."

"Does she now?"

"Just what are you implying?" Rufus Petersen broke the silence.

"A staff member that cannot be loyal to a Rector should resign. Frankly, I'm surprised that Father Austin has not fired your wife. Insubordination is not to be tolerated. It's grounds for dismissal."

Elmer Idle's face grew bright red. "Have you ever met Steele Austin?"

William Watkins shook his head. "No, I've never met the man."

"Believe me; if you ever met him you wouldn't trust him. He's as slick as snot on a doorknob."

Again, Mr. Watkins sat silently looking at each man. His gaze fell on Ned Boone. "Mr. Boone, isn't it?"

"That's correct. My name is Ned Boone."

"What do you have to contribute?"

"I don't understand."

"This meeting was called by the Bishop to seek my counsel. The accusation is that your Rector is misappropriating church funds. What is your role in all of this?"

"I don't care for the man."

"And that's it?"

"Yes sir."

"Do you have any evidence to substantiate these accusations against the Rector?"

"Nothing that would hold up in a court of law, if that's what you mean. I just don't care for the man."

"Oh. What in particular do you find so displeasing?"

"His every breath is displeasing. He has absolutely no redeeming qualities. He's not a spiritual person. I'm convinced that he's a thief. We only need to gather the evidence."

Henry Mudd interrupted. "I've personally seen his wife and him taking an extravagant vacation. They were staying in an expensive hotel and eating in an expensive restaurant. His wife is driving a brand new Oldsmobile. Now, you tell me just where they're getting the money to live so high on the hog if they aren't stealing it from our church."

Mr. Watkins again sat in silence. "Bishop, I fear that I'm wasting your time and mine. Based on what you've shown me, you can disagree with this priest's discretion if you choose. But that only means you disagree with or disapprove of his judgment. My hunch is that not everyone in the congregation would have found the professor to be anti-Christian or anti-American. You can even find your Rector guilty of poor record keeping and then again, maybe not." He paused, "Mister Holmes, I think you should standardize your check request forms. The Rector is not responsible for your record keeping. You are." William Watkins gave Ted Holmes a stern look before continuing. "Gentlemen, the bottom line is that you've not shown me one shred of evidence that this man has done anything illegal or even unethical. To the contrary, he is administering the funds in accordance with your very own policies for doing so. As for the way he chooses to spend his own money, frankly, that's none of your business." William Watkins looked around the table one more time. He looked deeply into each man's eyes. All made eye contact with him. Ted Holmes and Elmer Idle looked away. "Bishop, what I do think you have here is a group of people intent on discrediting one of your priests. As his Bishop, I think you should be defending him."

"Well, Mr. Watkins, you don't know him and we do." Henry Mudd was irate. "We're not through with our investigation."

William Watkins pushed his chair away from the table and stood. "Gentlemen, I wish you all the best in your inquiry. Bishop, could you drive me over to First Church before you take me back to Atlanta? I want to see this place."

"No problem." Rufus Petersen stood. "Thanks, men, for meeting with us. This is not over. Continue your work."

Henry beamed. "You can count on us, Bishop."

After the Bishop had shown William Watkins around First Church he asked if he could see the Rector's office. The Bishop introduced him to Crystal, the Rector's secretary. "Do you have a piece of stationary and an envelope? I would like to leave your Rector a note." Crystal handed him a piece of stationary and an envelope. Mr. Watkins wrote a note, sealed it in the envelope, and marked it confidential. "Please give this directly to your Rector."

The note inside the envelope read:

My Dear Father Austin,

We've never met, but I hope that you know me by my credentials. Having met with your Junior Warden, Business Manager, the spouse of one of your staff members, a disgruntled member of the parish and your Bishop on this day, I offer you the following counsel.

1. *Do not trust anyone in this building.*
2. *Watch your back at all times.*
3. *Get out of First Church as fast as you can. You are dealing with some very mean-spirited people.*

Call me if you need me to explain further.

William Watkins, Church Consultant

CHAPTER 26

"As you can see Steele, our Bishop has already signed it. I went by his house after the dinner party last night. You'll also notice that it's signed by every member of the Vestry." Steele handed the document to Randi. Randi took the file folder from Steele. Her eyes grew wide as she started to read it. She placed a hand over her mouth to silence the squeal that was building up inside her.

"Charles, this is very generous. We didn't expect anything like this."

"Steele, we want you guys. The Vestry of St. Jude's wants you here. Our Bishop wants you in his Diocese."

Steele threw his hands up in the air. "But Charles, I've not even met the Bishop. And...and...Charles, we haven't even seen your church."

Charles Gerard made calming motions with his hands. "Everything in due time. The Bishop wants to meet you after breakfast. Then we'll swing by the parish for a tour. After that, I've arranged with a realtor to show you some real estate. You don't have to decide on anything today, but at least you'll have an idea of what's available. We'll fly you back for a house buying trip."

"Steele, this is amazing." Randi handed the file back to her husband. "Charles, this is so much more than we're earning at First Church. Thank you, thank you so much."

"Don't you mention it, little lady." Charles stood and took his hat off the empty chair at the table. "Let's go see the Bishop. I think you're really going to like him. I know that I do."

The Offices of the Bishop for the Diocese of San Antonio were located in an office complex in downtown San Antonio. Charles pulled into the parking garage. "The Diocese used to own its own building, but when we elected Bishop Tucker he convinced us to sell it. He showed us that it was to our financial advantage to lease offices versus owning them. We also have plenty of parking for meetings."

Charles led Steele and Randi past the receptionist. She smiled at him, "Good Morning, Mr. Gerard."

"Good Morning, Rachel."

They walked directly into the Bishop's office. He was sitting behind his desk talking on the telephone. He waved them in. When he hung up the telephone he stood, "Charles, this must be Steele Austin and his wife. You told me she was pretty, but I had no idea."

Charles chuckled. "You be careful around him, Randi. He's a Bishop and all that, but he still knows how to appreciate a beautiful lady."

The Bishop came from behind his desk and shook everyone's hands. "Come; let's sit over here next to my window. Randi, you and your husband please sit on the couch."

Charles interrupted. "I'm going to wait for you all out there in your break room. You still have that fancy coffee machine?"

"It's still there. You can have anything from a Cappuccino to hot chocolate to plain coffee."

"I tell you that man is an absolute miser with the Diocesan funds on everything but that ga' darn coffee machine out there in the lobby."

The Bishop patted Charles on the back. "Go, have something expensive to drink. I'll come get you when we're finished."

When they were seated, the Bishop leaned forward in his chair toward Steele and Randi. He gave them a broad smile. "Well, Steele, I've heard a lot about you. You've exercised a pretty remarkable ministry in Falls City."

Steele blushed. "I fear that not everyone will agree with you on that."

The Bishop smiled again. "A leader can't lead without offending. It's impossible. And a faithful servant of Jesus is going to be challenged." The Bishop pointed to the crucifix hanging on the wall behind his desk. "I hang it here as a reminder. If you challenge the norms of society and religion like he did, you'd better get ready for a cross. When we start feeling sorry for ourselves, we need to remember what the religious people of the day did to Him."

Steele relaxed. "I was afraid that some of the controversy that has surrounded my ministry would be a problem for you."

The Bishop looked at Randi and gave her a soothing smile. "When is your baby due?"

She put her hands on her stomach. "Three months from now."

"Good, then we've got just enough time to have your child born in Texas."

She giggled. "That's been suggested by several people at St. Jude's."

The Bishop looked back at Steele. "A priest that hasn't created a little controversy is simply not doing their job. If everyone agrees with you, then you may be preaching and practicing something, but it's not the Gospel of Jesus Christ."

"I know you're probably right, but it's not much comfort when you're in the heat of battle."

"In this Diocese, I'm looking for priests to lead the congregations that will be faithful to the Gospel. If they're just interested in being in the religious entertainment business or in need of a group hug, then they're in the wrong place."

"I fear my current Bishop wouldn't agree with you."

"No, I suppose not." The Bishop grimaced. "I need to tell you that I've already heard from your Bishop. He wanted to know if you were here."

"And..."

"And I told him you were and that I hoped that he would issue your Letter Dimissory to me when I asked for it."

"How did he respond?"

"He wanted to tell me all the reasons that I don't want you in this Diocese."

Randi grabbed Steele's arm. "Oh..." She whimpered.

The Bishop smiled. "Don't worry. I'm very familiar with Rufus Petersen. I'm also quite familiar with his manipulations."

Steele and Randi relaxed. "Thanks, Bishop. That was a concern for us."

"If you're going to be in my Diocese I prefer to be called by my Baptismal Name. Call me Robert. Save the formal titles for formal occasions." The Bishop studied the two of them in silence. "I need to tell you that I also received a telephone call from a lay leader in your congregation."

"Oh boy." Steele whispered.

"His name was Ned Boone. Do you know him?"

"Yes, we know him. He's been planning our going away party from the day we arrived."

"Oh, I got the impression that he wants to give you a party, but I think he had a lynching in mind."

Steele sat forward on the couch and clasped his hands together. "He has given me some real drop dead looks over the past couple of years."

"Well, that may be, but I want you to know something about the Diocese of San Antonio. We don't tolerate that nonsense. Any group that goes after one of my priests has to go through me first. I deal with the abuse of my clergy in the strongest terms. I protect them at all costs. Now, don't get me wrong. One of my priests and me might have some pretty tough words, but they'll be in this office behind closed doors. No one else will ever know about them."

"That would be refreshing." Steele smiled at Randi and she smiled back. "How did you handle Ned Boone?"

"That's a fair question. I simply asked him if he was familiar with any court cases of people who had been sued for slander.

Steele raised his eyebrows. "And…?

"He hung up the telephone." They laughed. "Now do you have any questions for me?"

"I'm sure that if I come to St. Jude's I'll have an endless list, but…"

"First, let's get rid of that if. Now, I can tell there's something that you want to ask."

"I don't mean to be nosy, but Bishop I'm…uhr. Robert, I'm really curious. First, why aren't you wearing a purple shirt?"

"It's a personal preference. I walk in the shoes of a humble fisherman. I just don't think St. Peter would have worn the official color of the Roman Emperors. I also want my clergy to remember that when all is said and done I'm a priest just as they are. I wear the shirt of a priest of the Church."

"I find that really admirable. I like the way you think about your ministry." Steele smiled at Randi.

"Well…before you get too excited, you need to know that I'm fighting a losing battle. I think there are only three or four bishops left in the entire church that don't wear some shade of purple."

"Look at your ring. It's just a plain gold ring. I mean, Bishop Petersen's is the size of a baby's foot."

"My pectoral cross is the cross of my seminary. When I visit your parish, I will carry a wooden staff that is an actual shepherd's staff that I picked up on a trip to Israel. When I come for my visitations I won't wear the vestments of the House of Lords because I'm not in the British Parliament. I wear the vestments of a priest. I don't wear a Mitre on my head either because my wife says that pointed hat makes me look like a court jester. I will wear a cope if that's your parish custom."

"Wow, you must be the only Bishop in the Church that thinks this way."

"As I said earlier, I'm not but we are a dying breed."

The Bishop asked Randi and Steele to stand and hold hands with him. He prayed that God would guide them in their decision and give them a safe journey back to Falls City and a safe return to the Diocese of San Antonio."

The tour of the Church was all that they had hoped it would be. It was located in a suburban neighborhood on a busy street so it was very visible to the community. It was new and modern. There was lots of glass. It was beautifully landscaped. It was open and welcoming. It was quite a contrast to the dark wood, brass, and red carpet of First Church.

They spent the afternoon with a realtor. Randi fell in love with two houses in particular. They were in their price range. She wanted to sign a contract on the spot, but Steele persuaded her otherwise. "We need to go home and think about this, Randi. We shouldn't make a decision while we're caught up in the excitement of a new place. Let's go home, take our time, pray and see if God really wants us to come here."

She reluctantly agreed. "I know that you're right. But if those two houses aren't here once you decide, you're going to be in real big trouble with me, buddy."

Back at the hotel, Randi told Steele that she wanted to take a nap. Steele thought it would be a good time to go for a run. He changed into his shorts, t-shirt and running shoes. His run took him through the streets of downtown San Antonio. He ran past the Alamo and out to the Hemisphere Park. He returned to the hotel. As he was walking into the lobby he almost bumped into a blonde-headed young man. He went to the left and so did the young man. He went to the right and it was repeated. Finally, they both started laughing. Steele looked at the man. "I'm so sorry..." Then he remembered. "I know you. Don't you live in San Francisco?"

The young man nodded. "Yes, I do. How did you know that I'm from San Francisco?"

"I saw you at Grace Cathedral one Sunday when we were visiting."

Then a look of recognition crossed the blonde man's face. "You've got to excuse me. We're...I'm just checking out. I've got to get to the airport." He then pushed past Steele and rushed toward the door.

"Wait...please. I want to ask you..." Steele saw the man pass through the hotel doors and slide into the back seat of a taxi. Steele leaned over to look into the taxi. Sure enough, there was a familiar profile. His hair was dyed black and he now had a black moustache, but Steele was positive. He rushed through the doors to the taxi. The young man pulled the door shut. Steele pounded on the roof. "Chadsworth, it's me. Chadsworth, it's me—Steele Austin."

Steele leaned over to peer into the open taxi window. The young blonde man shouted back, "You've made a mistake. My name's not Chadsworth. I don't know you."

The older man looked back at Steele through his dark glasses. He smiled. "Driver, take us to the airport. Pronto!" As the taxi pulled forward the man continued to look at Steele and smile.

"Randi, I'm not crazy. I tell you it was Chadsworth. He looks a little different than when I saw him in San Francisco, but it was him. He told the taxi driver to take them to the airport. Randi, it was his voice. I'd know that voice anywhere. I know for a fact that it was him."

Randi sat wide-eyed on the edge of the bed. "Steele, how can that be? Chadsworth committed suicide. He left a suicide note. He was cremated and you buried his ashes. Steele, you just have to be mistaken. Chadsworth would not have choreographed such an elaborate hoax. I just don't believe that he would have done anything like that to Almeda."

Steele was pacing the floor. "I know. I know. But Randi, I'm positive."

"Okay, Steele." Randi spoke in a soothing voice. "If it was him...I mean, if he is alive, he's made one thing quite clear."

"Oh?" Steele stopped pacing and looked at his wife.

She nodded, "Steele, he doesn't want anyone to know that he's alive. He doesn't want any contact with his past. Honey, that includes you."

Steele sat down on the edge of the bed next to his wife. "But why? Why would he stage his own death?"

Randi took her husband's hand. "You never told me anything, my closed-mouthed husband, but I have a hunch you know the answer to your own question."

Steele sat in silence.

"And now, Father Austin, tell me about the young blonde that was with him. Is he still as hot as he was the last time I saw him?"

With that Steele gently pushed her back on the bed. "And for that question, you must now be punished."

She laughed and pinched her nose. "Please surh; before you punish me will you consider taking a shower?"

Steele smelled his running shirt and smiled, "I guess I am a bit rank, but you stay right where you are. You must suffer the consequences of your bad behavior."

She put her arms around him and kissed him. "Hurry, surh. I want everything that I have coming to me."

CHAPTER 27

"Howard, this is Henry Mudd."

"Yes, Henry. I was so pleased to hear my secretary announce you."

"How are your wife and daughters?"

"They're all fine, Howard. Thanks so much for asking. And your family, I hope everyone is in good health?"

"Oh, we're all doing well. You're so kind to think of us."

"Howard, I wish that I could restrict this conversation to our families, but I fear that I have a bit of bad news that I must share with you."

"Oh, I hope that it doesn't involve you or your loved ones."

"No, Howard. This is a legal matter."

"Oh?"

"Howard, are you still the Chairman of the Museum Board?"

"Yes, Henry. I'm the Chairman and my wife heads up the volunteer docents. Why do you ask?"

"Howard, I've been contacted by an attorney. It seems that a lawsuit is being filed against your Museum Director, the Board of the Museum, and the Museum. It's for several million dollars."

"What? What on earth for?"

"Alienation of affection."

"What?"

"Howard, it seems that your Museum Director has been having adulterous sex with a married woman."

"That slimy little Frenchman."

"The husband intends to file a civil suit against the Board and the Museum for millions."

"What kind of evidence does he have to substantiate these claims?"

Henry turned to his desk. He picked up the packet of photographs. He sorted through the video and audio tapes. "Irrefutable. He has photographs, video and audio tapes, telephone wire taps. He's got it all. Believe me Howard, the Museum does not want these made public."

"Why doesn't the man just divorce his wife? Why is he bringing us into all this?"

"That's where I think we can work together, Howard. I don't think the husband wants to involve the Museum. He just wants to hurt Jacque Chappelle."

"What do we have to do?"

"I think he'll drop the entire suit if the Board will do two things."

"I'm listening."

"First, fire Chappelle and do it today."

"And..."

"Get him out of Falls City for good."

"Tell your client to rest easy. The Board meets this afternoon before the Vestry gathers. As soon as I tell the Board about this, Chappelle will be fired on the spot."

"That's part of it."

"I don't know about the second part. I don't know if we have the authority to chase him out of town."

"No, I suppose not, but you can tell him that the husband will sue him personally and..." Henry fought to control his anger. "Tell him that the husband is looking for him. Tell him that the husband has some acquaintances that know how to hurt a man without leaving any bruises."

"Wow, it sounds like Chappelle is messing with the wrong man."

"You can tell him that. He's in for a real hurting if he doesn't get out of Falls City."

"Will he drop the suit if we fire him?"

"The Museum will not be considered in any lawsuit if the morning newspapers carry the story that Chappelle has been terminated."

"Done."

"Thanks, Howard. I told the husband that I would be able to work with you."

"Are you going to be at the Vestry Meeting tonight?"

"No, Howard, I think I'd better work with this client and try to keep the Museum out of it all. Will you call me as soon as your Board Meeting is over? My client won't call off the suit until I can assure him that Chappelle has been fired."

"I'll give you a call as soon as it's done."

"Thanks Howard."

"Henry."

"Yes."

"Consider it done. Chappelle is out of here."

"Thanks Howard."

When Henry had hung up the telephone, he leaned back in his chair and closed his eyes. There were so many signs and he'd chosen to ignore them, choosing rather to trust her. He thought back to the first time that he met the Frenchman. He thought that Virginia and Chappelle were awfully chummy at dinner that night, but he was engaged in a conversation with the Dexters and just really didn't pay any attention. And then, there was the time Howard Dexter's wife had dropped by his office to tell him that she was pleased to see that Virginia was taking an interest in the Museum. She had seen her talking to Chappelle on several occasions down at the Museum. He remembered just how Virginia seemed always to disappear at the big receptions at The Magnolia Club or the Country Club and he often couldn't find her until the reception or party was over. Then there were the lists. She was secretive. She never really told him where she was going or how she was spending her day. She'd played him for a fool and now he had the proof. Henry picked up one of the video tapes and put it in the VCR behind his desk. He pushed play. He watched the tape yet one more time. Tears rolled down his cheeks.

CHAPTER 28

"Before we begin, I want to welcome the Rector back from his trip." Howard Dexter was seated at the head of the conference table next to Steele. "I need to tell you, Father Austin, that my telephone has been ringing off the hook." Several of the other Vestry nodded and a chorus of "mine too" echoed around the room. "I know that this is not the way that you wanted this to happen, but Falls City is a close-knit community. We all know that you've been away looking at another parish. We don't know exactly which parish or where it's located, but we know that you've been looking."

Steele was uncomfortable. "You're right, Howard. This is not the way I wanted this to play out."

"Can you tell us if you've made a decision?"

Steele shook his head. "I can tell you that I haven't made a decision. Randi and I aren't going to rush into anything. We're going to take our time and try to listen to God. He'll tell us what to do."

Chief Sparks began applauding. Soon the entire table was applauding. Then the Chief spoke, "You realize that we're going to be praying that you stay. So let's just see who has the more powerful prayers. Us or the parish that's trying to steal you from us."

"It reminds me of a story." Stone Clemons had a Cheshire Cat grin on his face.

"Ohh...no!" Several of the Vestry shouted. "Stone, no stories, please."

Stone was not about to be deterred. "It seems this priest received a call from a parish in Mexico. Let's just call him, Father John." Several at the table slumped down in their chairs and gave each other knowing looks. "This parish in Mexico served all the rich patriots living down there. It was a plush position. Father John came back to his congregation and announced that he had received the call. Well, his parish was not going to let him go so easily. So they had a prayer vigil. They then went to see him. They said, "Padre, we've been praying and fasting and we've discerned that it's God's will that you remain here with us." Well, Father John, not wanting to go against God's will, wrote the congregation in Mexico and told them that the people in his current parish had convinced him that it was God's will that he remain as their Rector.

Stone stopped and looked around the table. He ignored the two members of the Vestry that were rolling their eyes at each other. "Go on Stone, we've got a meeting to conduct." Howard encouraged him to continue.

"The congregation in Mexico wasn't going to have anything to do with that. So they had a prayer vigil as well. They then sent him back a message. 'Father John, we've fasted, slept on the floors, and we've prayed. We've determined that it's God's will that you be our priest.' "

Stone looked around the table. He could now tell that he had everyone's attention. "Father John was confused. Both congregations were convinced that they knew God's will. He only knew that he had to make a decision. So he went into the church and threw himself down on the floor in front of the altar. He prayed, 'Heavenly Father, what am I to do? Both congregations confess that they know your will. Please tell me, what is your will for me?' The priest lay there in front of the altar pounding his fists on the floor. 'What do you want me to do? God, is it your will that I go to Mexico? Or, is it your will that I stay here in this parish?' He lay there in silence for just a moment and then, he heard a great voice from heaven. You know the kind—sounds like Charlton Heston. Kind of like Horace Drummond's."

Howard was growing impatient. "Stone, for goodness sake finish this story." The table broke out in applause.

"Oh...a prophet is without honor...Well, Father John was lying there pleading with God. 'Please tell me Lord, what do you want me to do? Do you want me to stay here with this parish or go to Mexico? Please God, what is it you want me to do?' Then to his utter surprise he heard this great voice shout down to him from heaven. *'Father John...I don't give a damn!'* "

The table erupted with laughter. "That's right. That's when the priest realized that God didn't care where the man chose to be a priest. That was his decision. God only wanted the man to be a good priest."

There were several 'Amens' in the room. "Father, we think you're being a good priest right here in Falls City. We hope you'll decide to stay."

Once again there was applause at the table. Steele noticed that Ned Boone was sitting in one of the visitor's chairs against the wall. The representatives of the School Board were there as well. Neither Ned nor any of the School Board were applauding.

"Before we begin, I need to tell this Vestry that a couple of us were at a meeting of the Museum Board earlier this afternoon. We just want you to know that we have fired the Museum Director. The news will be in the morning paper, but the reason for the termination will not. Off the record, we fired him in order to avoid being included in a lawsuit that most likely will still be filed against him for alienation of affection. It seems he has been engaging in sexual acts with a married woman. We had no choice in the matter. That's about all that I can tell you at this time. Of course, we will keep the actual reasons for his dismissal out of the news."

Steele asked, "Are we ready to begin?"

Howard nodded.

Steele noticed that Henry Mudd was not present. "Should we wait on Henry? Does he plan to be here?"

Howard shook his head. "No, Henry will not be here. He's actually working with the husband in an effort to keep the Museum out of the lawsuit."

Steele nodded. "Since we have a large group of visitors present this evening, I would suggest that we dispense with the Vestry Agenda for tonight and just focus on their petition. I believe everyone has a copy of it. "Mr. Barnhardt, would you like to lead us through this request?"

"First, this is not a request. Gentlemen, we're here to talk about the future of First Church School. You have two choices. The school can continue as a parochial school that will never be much more than a second-rate day school under the control of this parish, or it can become a first-rate private school that is supported by this entire community."

Howard Dexter cleared his throat, "If I read your petition correctly, you basically want the Vestry to sign over the school to the School Board. You want us to give up all control. You want us to give you the funds, the property, and the buildings. Now, if you don't mind my asking. Why should we do that?"

"As I said, you need to do this for the future of the school. Do you want this to be a first-rate community school or do you want it to continue as a second-rate parochial school?"

"Sir, I resent that!" The shouted objection came from Ned Boone. "Gentlemen, I realize that I'm no longer a member of this Vestry, but I just can't sit here and listen to this man disparage our school. Sir, do you have any idea the sacrifices that the people in this room have made for this school? I'm not just talking about money. I'm talking about hours upon hours of volunteer time. And now that it's growing and prospering you want us to just step away and give it to you. No sir, over my dead body."

Howard Dexter spoke in a hushed voice, "Now, let's just try to stay calm and rational. Mr. Barnhardt, Mr. Boone here makes some good points. What does the parish gain by giving the school lock, stock, and barrel over to the board?"

The School Board Chairman did not hide his disgust. "How many ways do I have to explain this to you? The choice is a first rate independent school supported by the community or a parochial school being controlled by a parish."

"What about being a first rate Episcopal School?" Chief Sparks asked.

Tom Barnhardt threw his hands up in the air. "That's part of the problem. Being an Episcopal school doesn't help us. We need to be an independent private school that can appeal to people regardless of religion. We want to be a school for people who don't even have a religion. We plan to keep the name of the parish on the school but control over school affairs will reside with the board."

Ned Boone smirked, "So this is about control. Just how would the school be improved for the students? Just what would your independent board offer that this parish can't offer?"

"We plan to raise the money from the community to build larger classrooms. We can then accommodate more students."

Ned rebutted, "And just how many students will you put in a classroom?"

"We plan to build classrooms large enough to accommodate thirty students."

"One teacher?"

"That's right. The ratio will be one teacher in a classroom with thirty students. That's about the only way we can make it work financially and still keep the school reasonably affordable."

Ned Boone snorted, "That's not a private school. I sent my children to this school and they never had a class with more than fifteen students in it. The classrooms here at the church could not accommodate any more than that. Now that's a private school. You're proposing the same student-teacher ratio that the public school has, but you want the parents to pay private school prices for it. You wouldn't be providing a private school education; you'd just be selling a label. What you're proposing is a public school education with a private school price tag. And for what? Just so that you can be in control!"

Tom Barnhardt did not try to hide his anger. "And you sir, you just don't get it. You're locked into a parochial vision. You need to think bigger."

Ned was not about to back down. "I don't necessarily think bigger is better. If you sacrifice the quality of education for buildings, the students are the losers."

Tom shot back, "It's just that kind of thinking that is holding the school back."

Ned's anger was now equally evident. "Oh, I can see exactly what this is about. It's not about the students. It's about people like you who don't like being accountable to this Vestry and this parish. You want complete control or you don't want anything to do with the school. Your ego just won't let you be a part of anything that you can't run."

"And this parish wants us to give you our money, but you don't want to give us a say in how it's spent."

Stone grimaced, "Forty-nine percent of the school board is made up of people who are not members of this parish. The board makes the budget. The board manages the budget. What more do you want?"

Tom Barnhardt pulled his checkbook out of his inside coat pocket. "If you want me and the people in this town to give money to this school, then the church has to give up control."

Chief Sparks let out a low whistle. "Father Austin, I would like to move the defeat of the request of the school board."

Howard Dexter quickly offered a second.

Steele looked around the table. It appeared that all were ready for the motion. "All opposed to the school board's petition raise your hands." It was unanimous. Ned Boone looked at Steele and nodded his pleasure. "Mr. Barnhardt, your petition is denied."

Tom Barnhardt and the board all stood to leave. Tom Barnhardt stopped and pointed his finger at Steele. "This is not over. We'll be back."

Steele just smiled at him.

After the meeting Steele decided to go down to the chapel to pray. He knew that he would need to make a decision about St. Jude's and he would need to do it soon. He slipped into the chapel. He didn't bother to turn on a light. The light over the altar was on. He stopped at the shrine in front of the statue to the Blessed Mother. He lit one of the votive candles. He then knelt in a pew and placed his face in his hands. His prayers were interrupted. In the distance he heard the sounds of sobbing. He was startled. He realized that someone else was in the chapel. He strained against the darkness waiting for his eyes to adjust. Then he saw him. He was holding a white handkerchief. He was kneeling in the back pew next to the door. It was Henry Mudd. He had not heard Steele enter the chapel. Steele stood and walked to where Henry was kneeling. He put his hand on his shoulder. Henry looked up at Steele as great sobs poured out of him.

CHAPTER 29

When Steele returned to his office, Henry was calmer. He was sitting on the sofa. He still had the white handkerchief in his hand. It had taken some convincing on Steele's part to get Henry to leave the chapel and go with him to his office, but ultimately he relented. Steele handed Henry one of the cups of hot tea that he had prepared for them in the staff break room. He sat down opposite Henry and took a sip of his tea.

Henry looked at Steele. His eyes were red and swollen. "I guess you see a lot of this sort of thing?"

"More than anyone really should."

"I don't know what else to tell you."

"How long have you suspected?"

"I hired the detectives about a month ago. I guess I've been in denial. I mean—there must have been signs that I just chose to ignore." Henry broke down again. Through his sobs he uttered. "I trusted her completely. I worshipped the ground she walked on. I thought she was my soul mate. I actually believed we had the perfect marriage. To me, she was the most beautiful woman in the world." Henry put his face in his hands as the grief poured out of him. "I never dreamed she would do anything like this. I just feel so stupid."

When Henry had stopped crying, Steele picked up the cup of tea that he had prepared and handed it to him. "Your tea is going to get cold. Drink this."

Henry took the cup from him and sipped the tea. "How could I have been so dumb? We had a charmed life. I thought I was giving her everything she needed. We were a Norman Rockwell Painting."

Steele looked at him. Clearly he was a broken man. "Henry, listen to me. Right now you're in a lot of pain, but there's one thing you must not do. You mustn't blame yourself for trusting her. You've done nothing wrong."

Henry started pointing toward the lighted church steeple that could be seen through Steele's office windows. "Can you believe the woman stood over there in front of that altar and lied to God, all our friends and relatives, and me. She promised all of us that she would always be faithful to me?"

Henry put his cup back on the table. "I must've done something wrong. I must not have met some need she had, but she never told me. I would have given her anything she wanted if she'd asked me. I thought she was happy."

"Life is about making choices. If there was something she needed she had other choices. She made the wrong choice."

Henry wiped his eyes with his handkerchief. He then blew his nose. Steele handed him the box of tissues. "I think your handkerchief is pretty well soaked. Why don't you use these?"

Henry stood and walked over to Steele's desk. He tossed the handkerchief in the trash can. He came back to the sofa and pulled a couple of more tissues from the box. "I just know that I hurt. I've never hurt like this in my entire life." He patted his heart. "She's already brought me more pain than I felt when either one of my parents died. My baby sister was killed in an automobile accident by a drunk driver when she was only eleven years old. I thought that grief was going to kill me, but having my wife do this to me hurts so much more."

"Henry, I'm so sorry. I know that you are in a lot of pain. And I know all of this is humiliating, but you need to keep talking to me."

Henry looked at Steele. "And what we say stays in this room."

"You're in a safe place, Henry."

"I guess the first thing that I felt was nausea. I actually got sick to my stomach. Can you imagine what it would feel like to not only see your wife embracing another man, but kissing him?"

"I think my reaction would be the same as yours, Henry. It would tear my heart out of my chest."

"That's not all. I've got tapes of them talking on the phone. She's saying things to him that a woman should only say to her husband."

"Did she call him from your house?"

He nodded, "And a disposable cell phone and a few pay phones. The detectives used their sound equipment to listen in on the conversations and record them as well."

"There's more, isn't there?"

"Henry looked at Steele and then cast his eyes to the floor. "The detectives used hidden cameras to record videos of everything."

Steele's heart went out to this man that had made his own life so miserable the past few years. He reached over and touched him on the hand. "Henry, I'm so sorry. I really hate that this has happened to you. You haven't done anything to deserve this."

Henry nodded. Tears streamed down his face. "It feels like she has driven a dull knife right into my heart."

"I think that's probably a pretty good description of the pain you feel."

Henry drank some more of his tea. "You know who the guy is, don't you?"

Steele shrugged. "Howard Dexter shared with us tonight that the Museum Board had fired its Director because he was having an adulterous relationship with a married woman. Then you weren't at the Vestry meeting. Then this...I think I've put two and two together."

"I just don't know where to go from here."

"You've confronted her?"

He nodded. "There were lots of tears. She says she's so sorry. She doesn't know what she was thinking. She was confused...please forgive her. Let's love each other enough to get through this. Oh hell, you know the lines. They're right out of a made for television movie."

"You don't believe her."

"Frankly Steele, she's lost all credibility with me. I don't believe anything she says. I don't know if she's upset because she got caught or because she hurt me." A blank look came over Henry as he stared off in the distance. "Or is she upset because she has to give up her lover now and she'll never be able to be with him again?"

"Do you want to save your marriage?"

Henry chuckled. "What marriage? Hell, haven't you been listening? I just discovered that my entire marriage has been a lie. It's been a farce. There hasn't been any marriage. I've been legally bound to a liar and whore. I don't even know if Jacque is the only slime ball she's been sleeping with. There might have been others. There may have been dozens of others. For all I know she could have been screwing on me for our entire married life. What marriage? The whole damn thing has been a farce."

Steele waited. "Go on."

"Go on. Go on with what?"

"Go on with your anger. Let's get it out."

"Oh, I'll get it out. I've already taken care of that Frenchman. Now I just have to decide what I'm going to do with my so-called wife."

Steele sat quietly with him. He watched Henry twist the tissues that he was holding around his fingers.

"You've got to turn off the videos."

"Huh?"

"You have the images of the two of them together in your mind. You've got to stop replaying them."

"Steele, I don't have to imagine anything. I have the tapes of the real thing."

"I know. But those images only fuel your pain. Do you still have the evidence that the detectives gave you?"

"No, I gave it all to a friend of mine that's a divorce attorney."

"Is that what you want to do? Do you want to divorce her?"

"No one would blame me. Not even the Church would find fault with that divorce."

"So that's what you want to do?"

Henry closed his eyes. "I don't know. I'm already humiliated beyond words. I don't want our daughters to suffer because of their mother's sin. Can you imagine the teasing they'll be subjected to if their school friends find out their mother is a whore?"

"I want to repeat something I said earlier. This is not information about you or your marriage or the type of husband that you've been. This is information about the choices your wife made in this marriage. It's information about her. There's absolutely no rational reason for you to be embarrassed or humiliated."

Henry pointed to his chest. "Tell that to my heart. Right now being rational doesn't seem to help. I have videos of my wife giving herself to another man. Rational just isn't working. I hurt too much to be rational. I'm angry, embarrassed, and sick to my stomach and those are just for starters. Do you know that it's taking everything in my power not to go over there and strangle that Frenchman and then do the same to the slut that pretended to be my loving wife?"

Steele studied Henry's face. He was a proud man. He was a man that liked to keep up appearances. He had worked hard to present the picture of the perfect family to the world. All that had been shattered. "You don't have to decide anything tonight."

Henry shook his head and looked at Steele through his tears. "Yes, I do. I have to decide if I ever want to look at her again. If I can't even stand to look at her, how can I even think about having sex with her? Every time she shuts her eyes I'm going to suspect that she's thinking about him."

Henry was silent for several minutes. Steele's office was like a tomb. Steele waited for Henry to collect his thoughts. "I really need to think through my legal options. The judges are tough enough on an adulterous husband, but in Georgia an adulterous wife doesn't have a prayer."

"So you're leaning toward a divorce?"

Henry smirked. "I don't know. Look at the mess she's made for all of us. She has spun a web of lies and deceit. Her lover is now unemployed and no longer in the picture. He'll never get a job as a Museum Director anywhere in this country. If I have anything to do with it, he'll never have a credible job of any kind again. So right now I'm thinking I just might let her soak in her own sewage."

"I don't follow."

"No, I didn't think you would."

Steele studied Henry's face. "What do you really think Virginia is thinking and feeling right now?"

Henry was caught off guard by Steele's question. "She's such a liar. I really don't know what she's thinking. Do you think she feels any guilt for what she's done? I mean, you're the priest. Do you think she feels guilty? I mean...do you think that she's really sorry for hurting me or is she just upset that she got caught?"

"Oh Henry, I don't know. I'd have to talk with her to try to determine if her contrition is real. If she doesn't find forgiveness, she could easily try to find other ways to compensate."

"Like what?"

"It's not unusual for people who are living with guilt to turn to alcohol, prescription medications, illegal drugs, overeating, spending, the list is endless. Wouldn't it be better to get everything out in the open? Otherwise, your secrets are going to be an unseen barrier between the two of you."

"Steele, I'm an attorney. A smart lawyer never asks a question he doesn't already know the answer to. I already know everything. The only way it's going to get out in the open is if she were to be completely honest with me. But frankly, I don't trust her to tell me the truth. The second she starts lying to me about so much as one detail or leaves one thing out...well, let's just say that it wouldn't help her case. And believe me, after all the lies that she's told me in order to run off and to be with that piece of slime..." His voice trailed off and he was silent for a minute. "But that's all moot anyway because I don't trust her to tell me the truth about anything."

"Forgiveness could change all that."

"That's easy enough for you to say. I've thought a lot about this. If I stay married to her I know that I'm going to spend the rest of my life questioning her every word. Every time she goes to the store, I'll wonder if she's going to telephone him. Every time she takes a nap will she be dreaming about him?" Henry shook his head. "Forgiveness...are you really that naïve, Steele? Do you really think forgiveness will wipe out my doubts about her every word—her every motive? I'm doomed to live a life of doubts and suspicion if I stay married to her. She cheated on me at least once; what's going to stop her from doing it again? Forgiveness? I'm sorry, parson. That preaches well from the pulpit, but I don't think it will work in this situation.

"Henry, I think marriages are built on truth telling. Honest and open communication is needed. This betrayal is like a giant chasm separating the two of you right now. How will you ever get close again if you don't completely unmask it?"

The tears were running down Henry's face again. "And just how do you expect me to take the word of a liar?" Henry stared off into the distance and was quiet for several minutes. "Don't you get it? I find her repulsive. Just how am I ever going to erase the memory of what she has done from my mind? If I ever try to have sex with her in the future it's going to take a monumental effort on my part. I'll never be able to completely open my heart to her again as long as I live. I can't. I have to protect myself. I just won't risk letting her hurt me like this again."

"So you have no warm feelings at all left for your wife?"

"She's dumped ice water all over those. Oh, I have feelings. All the hurt feelings I just described for you. If you mean love...well, I know that I'll never be able to love her the way that I did."

Henry stood and walked over to the trash can next to Steele's desk. He tossed the tissues he had been using into it. He walked back to the couch and pulled some more tissues from the box on the table. "I thought she was a real lady, boy…oh, boy…was I wrong about that. My so-called lady is a slut. I'd call her trailer park trash, but that would be an insult to trailer park trash."

"You're hurt and you're angry. Do you think with time and healing you could see new possibilities for your marriage?"

"Let's just do that, Father Austin. Let's think about the type of future I could have with her." Henry stood and started pacing around the office. It was as though he were addressing some unseen jury in a court room. "If I divorce her, it will destroy our girls. I just can't do that to them. No, the only way I can stay married to her is just to learn not to care what she does. I simply won't let her ever hurt me again."

"But Henry, that's not love."

Henry looked at Steele with a puzzled look on his face. He walked back to the sofa and sat down.

"The opposite of love is not hate. The opposite of love is indifference. The reason you hurt so badly is because you love her so deeply."

He nodded, "And if I don't love her so much, then she can't hurt me like this ever again. I think the only way I'm going to get through this is to just stop caring about her. I think it's the only way I'm going to stop hurting. I can stay married to her if I don't care so much about her."

"No, Henry, I'm not suggesting that as the solution. You need to have someone in your life that you can love. You need someone who loves you. Someone you can trust enough to completely open your heart to them. You deserve a soul mate."

"Well, I don't see how it can ever be her. I promise you I'll never give her my heart to shred into pieces again."

Steele did not like what he was hearing. "Henry, you're really hurt and you're getting in touch with your anger. You need to think about the type of life you're allowing her to sentence you to. You didn't do anything wrong, but yet you're allowing her to put you in a lifeless prison."

Henry looked confused.

"Have you thought about what your plan will do to you? Henry, it will turn you into a bitter old man filled with resentment and regret."

"Then that's the price I'll just have to pay. I've seen what divorce does to children. I'm not going to do that to my girls. I love them far too much to have their home ripped apart. The romantics may try to white wash divorce, but the pain the children live with paints another picture. Steele, I'm not going to do that to my girls!"

Henry was silent for a long period. Steele broke the silence. "Henry, keep talking. You need to think all of this through. Let me help you with that."

"I have thought about it, Steele. I haven't thought about anything else for the past month. If I divorce her, the reasons for the divorce will become public knowledge. Virginia will be painted with the Scarlet Letter that she deserves. But Steele, think about what that will do to my girls. Their mother will become the gossip of the town."

Steele could see that he was not going to convince Henry of anything just yet. "Let's allow a few days to pass and then let's talk about this again. In fact, I would like to walk you through this if you'll let me. But Henry, I want a happier ending for all of you. Virginia and the girls deserve better. Henry, you deserve better."

Henry spit the words out. "Virginia deserves to be stoned and then cast into hell. As for my girls, they'll never want for a thing, but I refuse to let them suffer because their mother's a slut."

"Listen to me, Henry. I would like to see you rebuild the trust in your marriage through forgiveness and communication."

"There's only one problem with all that."

"Oh?"

"I don't want it. You're a really good listener, but I don't think you understand just what I've been trying to tell you. I don't want to forgive her. I don't want to hear her lies. I know exactly what she's been doing. I have the proof. So why should I listen to her try to twist the truth? I wouldn't be surprised if she didn't try to blame me for her behavior. No, I now know what I have to do in order to stay married to her."

"Henry, listen to yourself. Think about the type of marriage you'd be modeling for your children."

"I'm a pretty good actor. The girls will continue to think that their parents have a happy marriage."

"Friend, I'm not sure any of us can act that well." Steele looked down at his wrist watch. "It's almost one o'clock in the morning. We both need to get home. Randi will be worried about me. Will you come back tomorrow afternoon? Let's talk this through some more."

Henry was silent for a minute. There were no tears. "You'd do this for me?"

"Why wouldn't I?"

"After everything I've said and done to you, you'd still be my pastor?"

"Henry, what's important right now is that you need a pastor. It just so happens that I'm in the business."

They both smiled. Then Henry whispered through a hoarse voice, "I may have misjudged you, Steele Austin."

"Let's put all that aside for now and let's just focus on getting you through this."

Henry stood and started walking to the door. Steele followed him. "Henry, I'm really sorry that this has happened to you. I think you've been a really good husband to Virginia. You didn't deserve to be treated this way."

Henry looked back at Steele. He gave him the warmest look that Steele had ever received from him. "Father Austin, the meanest bastard in the world doesn't deserve to have his wife do this to him."

Steele patted him on the back and the two walked out of the building into the dark parking lot.

CHAPTER 30

Steele Austin ran up the stairs of the Rectory. He could see that all the lights were on in the hallway and the master bedroom. "Steele, where have you been? It's almost 2:00 A.M. We've been worried about you." Randi was sitting up in the bed in the master bedroom. Travis was sleeping beside her on Steele's side of the bed.

"I'm really sorry, Honey. The Vestry meeting was relatively short, but then I got caught in a pastoral situation."

"Steele, I tried to call your office on your private line several times, but you never answered the phone."

Steele slapped his hand against his forehead. "Oh, I punched my 'Do Not Disturb' button on the phone earlier today. I guess I forgot to turn it off. It silences the ringer."

"Why didn't you phone me?"

"Oh, Honey, you wouldn't believe the counseling session I've been in for the past three hours."

"Well, tell me about it."

"I can't right now. It's under the seal. But Randi, if it becomes public and there's a very good chance that it will, I'll probably have to spend a lot of time separating fact from conjecture for you."

Steele walked over to his side of the bed. He looked down at Travis. A brand new puzzle box was lying next to him.

"He wanted to stay up until you got home. Remember, you'd promised to put this puzzle together with him tonight. He was so disappointed when you didn't get home in time."

"I'm sorry. I'll try to make it up to him."

"I put a big envelope for you on the desk in your study. It was delivered this afternoon. It's from the Diocese of San Antonio. I think it's some forms you need to fill out."

"I'm too tired to look at it tonight. I'll go over it tomorrow and then we can talk about it."

"Ned Boone stopped here after the Vestry meeting."

"He did what?"

"He said that you were supposed to have our bank and credit card statements ready for him to pick up. He wanted me to get them for him."

"He was lying. I never said I would give them to him."

"Steele, he wouldn't leave."

"What?"

"I said he wouldn't leave. He refused to leave until I'd given him our personal financial records."

"What did you do?"

"I tried to call you, but you didn't answer the telephone. I didn't know what to do. I was upset and scared. Travis was crying."

"Did you give him what he wanted?"

"I didn't give him anything. I told him I would have to talk to you. I had to finally threaten to call the police to get him out of the house."

"That's not going to happen again. I'll take care of Mister Boone first thing in the morning."

"Steele, why does he want our personal information?"

"Oh Randi, he's just off on another one of his investigations."

"Aren't you tired of all this, Steele?"

"I'm tired right now. I need to get some sleep. I have to get up and do the early service in the morning."

"That's just what I mean, Steele. We go away and you get rested and then you come back here and work day and night for a bunch of people who scrutinize your every move. Then you end up exhausted or sick. We go away again so you can sleep for three days or you end up getting sick." Randi started crying. She pounded the bed with her fists and yelled, "Steele, I'm sick of it."

Steele went back around the bed to her side. He started to put his arms around her so he could comfort her, but she stopped him. "No, Steele. Don't touch me. I simply can't take any more."

Steele was stunned. "Randi, what are you saying?"

"Steele, I know this has been hard on you. Some of the people in this place haven't done anything but criticize you since the day we arrived. They've done everything they know how to do to get rid of you. But Steele, it's been hard on me too. I can't stand any more. It upsets Travis to see us upset. Tonight is the final straw."

"Honey, I'll take care of Ned Boone. That's never going to happen again. Even if I have to get a restraining order from the court, he will never bother you again."

Randi wiped at her tears with her hands. "Listen to yourself. You're a priest and you're talking about getting a restraining order to protect your family from the very people that called you here to be their pastor. Enough is enough! I deserve better than this, Steele. Your babies deserve better. I'm fed up with Travis being disappointed and crying himself to sleep because that damn church is holding you prisoner."

Steele handed Randi a tissue from the side table. She threw it back at him. "I don't want it! I can take care of myself. If it comes to it, I can take care of these babies. You're more married to First Church than you are to me or this family anyway."

"Randi, you're tired and upset. You don't mean these things. I'm sorry that I'm so late getting home. I'm sorry that I disappointed Travis but more, Randi, I'm sorry I disappointed you."

"Steele, that's just not good enough. I just don't think I can take any more. I'm tired of the Ned Boones and Henry Mudds of this church. That damn little Bishop is supposed to be helping you, but he's actively worked to discredit you since the day we came to this god forsaken place. I'm worn out with all of it. I'm tired of what they're doing to you and I'm tired of what they're doing to Travis. I'm sick of what they're doing to me. And Steele, I won't let them do it to the baby I'm carrying."

"Randi, I know that you're right, but can we talk about it tomorrow?"

"Oh, there's always tomorrow. Do you have any idea of the number of things we keep postponing until tomorrow, but then something happens at the church and tomorrow never comes for us? Well, Steele, I've run out of tomorrows."

Steele looked at his wife. He'd never seen her so angry. "Randi, I love you. I'm sorry."

Randi looked up at Steele through her tear-stained face. "Steele, I love you too, but it just might not be enough."

Steele leaned down to kiss Randi, but she turned her cheek to him. So he kissed her on the forehead. "I'll carry Travis back to his bed."

"No, Steele, I'd prefer you let him sleep here."

Travis was stretched out crosswise on his side of the bed. So Steele nodded, "Okay, I'll sleep in the guest room."

"I think that would be best."

For the first time in their married life, Steele and Randi Austin slept in different beds in their house. Steele did not even bother to get undressed. He stretched out on the guest room bed. He set the alarm clock for 6:00 a.m. He closed his eyes, but in spite of his weariness, sleep did not come. Then he heard his alarm clock.

CHAPTER 31

Father Austin, you look like something the cat dragged in." Crystal was placing a fresh cup of coffee on Steele's desk. "Did you sleep in those clothes?"

Steele looked back at his secretary. She took the seat opposite his desk. He didn't respond. "My husband and I went to a late movie last night. We drove past the church and saw that the light was on in your office. Father Austin, that was after midnight."

Steele nodded, "I had a late night counseling session. Then I had to do the early service this morning."

She continued to stare at Steele. "Father Austin, you came back from your trip so rested and refreshed. Now you look absolutely worn out. You haven't even been back a week yet."

"Oh, I've just got a lot on my plate right now."

"I hate to bring you more problems, but yesterday afternoon Jennifer Samples came by the office. She wanted to know if we knew what had happened to her marriage license. She wanted to get a new passport, but her license was never filed at the courthouse."

Steele wrinkled his forehead. "We did mail it, didn't we?"

"Father Austin, I distinctly remember making a copy of it and putting it in her file. Then, I put it in the outgoing mail basket in the lobby for the mailman to pick up."

"Then what happened?"

"That's not all, Father Austin. I called the county courthouse this morning as soon as they opened. I asked them to check the marriage licenses for all of our weddings this year. Father Austin, the past six licenses for the weddings you performed were never received at the courthouse."

"What?" Steele was getting agitated. His chest was filled with anxiety. "How could this happen?"

Crystal leaned forward and spoke in a quiet voice. "Father, I think someone in this office has been taking the marriage licenses out of the basket and throwing them away. I think they're trying to get you in trouble."

"Who would do such a thing?"

Crystal's eyes grew wider. "I have a couple of ideas. If you think about it for a minute, you will too."

Steele slumped in his chair. "What do we have to do to fix this?"

"You're going to have to drive up to the county courthouse and sign duplicate marriage licenses for all of these couples. The bad news is that you personally are also going to have to pay a one hundred dollar fine for each license plus a new filing fee for each one."

Steele could feel the blood leave his face. He felt like he was going to faint.

Crystal's eyes filled with tears. "Father Austin, it's not my place to say anything, but I'm going to say it anyway and I want you to listen."

He nodded.

"This is a really mean parish. There are some really mean-spirited people in this building and in this church. This church is going to kill you. The rumor is that you've been offered a job at another church. I think you should take it. Now, don't get me wrong. You're the best boss I've ever had and I'd really miss working for you, but Father..." Crystal fought back her own tears. "Take your little family and get out of this place before it's too late for all of you."

The thought that Randi had called Crystal crossed Steele's mind. He liked Crystal and she had just made it clear that she really did have his best interest at heart. "Thanks Crystal, you're a wonderful friend and you're the best assistant I've ever had. I'll give serious consideration to your counsel. In the meantime, let's just hold onto all marriage licenses in the future and I'll personally take them to the post office."

"Well, you may not like what I've done, but I've rescheduled all your appointments for today."

"You did what?"

"Father, everyone was just fine with rescheduling. No one complained."

"I wish that you'd discussed it with me first."

"I didn't discuss it with you because I knew that you wouldn't agree to it."

"Fair enough."

"Now, I want you to go home, take a shower, and go back to bed. We'll handle everything down here. And for goodness sake, change clothes."

Steele chuckled. "Thanks, Crystal. I think maybe I'd better start listening to all the women in my life."

Crystal smiled. "I knew you were smarter than the average man."

Steele stood, "Do I have your permission to stop at the chapel and say some prayers before I go home?

"You did a service this morning. Wasn't that enough praying for one day?"

"No, those were prayers for others. I need to offer some for myself."

"Well go, but then go home."

Steele walked down to the chapel and knelt down before the altar. He prayed for Randi, he prayed for their marriage, he prayed for his children...and then he felt a tap on his shoulder.

"Father Austin, I just feel awful interrupting your prayers." It was Crystal. "There's a Charles Foster on the telephone. He's the manager at First Community Bank. He insists on talking to you. I tried to put him off, but he said it's urgent."

Steele stood, "I know who he is. I really do need to talk to him."

Steele hurried back to his office. Crystal transferred the call to him. "Father Austin, your Administrator transferred a quarter of a million dollars out of the Handley Endowment a few days ago into his personal checking account."

Steele felt his stomach do a flip. "What's the Handley Endowment?"

"You don't know about the Handley Endowment?"

"No, this is the first I'm hearing about it."

"Wow, this is serious. Mister Handley was a member of First Church. He never married and had no heirs. He left his entire estate to your church about three years ago. Father Austin, it came to 2.2 million dollars."

"How much is left in it?"

"This is the last of it. I'll have to pull the records, but my hunch is that your Administrator has taken all of it."

"Did the transfer go through?"

"I hate to tell you that it did. I called his bank to see if they would send it back. They said he'd already written some pretty big checks on it and they've cleared, so they can't send it back."

Steele thought for just a minute. "Tell you what I need to do, Mister Foster. I need to get my wardens and our chancellor to meet me over at your bank. Can you begin pulling all the records on this endowment? In fact, can you begin pulling all the records on any of the funds that have the First Church name on them?"

"It could take a while, but I'll put my people on it. Father Austin, I sure hope you plan to prosecute this guy."

"That's not my call, but I have a hunch that he'll be prosecuted. I'm going to try to get everyone to be at your office as soon as possible. Will that work for you?"

"I'll be here."

Steele walked into Crystal's office. "Have you seen Ted Holmes?"

She shook her head. "I don't think he's arrived yet. Do you want me to check?"

Steele nodded. "Don't tell him I'm looking for him. I just need you to keep track of his whereabouts for the next couple of hours. Can you do that for me?"

Steele could tell from the look on her face that she was curious as to just what was going on, but Steele also knew that she would not ask. She nodded.

He returned to his office and telephoned Howard Dexter and Stone Clemons. His third telephone call was to Henry Mudd. "Henry, I need to tell you something."

"No, Steele, I need to tell you something. I want to thank you for your pastoral care last night. You may not know it, but you gave me a lot of comfort. You also gave me a lot to think about."

"Were you able to get any sleep?"

"Not much. I slept in the guest room."

The thought quickly passed through Steele's mind. Whether a person is betrayed by a spouse or betrayed by a member of the church, it's not really very different. In both cases it led to separate bedrooms. "I'm willing to continue to try to help you figure things out, but right now I need to advise you of something in your official capacity as the Junior Warden."

"Oh?"

Steele then told Henry what the Bank Manager had relayed to him. Henry agreed to meet everyone at the bank within the hour. Steele considered calling Chief Sparks, but decided that would be premature and that it should really be a decision that he made with the Wardens. He started to dial the Bishop, but his instincts warned him against that as well. He left his office and walked the three blocks to First Community Bank.

The bank manager invited him to come into the office. He had several documents on his desk. They were soon joined by Stone, Henry, and Howard. "Here is a copy of the trust and a copy of the check for two million two hundred thousand dollars and some change. As you can see it was made out to Ted Holmes, First Episcopal Church. Here is the signature card. His is the only signature on the card. Then here is the canceled check that got our attention. As you can see, he made out the check to himself and signed it. We would have caught it, but he put it in the night depository of his own bank. The transfer of funds was processed electronically."

Stone asked, "Do you have the other canceled checks he wrote on this trust?"

"It'll take us a while, but we can get them for you."

Howard Dexter was thumbing through the other bank statements. "I didn't know anything about these other accounts. They've never been on any of our Vestry Statements. I know the Auditors have never seen them."

Henry Mudd had been standing silently with clinched fists. Steele put his hand on his shoulder. "Are you okay, Henry?"

"That little creep, he's been playing us all for fools. He's been orchestrating our investigation into you and all the time he was the one stealing from the church. Steele, I feel so foolish. No, I feel stupid. The man has made fools out of all of us. How long do you think this has been going on?"

Charles Foster shrugged, "It's hard to say, but as you can see some of these accounts are several years old."

"Henry, he took advantage of all of us." Howard Dexter placed the stack of bank statements back on the manager's desk. "He particularly saw his opportunity under Doctor Stuart. Poor old Doctor Stuart didn't want to know anything about the business affairs of the church. He preferred to attend to spiritual matters. He left the business affairs to the Business Manager and the Vestry."

'You're right, Howard." Henry nodded. "If it weren't for Steele here, it's no telling how long he would've kept stealing from the church. Steele, we—I mean, I owe you a gigantic apology. This church owes you a debt of gratitude for paying attention to the business affairs."

Steele smiled, "Thanks Henry, but right now we've got to decide what to do next. What do you advise us to do, Stone? You're the Chancellor."

Stone looked at the bank manager. "Can we use your telephone?"

He nodded.

"Steele, call the Chief and ask him how he wants us to proceed."

Steele got Chief Sparks on the telephone and brought him current on the events of the morning. "The first thing you need to do is secure his office."

"What do you mean?"

"Get him out of it and get someone else in there to safeguard all the records. You don't want him to get suspicious and start destroying records."

"I have most of the records myself, Chief."

"That may be, but you still need to secure what's left. Do that and I'll meet you at the church with a couple of my officers in about ten minutes. We have enough to bring him in for questioning. The next step will be up to the solicitor."

Steele hung up the telephone. "I need to make another call."

The bank manager nodded. Steele got Crystal on the line. "Crystal, is Ted Holmes in his office?"

"No, I've kept an eye on him. Right now he's down in Judith Idle's office. They have the door closed."

"Is Doctor Drummond there?"

"As a matter of fact he's sitting in my office. He's been waiting on you."

"Give the telephone to him."

"Hey Boss, where are you and what the hell is going on?"

"I'll tell you everything in a few minutes, but right now I need you to do me a big favor."

"Name it."

"I need you to go immediately to Ted Holmes' office and secure it. Do not let him back in his office for any reason. If you need to get a couple of the sextons to help you keep him out of his office, have Crystal get them for you. But right now go—go!"

"I don't need any help. I can handle it."

Steele hung up the telephone. "We need to go back over to my office. The Chief is going to be there by the time we get there. They're going to arrest Ted Holmes. We have to decide what we're going to tell the newspapers and we've got to put together a letter to mail to the members of the congregation."

"We want to thank you, Charles, for all that you've done to help us. You are a credit to this financial institution." Howard Dexter shook the bank manager's hand. "Do you have any suggestions on how we should proceed?"

"I'd suggest that you get a Forensic Auditor. We'll get you all that we can from this bank, but my hunch is that he was using other banks."

Henry nodded, "that's a great idea. We need to call an emergency meeting of the Vestry, Steele. Let's see if we can get everyone together tonight."

Steele rode with Henry back to the church. All of them arrived at the parking lot just as two officers were leading Ted Holmes out of the building in handcuffs. Ted shouted for Henry Mudd to talk to him. Henry walked up to the squad car, "Can you give us a second, officers?"

"Ted, why did you do this? Did you really need the money?"

Ted scoffed, "You don't believe all this, do you, Henry? I'm innocent. I didn't do this. Steele Austin is behind all this. He framed me. He's forged my signature and everything. They have the wrong man in handcuffs."

Henry shook his head. "Ted, I just saw bank records dating back over five years. We'd never even heard of Steele Austin back then. The records are in your name. Now, just how could Steele Austin have forged your signature and set up church accounts five years ago?"

Ted smirked, "He's just that good." Ted yelled over his shoulder at Howard and Stone, "I tell you men, Austin's the one you want. He's really, really slick."

Henry shook his head again and waved his hand at the officers. They opened the door to the squad car. As they pushed Ted's head down so that he could be seated in the back of the car he shouted one more time. "You have the wrong man." Then he yelled at Steele, "Steele Austin—you did this! You've framed me. I'm going to prove it."

CHAPTER 32

"Steele, I just feel awful about the way I treated you the other night." Randi was sitting in Steele's office.

"Don't give it another thought, Randi. You were upset and you had every right to be upset. You didn't say a single thing that wasn't true. In fact, you didn't say anything that I hadn't already thought myself."

"But things should be better now. I mean now that they have Ted Holmes."

Steele smiled, "I hope so, but you realize that he's not pleading guilty to anything. He continues to point a finger at me. I fear that there's still a handful in the parish that want to believe him."

"Did you talk to the Bishop?"

"Yeah, but I fear he still suspects me of something. He just doesn't know what."

"But you said Henry Mudd now believes you. He's on your side... right?"

"Henry has apologized. I think he believes Ted Holmes was behind all the insinuations and innuendos being cast on me. I guess he was trying to put my ministry under a dark cloud even before I arrived."

"Then it can't help but get better."

"Does that mean you want me to forget about San Antonio?"

"Oh, I don't know, Steele. That's such a wonderful call. I just don't know. What is your heart telling you?"

"I know that these people here have been crushed. Most every person that has ever served on the Vestry here feels a deep sense of betrayal. They feel like Holmes played them for fools. Some have said that they don't feel like they were doing their jobs."

"And what do you say?"

"What can I say? The last Rector did ignore the business affairs of the parish. He just wanted to focus on the spiritual. I fear that's not a luxury any Rector can enjoy. As for the Vestries...oh, I don't know. I don't want to sit in judgment on anyone. My job is to help these people get through this."

"What's next?"

"We have a Forensic Auditor coming in next week. He'll probably be here for six months or more. If Ted keeps pleading not guilty, then there will be a trial. This could go on for a year or two. If it does, it will keep this congregation in turmoil until it's all settled."

"Then, I say let's get out of here while the getting is good."

"Is that what you really want to do?"

"Steele, you have to admit that it's awfully appealing."

"And who's going to take care of these people who have had their trust betrayed?"

"That's the Bishop's job. He hasn't been much help to you or this congregation. Let him earn his keep."

"You really are fed up, aren't you?"

Randi held her hand over her head, "to here and then some. Are you happy with your sermon?"

"I think so. I hope it will bring some healing. I'd better get on over to the church. Are you going to come to this service or the next one?"

"Both. I think I need to hear your sermon both times."

They walked together over to the church. Steele left Randi at the front door of the church and he walked around to the sacristy door. He was relieved to see that all the other clergy and lay ministers had already vested. He put his vestments on in silence.

During the readings from scripture that were appointed for the day, Steele studied the congregation seated before him. The church was packed to overflowing. He spotted a couple of reporters and a camera crew from the local television station. The news of the embezzlement had made front page in the local paper and had been on the local television news each night. Steele's eyes fell on the Henry Mudd family. They were seated in their usual pew, but the seating arrangement was different. Usually, Henry sat next to his wife and he would put his arm around her for most of the service. The girls would sit on either side of their parents. This morning, however, the girls separated their parents. Virginia Mudd was as white as a sheet. To his knowledge, no one knew anything, but Steele thought she might as well have been wearing a Scarlet Letter. Henry looked equally uncomfortable.

Steele noted that the hymns were sung with less gusto and the verbal responses to the prayers were more subdued. He had been dealing with his own feelings of betrayal. He had felt like a victim fighting against an unseen enemy. Now, everything was out in the open. Now the truth could be told. The master of the game had been revealed, but not everyone shared his sense of relief. He was looking out at a proud people who had been humiliated. Their trust had been betrayed and made public for all to see. They were embarrassed. They were angry. He and the people he served were united by emotions that none of them wanted and none could really understand.

He glanced back at Henry Mudd. The thought crossed his mind that the congregation was feeling all the emotions of betrayal that a husband would feel if his wife's adultery were to be made public. He suddenly understood Henry's struggle. Virginia's shame was now Henry's shame. If he chose to keep her betrayal secret, he would be held prisoner by that awful secret for the rest of his life. Steele wondered how he could do that without becoming bitter and resentful. But Henry was a proud man. He had thought he had the perfect marriage and family. He had believed he was married to a lady. If he made her adultery public, then all of that would be shattered. He would have to come to terms with the fact that everything he had cherished was a lie. Henry may be right. It just may be more then either he or his daughters could withstand. If Virginia's betrayal was revealed, she would become the object of public gossip and scorn. Most likely her daughters, their friends, and the people in the church would turn against her. Any decision that Henry made would continue to bring pain into his life and potentially that of his children. His wife's sin would haunt Henry for the rest of his life. He really didn't have a good choice. Steele closed his eyes and asked God to help him help all of them.

Steele stood in the pulpit. He smiled, but no smiles were returned. He realized that many in the congregation were not even looking at him. They were looking down. "Last night," he began in a soft voice. "I was helping our son Travis with his pre-school homework. I'm sure we can all remember learning to print our letters. The paper the teachers use today has not changed much from that which I used as a child. It has bold blue lines, top and bottom, with a dotted line in the middle. The idea is to keep each letter within the bold lines. If the letter has a secondary part to it, like a small 'b', then you try to round off that portion of the letter so that it is between the dotted line and the bottom solid line. Of course, it's next to impossible for a beginner to print every letter perfectly. Like all of us, my son grew frustrated with some of his letters and wanted to cross through them or erase them. But when he crossed through them or erased them, the marks of the eraser were left on the paper. It was less than perfect.

The entire exercise started me thinking about the effort that most all of us put into writing a note or a letter. We want it to be perfect. We want every word spelled correctly. We want it to be punctuated correctly. We want our letter to be without error. We want it to be picture perfect. We resist crossing out our mistakes. And if we try to erase them, the marks of the eraser remain on the stationery.

Can we not say the same thing about our lives? Don't we all want to live the perfect life? Wouldn't it be wonderful if there were no parts we wanted to erase or draw a line through? Can you imagine a life so proficiently lived that there would be no desire to correct any of it? Most every Christian would like to live the perfect life. No Christian wants to intentionally violate one of the commandments of God. All of us would like to stand before the Almighty on that great day in eternity and hold before Him a perfectly lived life, a perfectly written letter free of all cross-outs and eraser smudges."

Steele stopped to look out at the faces of his congregation. He had everyone's attention. They were all looking at him. "That's our desire, but we suffer from the same infirmity that afflicted the Apostle Paul. The blessed Apostle wrote, 'I do those things I do not want to do and leave undone those things that I desire to do.' Not a single one of us will be able to stand before God with a perfectly written letter. All of our life scripts will have those portions we would have rather crossed out or erased. In spite of our best efforts the crossed through lines will still be there. The parts we attempted to erase will still be evident."

Again, he stopped and smiled at his congregation. Several now returned his smile. He made eye contact with Virginia Mudd. She looked at him with a desperate look. It was as though she was pleading with him to help her. "Did you happen to notice our big magnolia tree in front of the church as you entered this morning? It has a new look. Almeda Drummond is in charge of our church grounds. She advised me that the tree needed to be pruned. It needed to be cleaned up. She had the lower branches removed so as to expose the trunk of the tree. She also had all the dead debris underneath it removed. Now the area underneath the tree is neat and clean. If you look on the altar this morning, you will see that the flower vases and the altar itself are adorned with branches of magnolia. Those branches were pruned from the tree in front of our church."

Steele turned to look at the altar. The eyes of all in the congregation did so as well. He turned back to face the congregation, "Unlike the magnolia tree, we cannot prune away the parts of our lives that we regret. In spite of our best efforts, we cannot completely erase them. The marks of our pencils and our erasers will always be evident on our life's script. But like these branches which were pruned from the tree out front, we can lay those parts of our lives on the altar of God. We can offer them to God. Through the cross of Jesus, we are given the assurance that the Almighty will welcome us home on that great day, in spite of our imperfections.

Like the good apostle, we all do those things that we do not want to do and we leave undone those things that we would like to do. There is no such thing as a life lived without error or regret. They put erasers on the end of pencils because people make mistakes. There is a delete key on our computer keyboard because we make mistakes. We do not, however, have the luxury of hitting the backspace button and starting all over. Words once spoken cannot be reclaimed. Deeds once done cannot be undone. Opportunities once passed may never be presented again. Almeda had to carefully supervise the pruning of the magnolia tree. A branch once cut cannot be reattached.

The good news of the Gospel of Jesus Christ is that God can take the errors, mistakes, and parts of our lives that we would like to erase or do over and use them to make better people of us. We can learn from our mistakes. We can allow the errors of our ways to motivate us to be better people. The acceptance of our own frail weakness can lead us to be more understanding of the weak moments we see in the lives of others. The repentant heart is the compassionate heart that hears the prayers of our fellow sinners."

Steele stopped again to look out at the congregation. There was no movement. The congregation was silent. They were listening. "Now, let me speak very directly to the current trauma that we are experiencing. As Christians, we are called on to forgive those who sin against us. We do so even as God forgives us our own sins. We must do this for our spiritual health. We must do this even when those who sin against us fail to repent of the hurt and pain that they've brought into our lives.

Forgiveness is a gift that we give to them to be sure, but it is a greater gift that we give to ourselves.

My brothers and sisters, the Church of Jesus Christ is in the forgiveness business." He paused. "The state of Georgia is not." He paused again. "There's going to be a trial. There will be a verdict. There will be a sentence. The sentence will have to be served. Those decisions are now out of our hands. We cannot cross out this experience from our congregational letter. There is no way to erase it. We cannot hit the backspace key in our parish history and try to do it over. We can, however, learn from it. Your Vestry and I are committed to doing the things necessary to minimize the chance that something like this will ever happen in our congregation again.

I would like to suggest to you that we use the magnolia tree standing in front of this church as a symbol of a new day in the life our congregation. The tree standing out there is the same tree that's been there for over one hundred years. It has stood as a silent sentry overseeing the things that the people who worship here have both done and left undone. That tree, however, has a new look. It has been pruned. The branches have been laid on the altar and now adorn it. Our congregation has experienced a pruning as well. That tree reminds us that we will now have a new look, but we are the same people who are going to continue to grow in our service of Christ. We are going to look different, but we are the same people. But because of the events of this past week, we are going to be an even better people. We are going to be a more compassionate people." Steele stood silently looking out at his flock. Then, to his surprise, the congregation exploded with applause. The choir stood first and then the people in the pews. The entire church roared with the sound. Steele turned to face the cross. He pointed to the altar and joined in the applause.

CHAPTER 33

Father Austin, Horace Drummond is on the telephone."

"I thought today was his day off."

Crystal smiled and shrugged, "I guess so. He says he needs to talk to you."

Steele picked up the telephone. "Can't you stay away from this place? Go do something fun with your wife and forget this place for at least one day a week."

"Hey brother, I wish it were that easy. I hate to ask you, but I need you to come over to our house."

"When?"

"As soon as you can get here."

"Is there something wrong?"

"I'd rather tell you when you get here."

"I guess I can come now. I don't think I have anything scheduled until later this afternoon."

"You don't need to break any speed limits, but don't waste any time. I need you up here right away."

"I'll be right over."

Steele turned on to the street leading to Horace and Almeda's house. It was packed with cars. There were cars on both sides of the street. The circular drive in front of the house was lined with cars. Then Steele spotted a sign pointing to valet parking. He pulled up to the sign. Horace was waiting on him. "What's going on, Horace? Are you guys having a party?'

"Oh, you might say that. Give the valet your keys and come on in."

When they entered the house it was filled with women. Steele could see that they were overflowing onto the patio and around the pool behind the house. Horace announced in a loud voice. "Look, I have the proud papa with me."

Then Steele spotted Randi. She ran up to him and hugged his neck. "Steele, it's a surprise shower. You won't believe all the stuff the ladies of the church have given us for the baby. She's going to be the best dressed little girl in Falls City."

Just then Steele felt someone hugging him from behind. He turned around to see Melanie and Rob. "Hey daddy!"

Steele hugged each of them. "What are you two doing here?"

"The ladies of your church sent us airplane tickets. They wanted us to be here for your baby shower."

"That's just wonderful. It's so good to see the two of you. You look like you're still in love and happy."

Rob smiled, "We're on a honeymoon without end."

Randi was pulling on Steele's arm, "Come on outside. You have to see these gifts."

There were three large tables covered with baby clothes, blankets, shoes, toys, and furniture. "Steele, isn't this wonderful? Can you believe all this stuff?" Randi was glowing. "I just can't believe the ladies of the church did all this for us."

Steele put his arm around Randi and kissed her. "It's just wonderful. But how are we going to get all of this stuff home?"

"No problem, man." Horace walked up behind him. "Almeda hired a panel truck and two drivers. They're here now to load everything up. They'll also carry it into your house for you."

Steele whistled, "You guys have thought of everything."

"Here's a cup of punch. Now I need to ask you and Randi to go with me to the study. There's a group of people in there that want to have a word with you."

"Huh? Who?"

Horace chuckled, "Never mind who. Just follow me."

He led them into his study. When they walked in they were greeted by Howard Dexter, Henry Mudd, Stone Clemons, and Chief Sparks. "What's going on, guys?"

Howard smiled. "Why don't you and Randi have a seat over there on the sofa? We want to make you an offer."

"What kind of offer?"

"We would like to extend a new call to you to serve as Rector of First Church."

Steele looked at Randi. "I don't understand."

Howard continued, "We all know that a parish in Texas has extended a call to you. They've even made an offer. This Letter of Agreement is our counter offer. We will meet their offer dollar for dollar and term for term plus ten percent."

Randi squeezed Steele's arm. "Mister Dexter, do you know that they will let us buy our own home?"

"No, I didn't know that. In fact, we don't know any of the terms in their proposal to you. The Vestry has authorized us to meet their terms, whatever they might be, and add ten percent to their offer. If that means we have to sell the Rectory so that you can buy your own home, then we agree to it."

Steele took the piece of paper from Howard and studied it. "I don't know what to say."

Stone chuckled, "Well Father, it would make everyone in this room and in this house very happy if you'd just say 'yes'. We love you, Father. We don't want you to leave."

Henry Mudd nodded. With a shaking voice he said, "That goes for all of us Steele. I want you to stay as well. I don't want First Church to lose you. I don't want to lose you."

Steele smiled, "that means a lot to me, Henry. Thank you."

"And you, Chief, how do you feel?"

"If you leave, who's going to run this place while Stone is on all of his fishing and hunting trips? If you don't stay and do the job, then it's going to be left for the rest of us to do."

Howard Dexter snickered, "I second that." He handed Steele an envelope to put the offer in. "We know that this is a big decision and that you and Randi need to talk about it. Just know that our offer is genuine. And Steele, this time I will personally insure that every iota of the agreement is met. No one will try to rewrite the terms of your agreement once we've signed it. That won't ever happen again. You have my word as a gentleman and a southerner. There's no greater guarantee."

EPILOGUE

Steele and Randi invited Rob and Melanie to go with them for a long weekend in Savannah. In addition to having a great weekend with their friends, they wanted to seek their counsel on the decision they needed to make. After all, they were going to be their baby's godparents.

The guys decided to drive up to Hilton Head on Saturday. Rob wanted to teach Steele his newfound sport. He wanted to teach Steele how to play golf. Melanie and Randi stayed behind in Savannah. They would spend the day shopping.

Randi and Melanie found a cute little restaurant for lunch right on the riverfront. The maitre d' led them to a table. Randi failed to notice a familiar face at the bar, but the man recognized her. He turned to watch the two women. He was not happy to see them. He remembered Melanie's face, but it took him a minute to recall just who she was. He turned his attention back to Randi. She was laughing and talking with Melanie. The very sight of her reminded him of just how much he detested Steele Austin.

He turned back to face the bar, but he could still see the two ladies in the bar mirror. He had heard that Steele Austin had received a call to a parish in Texas. He wanted him to take it. He wanted him out of Falls City. He had also heard that the incompetents at First Church had agreed to meet the Texas offer. This infuriated him. He wanted to make sure that Steele Austin left his town and his church. If he didn't, he wanted to make sure that he would regret the day that he didn't. He continued to watch Randi in the mirror. She's a pretty little thing, he thought. She's just the type of woman that could tempt most any man. Then it hit him.

He turned so that he could look at Randi one more time. He knew exactly how he would get rid of Steele Austin. They had been going at him all wrong. He needed to go for Austin's underside. He would attack him where he was most vulnerable. He smiled as his vindictive plan began to unfold in his mind. He wondered why none of those other idiots at the church hadn't come up with this idea before now? It was perfect. Yes, he would go after that sorry excuse for a priest one more time. Only this time, his work would not be in vain. He glared at Randi. He whispered, "It's a pity, but for the good of First Church, little lady, you're going to have to suffer. In just a few weeks you won't be smiling and laughing. When I'm finished with you and that Okie you're married to, you both are going to fold like paper dolls."

"Did you say something, sir?" the bartender asked. "You want another?"

Ned Boone turned to look at him. He smiled even more broadly. "Yes surh, I do. Make it a double. I finally have something worth celebrating."

CHAPTER 1

The Right Reverend Rufus Petersen was sitting in his favorite purple arm chair. He had placed it next to the window in his office overlooking the cathedral gardens. He had returned all of his telephone calls before lunch. He had no appointments for the day so he was able to catch up on his correspondence. He was particularly pleased with the letter that he'd written to the Rector of First Church in Falls City. He was so proud of it that he'd had his secretary both fax a copy to him in Falls City and send him a hard copy through the mail. Finally, he felt like he'd put that sorry excuse for a priest in his place. For lunch he'd walked across the street to a little bistro. As he settled in his chair to read one of his favorite mystery novelists, he felt like the Reuben sandwich he had eaten was still lodged in his throat.

He pushed the intercom button on the telephone sitting on the table next to his chair. His secretary answered, "Yes, Bishop. What can I do for you?"

"Do we have anything carbonated out there? I need something to help me digest that damn sandwich."

"I'll look in the refrigerator, Bishop. I think I saw a Coca-Cola earlier. I'll bring it to you."

Rufus sat back and picked up the novel. He tried to belch, thinking that would bring him some relief, but he couldn't get anything to come up. He started reading. He was excited about this particular book. He had scanned the pages when he purchased it at the neighborhood bookstore. The murders were described in a particularly gruesome detail. Bishop Rufus Petersen anticipated reading the descriptions over and over again. He tried another belch. He found no relief. Instead, he felt a sharp pain in his left jaw that shot up the side of his face. It radiated down his neck into his left arm. He broke out in a cold sweat. He was having difficulty breathing. He tried to stand but fell forward onto the floor. His neck and arm were now numb. He felt as though he was going to vomit.

Then the Bishop of Savannah heard a ringing in his ears. It was deafening. He felt himself being drawn through a tunnel. There were swirling multi-colored lights all around him. He was flying at lightning speed toward a bright light at the end of a tunnel. He exited the tunnel and realized that he was outside his own body. The ringing had stopped. There were no bright lights. He was floating over his own body. His body was lying on the floor of his office. He could see his secretary pushing on his chest and blowing into his mouth. Her face was covered with tears.

"Rufus…Rufus," he heard a familiar voice calling to him. He looked to his left and saw his sainted mother. She was absolutely radiant. She was more beautiful than he remembered her. She was extending her hand toward him. She was smiling. "Rufus, take my hand. I've been waiting on you."

COMING IN THE AUTUMN OF 2008
BOOK FOUR
IN THE MAGNOLIA SERIES
<u>THE PINK MAGNOLIA</u>
BY
DENNIS R. MAYNARD

ABOUT THE AUTHOR

The Reverend Doctor Dennis R. Maynard has been a priest in the Episcopal Church for thirty-eight years. He has served parishes in Oklahoma, Texas, South Carolina, and California. The author of eight books, he is often requested to be a guest speaker or preacher in congregations and communities throughout the nation. He has also served as a consultant or retreat leader to some sixty parishes and Dioceses.

Doctor Maynard and his wife, Nancy, have parented four children. He retired from full-time parish work in 2003. He lives in Rancho Mirage, California.

All of Doctor Maynard's books can be ordered through his website at www.Episkopols.com, through Amazon.com, or any of the online bookstores. If you would like to have Doctor Maynard visit your parish or organization as a guest speaker or preacher, please visit his website or e-mail him at Episkopols@aol.com.